One
Summer
Day
in Rome

One Summer Day in Rome

MARK LAMPRELL

FLATIRON
BOOKS
NEW YORK

ONE SUMMER DAY IN ROME. Copyright © 2017 by Mark Lamprell. All rights reserved. Printed in the United States of America. For information, address Flatiron Books, 175 Fifth Avenue, New York, N.Y. 10010.

www.flatironbooks.com

The Library of Congress Cataloging-in-Publication Data is available upon request.

ISBN 978-1-250-10553-0 (hardcover)
ISBN 978-1-250-10555-4 (e-book)

Our books may be purchased in bulk for promotional, educational, or business use. Please contact your local bookseller or the Macmillan Corporate and Premium Sales Department at 1-800-221-7945, extension 5442, or by e-mail at MacmillanSpecialMarkets@macmillan.com.

First Edition: August 2017

10 9 8 7 6 5 4 3 2 1

FOR KLAY, ALWAYS

One
Summer
Day
in Rome

Prologue

EACH PERSON IS BUT A WAVE PASSING
THROUGH SPACE, EVER-CHANGING FROM MINUTE
TO MINUTE AS IT TRAVELS ALONG.
—Nikola Tesla

Let me tell you about Rome, my beloved Roma, so ancient she is called *eternal,* the city that has always been and will always be. Assured of her own magnificence, her venerable significance, she does not seek comparison—and yet I find it almost impossible not to compare her.

New York, Paris, London—every grand metropolis—has its own irresistible attraction, but Rome so swirls with stories of saints and sinners, martyrs and monsters, lovers and fighters, that she compels you toward her, like gravity. If you linger long enough among her piazzas and monuments, you will find yourself simultaneously lost and found, swept away by her grand cavalcade of history, captivated by her crumbling beauty. Built of grandiose and preposterous dreams, Roma lays bare the delusion that reality is shaped by realists. No one leaves her unaltered. Part of you always loves her.

Listen carefully and you will hear her columns humming like harp strings, plucked by those who have been enchanted before you, among them Caesars, popes, despots, dreamers, scientists, artists, and lovers. Look carefully, beyond the masterpieces and marvels, and you will see that there is not a single mundane sight to be witnessed. Here, even the gutters are beautiful.

This is the place where passions are aroused, senses inflamed, and lovers fall into each other's arms. It all appears to unfold like magic, but I will tell you what really happens.

How do I know?

I have been here since the beginning.

I was here when Romulus killed Remus.

I was here when Augustus draped the city in marble.

I was here when Peter died upside-down for the love of his Christ.

I was here when Michelangelo battled the pope for the love of his ceiling.

I was here when Christina surrendered her kingdom for the love of her faith.

I am here now and will be here long after you leave.

My business card, were I to have one, would read: Quantum Mechanic. The classicists among you might have guessed my purpose. I am long forgotten in the modern world, but the ancients knew me as a genius loci—a spirit of place—assigned to inspire and challenge the people within it. Some of my colleagues lay claim to elevating Leonardo or Caravaggio to brilliance of expression. I, alas, cannot. I oscillate within the floors and walls of Rome, and while my presence accentuates her beauty, this is merely a by-product of my specialty, which is, and has always been, the labyrinthine machinations and mysteries of the heart. I am, to be specific, a Genius of Love.

Come with me, if you will, and observe my labors.

First step, we gather our players. First stop, the corners of the earth. . . .

New York, New York

"WOULD YOU TELL ME, PLEASE, WHICH WAY I OUGHT
TO GO FROM HERE?"
"THAT DEPENDS A GOOD DEAL ON WHERE YOU WANT
TO GET TO," SAID THE CAT.

—Lewis Carroll, *Alice's Adventures in Wonderland*

Specks of dust slow-danced in the sunlight streaming through the tall southern windows. Above the old man's head, they tumbled and collided, equal parts chaos and choreography, at once permanent and fleeting. Some moved earthward, but just as many climbed heavenward with no visible means of propulsion. *Why don't the laws of gravity apply to them?* Alice wondered.

She could hear New York humming and honking beyond her professor's studio, and although she felt reasonably certain that the city was in fact actually *there,* she had often suspected that another city, very close but obscured by some deficit in her perception, also existed. In that Other World, she could not be judged or derided for being clever or dull because the rules—like the law of gravity currently disproving itself before her very eyes—did not apply. In that place, there simply were no rules. How she longed to go there sometimes.

Professor Stoklinsky looked up and smiled with his eyes, all wild hair and wisdom. She braced herself for him to speak. But he said nothing and returned his attention to her work.

She dreaded this, his scrutiny. He expected so much of her. He treated her as if she were special, and if there was one thing Alice was certain about at the ripe old age of nineteen-almost-twenty, it was that she was not exceptional. She knew this because she had been born into a family of unequivocally exceptional people.

Her mother had been a rising star at the BalletMet in Columbus, Ohio, until she fell through an unsecured trapdoor in the stage floor during a rehearsal of *The Nutcracker* and shattered thirty-nine of the fifty-two bones in her feet. During her long recuperation, she began to study law and was now managing partner in a prosperous legal firm on Wall Street. Her father, a celebrated ophthalmologist, spent all his spare time in India restoring sight to those who could neither access nor afford proper care. Her older brother followed her father into medicine, had been a Rhodes Scholar, and was currently specializing in renal surgery at the Mayo Clinic. Her younger sister had recently distinguished herself in her freshman year at Harvard by winning the Jacob Wendell Scholarship Prize. Each member of her family effortlessly excelled at most things they did.

Alice, on the other hand, did not. She did not have a grand passion for anything in particular, although it was her habit to carefully observe the hue, saturation, and intensity of color in just about any object that she came across. Her earliest memory was of hiding in her mother's voluminous walk-in closet, arranging the clothes according to their proper place on the visible spectrum. She had begun with the blouses. Purple blouses, violet, blue, green, lime, yellow, cream, orange, red, burgundy. She put the white blouses between the yellow and cream ones, even though, strictly speaking, white was not part of the spectrum. Her mother had been charmed initially, but when Alice repeated the exercise with her siblings' wardrobes, she had her tested to see if she was autistic.

At fourteen, Alice lied about her age and secured a part-time job in a clothing boutique, three shops down from the corner of Eighty-third and Madison. Nadine, the owner of the eponymously named boutique, soon recognized Alice's flair with color, as did her customers, who would always solicit Alice's counsel before making purchases. Nadine even took Alice on a buying trip to the Say Yes to Life, Love, and Style Fashion Week in Chicago. Alice liked being good at something. As her confidence grew, so did her circle of friends.

In her final year of high school, Alice plucked up the courage to ask her new best friend, Manuela, home for dinner. After she had left, her mother observed that Manuela had thick ankles. It was her sole comment about the evening. The next day in the canteen, Manuela performed a highly entertaining monologue about how their feisty friend Alice turned into a mouse at home. Alice rolled her eyes and laughed along, but her cheeks burned bright.

At a cocktail party to celebrate her brother's return from Oxford, a colleague of her mother's mentioned he had seen Alice walking into a shop on Madison Avenue. Alice was on the verge of explaining that she had been working there for almost four years when her mother interjected, telling him that Alice was applying to volunteer as a guide at the Metropolitan Museum of Art, which is why she was on the Upper East Side. This was a fabrication—Alice and her mother had discussed the possibility of it once, briefly—but that was all. Alice was about to protest when a steely matriarchal glance silenced her. She nodded impassively, choking on the sudden and certain realization that she was actually a slight embarrassment; that in comparison to the daily activities of the rest of her family, what she was doing was trivial, that therefore *she* was trivial, that she was *letting the side down*. It all arrived in one brief but devastating epiphany.

When she handed in her notice a few days later, Nadine pressed Alice to her impressive bosom and cried. Alice had a distant memory of being hugged like this as a child, but she could not place where or when. She finished her final year of school with mediocre grades and did not attend her prom despite having sourced eight yards of Yves Klein blue shot silk fabric for a dress.

On a brief visit home, Alice's father noticed that she was somewhat withdrawn and mentioned this to her mother, who responded by arranging a blind date for their daughter with a young man from her firm who had just been promoted to junior partner. Daniel was ten years older than Alice, a clever litigator with the remnants of a childhood stutter. He had disconcertingly long eyelashes and would have been darkly handsome if not for his unusually large ears. *If he's prepared to forgive my red hair,* Alice thought, *I'm prepared to overlook the ears.*

Alice's mother was uncommonly pleased by the match, and

Alice could see that Daniel's affection had not only redeemed but elevated her. Basking in the sunshine of her mother's newly dawned approval, Alice realized how cold she had felt without it and was enormously grateful to Daniel as a consequence. When the time came for Alice to embark upon a course of tertiary study, it was Daniel who gently encouraged her to set aside her plans for a degree in fashion design at IED Milan and instead pursue a course at the Parsons School in New York City where they might still see each other every day. Unfortunately, Alice was so nervous that she botched her entrance interview and did not receive the offer of a place. Daniel wanted to sue, but Alice, not wanting to make a fuss, quickly enrolled in a fine arts course at a local college that specialized in 3-D modeling and printing, the principles of which she thought she might later apply to the design and manufacture of clothing.

And so it was, two years later, that Alice had left the warm bed of the loft she shared with Daniel and found herself standing in front of Professor Felix Stoklinsky with her stomach flipping. Once again, the old man looked up from her work. This time, his look demanded some kind of response.

She had submitted three shoe box–sized maquettes as her major work for her second-year sculpture class. With the professor's approval, they would become much larger bronze pieces during her third and final year of study. The first maquette, of a young couple intertwined, suddenly looked like the rip-off of Rodin's *The Kiss* that it actually was. Alice steadied herself. Now was not the time to panic. She had rehearsed this with Daniel. It was his big idea in the first place. She'd had no clue what to submit as her major work until he had browsed her previous year's efforts and helped her write a list of pros and cons for each piece. Having chosen three figurative sculptures, the next trick, Daniel explained, was to find some concept, some overarching idea, to connect them.

Alice cleared her throat and swept her hand in front of the Rodin maquette, feeling for all the world like a sales model on the Shopping Channel. "Bliss. The first stage. Two people meet. Fall for each other. It's . . . bliss," she said.

The professor did not appear to respond. She moved on to the second maquette: two middle-aged lovers, their arms wrapped around each other but their faces turned away, blank. Alice suddenly wondered what on earth had possessed her to suggest this awkwardly realized piece. But she stuck to the plan.

"Doubt. The middle stage," she said. "Euphoria wears off. They have to work at making it work. Jealousy, boredom, disappointments . . . fill them with doubt."

The professor nodded. A smile flickered across his face. Clamping both hands behind her back, Alice moved on to the third statue—an old man, his face contorted with pain, held the lifeless body of a woman. Michelangelo's *The Pietà* with a role swap and postmodern twist. It suddenly seemed so lame. She suppressed her horror and plowed on.

"Loss. The final stage," she said. "One person always loses the other."

"Always?" the professor inquired.

"Always," she said. Either they find another person, or they leave, or one of them . . . dies."

"So this is your thesis?" he said. "That love ends badly?"

Alice's stomach appeared to be planning an exit strategy via her mouth. She pursed her lips and nodded.

The professor looked into her pale gray eyes. They were all lovely at this age, but this one was particularly so. She reminded him of a marble-eyed Venus, not quite present, not yet vividly alive the way most of her rambunctious classmates were. Years of experience told him there were fires flickering in her unexplored depths, but he worried that she would never go exploring because there would never be a need; hers was the kind of beauty that opened doors, that would allow her to skim lightly across the top of life for as long as it suited her.

"What are you doing for the vacation?" he suddenly asked.

"I'm . . . sorry . . . ?"

"What are you doing? Where are you going?"

"I . . . I don't know."

"I want you to go somewhere different. And I want you to do something . . ." The old man grabbed her hands from behind her back. For a beat he held them in his grasp then flung them high above her head. "Something *voosh*!"

He was smiling kindly at her, but she felt tears sting her eyes. She had disappointed him, too. Well, she was sick of it. She was sick of disappointing people. She was sick of being an idiot. Suddenly Alice knew exactly what she should do and right there and then determined to do it.

In that moment, she believed that the inspiration to go abroad was completely hers. She had no conception that forces greater than her were calling her to Rome—that she had, in fact, been summoned to the eternal city. By me.

TWO

London

NOT EVEN OLD AGE KNOWS HOW TO LOVE DEATH.
—Sophocles, *Fragments, Volume 3*

The Eiffel Tower trembled and shuddered and began to move down Holland Park Avenue. Lizzie watched from the enormous bay windows of her dead brother's pied-à-terre as a bright-red double-decker bus, on which the poster of Paris was plastered, plowed toward a flock of pigeons. They exploded into the air, scattering to the winds. One particular pigeon shot over the top of a plane tree and headed straight for Lizzie. She reeled back slightly, fearing that it might fly into the glass, but the bird stopped in an elegant flutter and landed on the stone ledge directly in front of her. Lizzie and the pigeon regarded each other, tilting their heads this way and that.

She was not, and never had been, a beauty, but there was nonetheless an irresistible sparkle about gray-haired, seventy-nine-year-old Lizzie Lloyd-James dressed in mourning purple. Okay, she had conceded just this morning, there was no such thing as "mourning purple," but she looked like a cadaver in black, so that was that.

Lizzie addressed the pigeon. "Henry wants to go to Roma." When she spoke, it was with the cut-crystal ring of the British upper class. The bird cocked its head.

Behind, in the dark gleaming room, a woman's voice responded, a trace of the rural west betraying her Bristolian roots, "A Roman sojourn. Something to blow the wind up our skirts."

Lizzie lifted the dog-eared, hand-typed document and angled it toward the light. She searched her pockets before she realized that her reading glasses were hanging on a chain around her neck and put them on, pushing and pulling them up and down her nose until she achieved focus.

"He wants to go to some bridge . . ." said Lizzie.

Again, the voice: "Ponte Sant'Angelo."

"Yes, the Bridge with the Angels," said Lizzie, squinting at the document. "According to this, it's where you met."

"Yes, it is," said Constance. "Good God."

Lizzie turned and peered over the top of her glasses to see a bejeweled, blue-veined hand rise from the depths of a wing-backed chair. Leaving the pigeon to his own devices, she crossed the room and placed the document in the hand of her dead brother's wife.

Seventy-eight-year-old Constance Lloyd-James, in contrast to her sister-in-law, had been, and still was, a beauty, despite the recent ravages of grief. She had been born to entrepreneurial working-class parents who had made a fortune redeveloping the Bristol docklands when the floating harbor began to lose its place as a major port for English merchant ships. The money had afforded Constance a tertiary education in London and Rome, while her beauty allowed her to marry "up" into a minor aristocratic family at the beginning of the Swinging Sixties, a time when all levels of society were pretending that social class no longer mattered, even though it really did.

Harnessing her own family's gift for property development, young Constance helped turn the dwindling fortunes of her husband's estate around. As their wealth grew, both husband and wife engaged in a campaign of supporting living British artists by purchasing their works. As a consequence, they now owned a priceless collection of paintings, sculptures, and installations as well as large tracts of London property and a number of organic farms in Devon and Cornwall.

"Are you okay there, girlie?" asked Lizzie. They had called each other "girlie"—she couldn't recall why exactly; perhaps as some ironic prefeminist diminutive?—ever since they had met in their early twenties. Lizzie had instantly liked the bright young beauty. She liked the way her big brother radiated happiness whenever Constance was near, but she especially liked the way her father spluttered his tea into the Wedgwood when Henry announced his intentions to marry her, and she would never forget the consternation on the mother's face. "But she talks like a *pirate*," she had protested.

Lizzie patted the top of Constance's head and peered into the gloom of the room. She could see her own dim reflection in the vast Venetian mirror hanging over the fireplace, and it did not give her pleasure.

"Who is that old lady?" Lizzie asked the ghost squinting back at her.

"Sometimes I look at my laughter lines and wonder what on earth could have been that funny," said Constance.

Lizzie laughed.

Constance hauled herself out of the chair. At once, her reflection appeared next to laughing Lizzie's. Constance frowned.

"What?" asked Lizzie.

"That laugh of yours. Reminds me so much of him," said Constance.

Lizzie took the document back from Constance. "He's very specific about where he wants us to go and what he wants us to do. All a bit odd, really."

"He was an odd man," said Constance plainly.

"Indeed."

"That's why we love him."

"Indeed."

Lizzie's bottom lip trembled. She turned quickly, hoping Constance might not catch her lapse in decorum. But Constance did.

"Come now, girlie," said Constance briskly. "What's that going to achieve?"

Days later, Henry's driver, Robert, negotiated the dark-blue Jaguar through the roads and roundabouts that surrounded Heathrow like a network of modern moats, delivering Lizzie and Constance to the ramparts of the departure gates. Robert carried Constance's luggage inside, and Constance followed. When a nice young man opened the entry door for Lizzie, she instructed him to follow Robert with her luggage. The young man began to explain that he was a fellow traveler—not an employee of the airport—when Constance shot past her in a panic. Lizzie abandoned the young man and followed.

"What's up, girlie?"

"Henry. I left him in the Jag."

Indeed she had. Henry's ashes had been waiting in a plain brown recyclable cardboard box—his own premortem selection—seat-belted into the front passenger side of the Jaguar. And that is exactly where they found him a few moments later. Robert arrived, mortified that he, too, had not only forgotten his esteemed incinerated employer but left the car unlocked and the box vulnerable to theft. Constance calmed Robert and warmly offered him absolution. They were all nervous. It was a big day. Robert took the liberty of hugging Constance, which Lizzie noted she endured with grace. Next there was a brief and slightly unseemly tussle over who would carry Henry into the terminal. Yes, he was heavy, Constance conceded, but she was perfectly capable of carrying him, *thank you, Robert*. As soon as he registered the steely pirate in her tone, Robert surrendered the box to Constance.

High above the Alps, Constance and Lizzie sat in their voluminous first-class seats, sipping DOCG Prosecco di Conegliano-Valdobbiadene, as instructed by Henry. He had been retrieved from the overhead locker where he was secured for takeoff and now sat comfortably on the wide walnut-trimmed armrest between them.

A young flight attendant approached, rubbing errant lipstick from her teeth. She addressed them with a deep-fried Southern American accent that would have been charming had it not been for a note of disinterest that would not have been detectable, they suspected, had she been speaking to two handsome young businessmen.

"Can I put your box away for you, ma'am?" She started to reach over Constance toward the box, making it clear that she wasn't really asking, more informing them of her intentions.

"No, thank you," said Constance brightly but so loudly that the flight attendant reeled back.

"That's not a box," said Lizzie enthusiastically. "That's my brother."

"And my husband," added Constance.

"Henry!"

"We're taking him to Rome."

"Henry adores Rome."

The two old ladies grinned manically at the flight attendant.

"Oh. Okeydokey," said the flight attendant. "Um. You just holler if you need anything."

"*Grazie,*" said Constance in her steely pirate voice.

The flight attendant scurried away.

Constance took a sip of her prosecco. "I think we frightened her."

Lizzie took a sip of her prosecco. "I believe we did."

"We're scary old ladies," said Constance.

"I believe we are," said Lizzie.

Constance turned and raised her crystal flute to Lizzie. "To scary old ladies."

Lizzie clinked her flute against Constance's, and a *tring* rang out.

THREE

Leonardo da Vinci

THE LONG, DULL, MONOTONOUS YEARS OF MIDDLE-AGED
PROSPERITY OR MIDDLE-AGED ADVERSITY ARE EXCELLENT
CAMPAIGNING WEATHER [FOR THE DEVIL].
—C. S. Lewis, *The Screwtape Letters*

A tanned man with an easy smile that made him look at home wherever he went ambled down the business-class aisle of the Airbus 380 bearing two bottles of water, one sparkling, one still. At forty-six Alec Schack was just beginning to allow himself to enjoy the fruits of his success. He had graduated with a degree in architecture at the tail end of a building recession and finding himself virtually unemployable gratefully took a job in his uncle's modest lighting shop in Cincinnati. When his uncle was electrocuted installing a Christmas window display, Alec's grieving aunt asked him to take over the business. It was not his chosen profession; he didn't love lighting, but he liked it and evidently had a knack for it. Within three years the store expanded to two more locations in Cincinnati, and within ten years there were stores in Cleveland and Toledo as well. Strategizing his way through the housing crisis and riding the back of the renovation boom, Alec had just opened his twenty-ninth and largest store at Westfield Century City in Los Angeles.

This was the American dream, and Alec knew he was lucky to be living it. Many of his competitors had folded, but he was of the few who had survived and thrived. He knew he should be grateful, and most of the time he was. But some of the time he wasn't. Some of the time he suspected that his life looked a whole lot better from the outside than it was on the inside. Not that he was dogged by a desire to toss it all in and become a professional golfer or a rock-and-roll guitarist. But sometimes, on the rare occasions when he woke at 3:00 A.M. and could not get back to sleep, he wondered if maybe he'd *missed* something.

Reaching his seat, Alec handed both bottles to his wife, Meg. "Still and sparkling," he said, infusing the announcement with just enough resentment to be sure it would register, "just in case you change your mind."

Meg turned to her husband but, as was her habit, directed her attention to midair as if she were addressing an unseen stranger sitting between them. "Why would I change my mind?" She had lived in the United States most of her adult life, but a nasally Australian twang lingered.

Alec shrugged.

"Why are you turning this into a big deal?" she said. "I asked for water. I happen to believe in getting what you want."

You mean getting me to get you what you want, thought Alec.

Knowing what he was thinking, she said, "I divorce thee, I divorce thee, I divorce thee."

"If only it were that simple," he said, addressing the in-flight entertainment guide.

Meg opened the water and took a swig. "You've grown tired of me. I've lost my allure."

"Why do you think I'm sitting here next to you?"

"Habit?" said Meg. "I don't know. Why are you sitting here next to me? So you can snipe at me about how demanding I am?"

Alec looked out the window at the wing, bouncing slightly in the tumescent white clouds. "If I kicked this window out, we'd both be sucked into oblivion."

"You shouldn't have come. You have no faith in our mission."

What mission? thought Alec.

There was a mission of sorts. Years ago when their eldest daughter, Sydney, had transitioned from toddlerhood to little-girldom, Meg had begun a blog chronicling the redecoration of her room. Essentially it was a marketing exercise to promote Alec's new range of children's lamps and night-lights, but Meg's way with a funny anecdote saw it quickly expand and rebrand as *Megamamma,* one of the most popular, we're-all-in-this-together-and-most-of-us-are-sinking homemaker blogs on the Web.

Meg's latest project was reporting on the rejuvenation of their large Spanish Mission house overlooking the Silver Lake neighborhood of Los Angeles. She had sourced a particular sky-blue tile that appeared to come from a boutique manu-facturer in Rome. Because it had emerged from a jumble of tiles minus its sticker, no one could be 100 percent sure of its provenance. She had e-mailed photographs and even Skyped but in the end decided the best (and most fun) course of action would be to fly to Italy and have a conversation with the tile-maker in person.

Her next step was to bully her husband into accompanying her. Since he had forgotten their last anniversary as well as her most recent birthday (the enormous bouquet of Australian native flowers delivered late afternoon by his terrified PA had only made matters worse) she felt fairly confident that Rome would prevail.

Rome did prevail, but not because of forgotten birthdays or anniversaries—he had forgotten that he had forgotten these—but because, as Alec recollected, they always seemed to have especially amorous encounters in the eternal city. And since it had been an eternity since they had enjoyed any encounters at all, he leaped at the opportunity to address the situation.

The plane began its descent. Meg dug her fingernails deep into Alec's wrist. It was their unspoken understanding that she was allowed to express her terror of takeoffs and landings by mutilating his nearest hand and forearm. Alec winced and stroked her ravaging hand. She smiled gratefully, not quite directly at him, but as close as she ever got. He tucked an errant strand of hair behind her ear and noted that, despite the bone-dry atmosphere of the cabin, her ruthlessly straightened golden hair had begun to curl.

Tossed in a colorful sea of gesticulating Mediterraneans, they jostled for position at carousel number three, waiting for their bags to spew forth. Alec formed a picture of laconic

Roman baggage-handlers lolling over their luggage, macchiatos in one hand, cigarettes in the other. He felt a surge of irritation.

"If we were in search of some amazing fresco," he said, "I'd call that a mission. If we were helping excavate some ancient temple, I'd call that a mission. If we were on some kind of spiritual—"

Unfazed by what she knew was simply redirected anxiety, Meg cut through the diatribe and pointed out that his bag had appeared. Alec pushed through the almost impenetrable wall of passengers crowding around the carousel and reached for the suitcase at exactly the same time as a solid old nun in a classic black habit with a white wimple.

Meg watched with glee as Alec and the nun tussled over the bag. A brief but heated discussion led them to consult the name tag. Wisely, Alec let Soeur Luc-Gabrielle do the reading. Her silver crucifix dangled from a blue ribbon around her scapular, waving back and forth across the luggage in a private benediction. The nun spoke firmly to Alec, who bowed and babbled in return. He retreated sheepishly through the crowd and stood next to Meg, taking care not to look at her.

"If you say a single word," he said, "I will not be held responsible for what happens next."

"Oh, I believe you," said Meg. "You were so terrifyingly assertive with that seventy-year-old nun. I shall not utter another syllable."

Alec watched the luggage birthing onto the carousel, reminding himself to be patient; he was no longer in a land where customer service was paramount. While Italy had many areas of excellence, baggage retrieval was probably not one of them. "They should be here by now," he said. "Business luggage always comes before coach."

"Unless, of course, it's lost," said Meg.

As the carousel emptied and the crowd dispersed, it became evident that their bags were, indeed, missing. This was supposed to be a fun, duck-in-and-duck-out-adventure-slash-mission; a day in Rome to source floor tiles then back to business in LA. Meg's feet had barely touched the ground, and already she was being derailed. Quelling a surge of childlike disappointment, she refrained from stamping her foot.

"This is not part of the plan. *This is not part of the plan*," she said louder the second time, permitting a petulant eruption from the cross little girl inside her.

Two airport guards, wearing black berets and bearing submachine guns, paused. Alec noted that they had black pistols holstered to their thighs as well. He lowered his voice. "If you're planning on getting us arrested before our vacation begins . . ."

"This is not a vacation," Meg protested. "We're on a *mission*."

After a few wrong turns and some more cross words, they located the lost baggage counter and joined a long line of disgruntled passengers. As they waited, his wife's conviction that they were on a mission stuck like a burr until Alec could contain his irritation no longer, and once again thoughts burbled into words.

"We're not on a mission," he said.

"Don't trivialize it."

"I'm not trivializing it—it is trivial. We're spending a day in Rome to find tiles for our house."

Meg sighed.

"On the scale of Vacuous and Unimportant Things to Do,"
he continued, "what we are doing earns maximum points."

"I do not consider building a nest for our little chicklings
vacuous and unimportant."

Alec looked hard at his wife; maybe it was early meno-
pause. *What chicklings?* he thought. *We have evil teenagers plot-
ting against us.*

"Please don't do the Mr. Misery routine," said Meg.
"We're in the eternal city. The city where we met and fell in
love . . ." Here she paused to calculate exactly how long ago
that had been. At precisely the same time that she said,
"Nineteen years ago," Alec said, "Eighteen years ago."

"Nineteen."

"Eighteen."

"Nineteen."

"Does it matter?"

"Obviously not to you."

FOUR

All Roads

RIGHT AS DIVERSE PATHES LEDEN DIVERSE FOLK
THE RIGHTE WEY TO ROME.

—Geoffrey Chaucer, *Treatise on the Astrolabe*

Elsewhere in the airport, Alice found herself in a similar predicament to that of Meg and Alec Schack. Her flight from
New York had landed moments after their flight from Los
Angeles. Arriving at the luggage carousels, she had been
overwhelmed by brilliant reds, yellows, and blues in every
combination of hue and luminance imaginable. She had left
the charcoals, browns, and grays of Kennedy Airport to be
greeted by this kaleidoscope of color, as if all the passengers
had conspired to a midair wardrobe change in celebration of
their arrival at Leonardo da Vinci airport.

It felt like a gift, this polychromatic symphony, an auspi-
cious omen. She had left Professor Stoklinsky's studio resolved to reinvent herself; no more insipid acquiescing, no
more scrambling to please. She would be decisive and assertive, strike a course, and boldly navigate it. This was her first

trip abroad without her family. She had never been to Italy, but she spoke a little Italian, having studied it in high school. She wondered if she might further reinvent herself in this place.

Perhaps she would introduce herself as Alicia. Or a new name altogether. Maybe she would cloak herself in an entirely new identity. She could pretend to be her friend Manuela. Waiting at the carousel, her thoughts ranged so wildly that it was a long time before she twigged that her bag had not appeared. This had never happened before. What would she do? A man in a uniform approached and asked her if she was okay. Alice was so scattered that she failed to notice that she had managed to plumb the depths of her schoolgirl Italian to both understand what he was saying and communicate her predicament.

Following the kind man's directions to the lost baggage counter, Alice gave herself a good stiff talking-to. Losing one's backpack was not a catastrophe; it was a setback. In fact, it wasn't a setback, it was a gift; this was her opportunity to launch the new capable, assertive Alice. If she couldn't manage this small speed bump, well, what was the point of coming in the first place?

She turned a corner and saw a crowd of people, among them the Schacks, waiting at the counter. Had she seen the Schacks or had the Schacks seen her, there would quite likely have been a moment of mutual recognition and some *what-are you-doing-here*s. This would have been genuine coincidence and not a meeting initiated by me or any other of the genii of Rome. There was no need for them to meet. Indeed, a meeting may have altered their trajectories. So they did not meet.

Taking in the long line at the counter, Alice's heart sank.

The old Alice would have meekly joined the back of the line and called Daniel for consolation. The new Alice did precisely that. But as she dialed Daniel's work number, Alice felt such a depth of self-loathing that it startled her. Something *voosh,* the professor had said to her. *I want you to do something voosh.* Alice hung up before Daniel could answer.

At the head of the line, a group of five scruffy young men were about to approach the counter. Propelled by an inner force as sudden as it was mysterious, Alice sashayed, actually sashayed, toward them. She could tell from their accents that they were British. Her heart raced. Sweat beaded her upper lip. She heard a voice speak with an Italian accent and realized that it belonged to her. "*Scusi, signore,*" said Alice, targeting the most confident and handsome of the lads.

They all turned, almost sputtering with delight that this red-haired goddess had approached them. Rick, the handsome one, made an effort to look calm, as if beautiful women spoke to him all the time. "Hi," he said slickly. "How can I help you?"

Alice faltered then smiled to cover her loss of nerve.

A series of responses tumbled out over each other.

"Well, *hello,*" said one boy with a posh accent and a Prussian-blue backpack.

"Let's make babies together," said a large oaf wearing a coral-pink polo shirt.

"*Lads,*" chided a guy in a pea-green T-shirt.

"She has no idea what I'm saying," said Pink Polo. He turned to Alice. "Do you, sweetie?"

Alice pressed on with her fake Italian accent, "I in big hurry. I go before you?"

"You can go wherever you want if I get to look at that spectacular arse," said Pink Polo.

Green T-shirt thumped Pink Polo on his shoulder.

"Of course. You go right ahead," said Slick Rick to Alice.

"Ow, ow, ow," complained Pink Polo.

Alice stepped up to the counter. A woman wearing a navy-blue uniform and a lot of orange-tinted makeup said, "*Dimmi.*" Alice wasn't exactly sure what this meant. She wavered; her bravado fractured. She was also aware of being ogled from behind and suddenly felt a surge of fury for putting herself in this position. Her capacity for artifice abandoned her, and she explained plainly in English that she had just come from New York and her backpack was missing.

Alice knew that the boys were listening to her American accent. The jig was up. She hoped they wouldn't be too angry or seek any kind of weird retribution. She resolved to apologize for deceiving them and be on her way.

"Can you give me a description of the bag?" said the orange-tinted lady, as comfortable in English as she was in Italian. At that moment, the man from the carousel appeared in Alice's peripheral vision. "*Signorina, è suo questo zaino?*"

She turned. He was holding her avocado-and-lime backpack.

As the man helped her strap the backpack on, Alice took care to keep her eyes averted. She thanked him and finally turned to face the faces of those she had deceived. To her surprise, she was greeted by admiration, not accusation. These guys clearly thought she was *the bomb*. New Alice seized the reigns from Old Alice. She smiled broadly at her audience and said throatily, as if she smoked fifty cigarettes a day, "Good luck with your bags, boys. And have a nice day." This time, she did not sashay away. She sauntered.

In the arrivals hall, she began to calculate the costs and complications of taxi, bus, and train transport into Rome when it struck her what New Alice would do: hitchhike, of course. She had never hitchhiked in her life, but suddenly it seemed like a thrilling and appropriate next step.

Declining the offers of several heartbroken taxi drivers, Alice made her way out of the airport on foot. An abrupt end to sidewalks and pedestrian access soon made it very clear that this was an irregular undertaking. She found herself standing on the cracked asphalt shoulder of a four-lane highway. Being a native New Yorker, Alice was accustomed to edgy driving, but she had never seen anything like this. Without any regard for the orthodoxy of the dividing lines, cars sped and swerved around one another, drivers honking and gesticulating. For one terrifying moment, six cars drove parallel to one another in the four lanes, millimeters from shredding one another's side mirrors.

New Alice consulted Old Alice, and together they decided it would not be admitting defeat to retreat at this point. Waiting for a break in the traffic, Alice saw five *motorini* putt-putting slowly toward her. Judging from their pace and a certain lack of technique, she concluded they must be a group of learner-drivers.

The first driver passed her and waved. It was Slick Rick, looking as surprised to see her as she was to see him. The other British boys passed in quick succession. The last of the drivers was Pea Green T-shirt, apparently so astounded by the vision of Alice that he literally could not take his eyes off her, causing him to miss the crucial fact that his compatriots were slowing in front of him.

Alice suddenly saw what was about to happen and began to point and motion wildly. Pea Green T-shirt turned and saw what Alice was seeing: his stationary friends, screaming, shouting, and waving, directly in his path. A surge of adrenaline prompted him to squeeze the brakes so hard that his *motorino's* tires locked. In a screeching puff of rubbery smoke, the bike stopped. The boy gripped the handlebars, but his feet lost their purchase and momentum propelled them skyward, as if he had been catapulted from the saddle of a bucking bronco. Several structures in his brain simultaneously registered that the inevitable resolution of his trajectory would be to slam directly into his friends. He gripped tighter to the fulcrum of his handlebars, injecting all the will he could muster into reconfiguring the physics of this rapidly unfolding equation. His feet stopped midair, almost directly above his hands. Ceasing his trajectory, he bounced back onto the seat. There was a moment of silence. Clapping and cheering ensued.

Alice shouted at the boys to get off the road as a massive semitrailer led a fresh cluster of traffic toward them. The boys scrambled to the edge of the asphalt. Alice lugged her backpack over to them. Pea Green seemed particularly pale, but in a bluster of chortles and backslaps they assured her that they were all hunky-dory.

Slick Rick offered Alice a ride into town, and she accepted. She explained that she would only be staying overnight in Rome before catching a train to Florence the following afternoon and had hence chosen a backpacker hostel near the Termini station. Rick, who professed to know Rome like the back of his hand, consulted a map and located her hostel. He pronounced that the area around her hostel was dirty and dangerous and suggested she try to get a room in the "authentic" old-school guesthouse where they were staying.

It flashed through Old Alice's head that this could be part of an elaborate revenge strategy, but New Alice looked at the five pairs of puppy-dog eyes waiting eagerly for her response and decided to risk it. Moments later, the small fleet of *motorini* was back on the road with Rick bringing up the rear, Alice clinging tightly to his torso. The wind whipped her hair around her face. It was the first time she had ever been on a motorbike, and she found it completely and utterly thrilling.

"You okay?" Rick shouted to her.

"Fine!" she shouted back, smiling so broadly her jaw ached.

"You can hold on tighter if you like. I won't break."

Alice liked him flirting, however tame it was. On reflection, she liked the flirting precisely because it was tame; somehow this lack of genuine frisson meant she was not being disloyal to Daniel.

"How come just one day in Rome?" said Rick.

"I'm meeting someone tomorrow night in Florence," she answered.

"Male or female?"

"I know it's hard to tell but I'm female," said Alice, hijacked by New Alice.

"No, your friend in Florence."

Not a great sense of humor, thought Alice. "Sorry? What was that?"

"I was asking about your friend in Florence."

"Sorry?"

"I was . . ." Rick gave up shouting into the wind. "Doesn't matter."

"You staying here long?"

"A week or so. To see the buildings. We're architects," he said, perking up again.

"You mean architecture students?"

"Yeah, students," said Rick, digesting the unintended put-down.

He had asked for it, of course. It was obvious they were students—scruffy, foul-smelling, backpacking students. They were all on summer break from the University of Sheffield and had left it too late to book accommodations in San Sebastián with the other half of their architecture chums. An opportunity had come up in Rome because, fortunately or unfortunately, Rick's sister's fiancé had balked at marrying her four weeks before the wedding, and Rick's sister's Roman bachelorette event was suddenly canceled, leaving rooms available near Piazza Navona. It wasn't a Spanish beach party, but at least it was Latin.

"Maybe we could meet up in Florence," said Rick.

Alice smiled into the wind. "Let's see how we do in Rome before we make any major commitments," she said.

They drove in silence for a while. When Alice turned again, she discovered Pea Green riding parallel, watching her. It startled her. Not because he was watching but because there was something deeply familiar about him. Why had she not noticed this before? Pea Green smiled and waved. She waved back but, unable to hold his gaze, turned away and looked over Rick's shoulder. In the lane next to them, directly in front of Pea Green, the brake lights of a black limousine lit up. For the second time in less than twenty minutes, Alice motioned madly to Pea Green. He turned back to the road and, clocking the slowing vehicle, swerved around it, narrowly avoiding a collision with Rick and Alice.

Jesus, thought Pea Green, *I've nearly crashed twice and fallen in love with the most beautiful girl I have ever seen in my entire life. What a day.*

FIVE

Saint Christopher and the Vicolo del Polverone

WE DO NOT SUFFER BY ACCIDENT.

—Jane Austen, *Pride and Prejudice*

Inside the black limousine, the Sardinian-born driver, Jean-Paul (whose mother had been a devoted Francophile), glanced in the rearview mirror at his two wealthy American tourists. Each stared bleakly out their respective windows, which gave him a chance to gawk at them. Despite the fact that they were obviously unhappy, Jean-Paul felt quite satisfied that they belonged together. They were a handsome pair, these two—they *matched,* and not in the creepy brother-and-sister style of some couples; they would make nice babies. It occurred to him that he would quite like to watch them making babies.

Jean-Paul glanced apologetically at the small medallion of Saint Christopher bobbing just below his rearview mirror, hoping that the saint had not intercepted his lascivious thought. Of course he knew this was ridiculous—Saint Christopher knew everything he was thinking—but instead of submitting to his default guilt position, Jean-Paul felt a small flash of rebellion. Christopher had been letting him down all morning, leading him from one traffic jam to another; maybe it was time to remind the holy big cheese who was driving whom around Roma.

In the backseat, Meg watched the ancient ruins whizzing by, planning the menu she would have served had her sixteen-year-old son, Campbell, submitted to her plans for a sit-down six-course birthday dinner on the tennis court for 120 rather than the small Australian-themed barbecue by the pool on which they eventually compromised.

The shape of the large field that they were passing penetrated her consciousness. "Circus Maximus," she said to no one in particular. The elongated oval-ended racetrack was almost obscured by overgrown grass, but she could still imagine the thundering of the charioteers. She turned to Alec and registered the slight sagging of skin around his jaw. No point mentioning it; he'd never agree to a nip and tuck. She was going to say, "This is what I love about Rome. You can drive through two thousand years of history like it's an everyday event." But she didn't. Instead she said, "Maybe we should try to find that hotel with the kissing concierge. What was his name?"

By the time Alec turned from his window, she was looking out hers.

"Bronco," he said.

"Bronco!" she exclaimed to her own reflection.

"Please don't pretend to forget. It's extremely irritating."

Ah, we're playing it like this, she thought.

In the driver's seat, Jean-Paul was also extremely irritated.

He had already turned off the Via Appia Nuova to avoid a traffic jam, only to get stuck in a crawl on the Via Appia Pignatelli. Now he was having to duck and weave through traffic one might expect in peak hour but not in the middle of the day. Up ahead, cars were grinding to a halt, unraveling his brilliant plan to skirt around this side of the Centro Storico. Jean-Paul avoided looking directly at the saint dangling in the peripheral vision of his left eye, but clearly *someone* had heard someone else thinking things they didn't mean to think and were now being punished for thinking. Well, he (Jean-Paul) wasn't taking it. Particularly from someone who wasn't a real saint anymore anyway.

Abandoning his plans for the Via Luigi Petroselli, Jean-Paul changed gears, threw a left and a right, and roared victoriously onto the Lungotevere that shed its name for a new one every block or so as it curled its way along the banks of the river Tiber. Meg noted the Tiber on her left and could hear the roar of the current as the river split into rapids around both sides of Tiber Island. They were a little off-course, weren't they? *Ah, what did it matter?* She had already paid for the limousine online; this was on the driver's dime, not hers. She was happy to enjoy the sights. And besides, she was not going to be distracted and let Alec's mean little comment fall by the wayside. She knew he had been waiting for her to respond and had deliberately left him hanging in the air.

Finally, she turned and, smiling at a point slightly above the top of his head, said, "Are you sure it was *Bronco*?"

"You know what his name was," he said.

"I prefer you when you're jealous. You get this really interesting edge."

"This is not an interesting edge," he replied. "This is fear of death."

Indeed, Jean-Paul was driving very fast, even for a Roman. When the traffic once again slowed before him it was the last straw; Christopher was clearly toying with him, and he would not be toyed with. So he peeled the limousine down the Via Giulia, running a red light and beeping at two young nuns in battleship-gray habits who had stepped onto the pedestrian crossing. The sisters leaped backward onto the sidewalk. *Ha!* thought Jean-Paul, smiling into his rearview mirror.

Catching his eye, Alec said, "Slow down please, driver." And then, recalling their initial exchange in broken English, searched for some Italian words that he hoped meant *slowly* or *softly* and added, "*Dolci, dolci.*"

Why is he saying "sweets"? Jean-Paul wondered. Did the American signore want to stop at a bakery? There was a very good *forno* not far in Campo de' Fiori. Without slowing, he turned to look at Alec. "Signore?"

Meg was no less concerned that the driver had completely turned away from the road to address them, but her pleasure in Alec's fear was greater than her own fear. Smiling at her reflection, she said helpfully, "You appear to be ordering dessert."

Alec signaled frantically at Jean-Paul, gesturing in staccato circles. "*Regardez la rue! La rue!*"

Making a mental note to treasure this moment always, Meg said, "I don't think he speaks French."

This was correct. If only Jean-Paul's mother had been with them, she would have been able to translate perfectly.

Realizing his error, Alec scrambled for some more Italian. "Um. *Via. La via dolce!*"

Finally, Jean-Paul turned back to the road but continued the conversation in the rearview mirror. "Ahh. *La Dolce Vita!* Si, signore, they make this film in Roma. Not here. On the other side, the other side!"

Alec looked across at his wife; she was limp with laughter.

"Help me," he said.

"Oh, don't be such a baby. This is how everyone drives here. When in Rome, you know."

"Signora?" asked Jean-Paul, assuming she had been talking to him.

"My husband was saying how he enjoys your driving. He likes going fast."

"Oh, fast, vroom, vroom," said Jean-Paul. Then, as an afterthought, he added, "Faster?"

"Oh, yes, please," said Meg.

Jean-Paul put his foot down; Meg felt the exhilarating acceleration; Alec looked slowly, murderously across at his wife.

Up ahead, a busload of French Jesuits stopped and started to disembark, smack-bang in the middle of the Via Giulia. There was no way around them without running over a few, an idea that Jean-Paul entertained for the briefest of moments. He knew that Christopher was behind this latest obstacle and frankly found the gaggle of black-frocked priests in white collars a tad predictable. Not to be outdone by his meddlesome saint, he suddenly turned the wheel, and the limousine's tires squealed across the cobblestone as they roared in to narrow Vicolo del Polverone.

This is where disaster struck.

Thirty meters up the Vicolo del Polverone on the left-hand side, a dusty blacksmith's window displayed a beautifully forged baby's cradle and a set of portable iron steps, ideal for accessing the top of a tall bookcase. Next door, a cavernous store sold vintage furniture, mostly art deco, but with some pieces dating back to pre-Christian times.

At that moment they were taking delivery of a large Chinese urn of uncertain and possibly scandalous provenance. The current owner of the urn, who identified herself only as "Maria" to the owner of the vintage store, had inherited it from her father, who claimed it was a gift from Princess Orietta Pogson Doria Pamphilj. Maria's father had worked as a domestic, specializing in hand polishing (with beeswax harvested from the family estate) the floor of the Palazzo Doria Pamphilj that took up an entire city block on the Via del Corso in the center of Rome. One day, in 1956 or 1963—Maria's father had forgotten which—when part of the roof collapsed after a heavy snowfall, Maria's father worked tirelessly through the night (with the other servants presumably) to clean up and rescue what was left of the broken antiquities below. As a sign of her undying gratitude, the princess presented him with a large blue-and-white Ming Dynasty urn.

Even as a little girl, Maria felt there was something fishy about this story. As an adult she suspected her father had probably pilfered it in the chaos after the ceiling collapsed; it would not have been out of character. All these years later, more than half a century after it had been "gifted," the urn remained uninsured. This puzzled Maria until it came into her hands, and she realized that to insure it, she would need to have it appraised—and if she had it appraised, certain unorthodoxies about its provenance might be established. So the giant urn sat in a corner of Maria's small apartment until, like many of her contemporaries, she started to feel the financial pinch of living in Rome and decided to sell it. Discreetly.

Which is how it came to be carried from a van by a sweating, round-bellied courier, just as a black limousine screeched around a corner and hurtled toward it.

Jean-Paul could see a large man grappling with a big vase inside the van. He could see the wooden ramp reaching from the ground to the van and made a quick estimation that he could squeeze past, clearing a couple of centimeters on each side. He did not, unfortunately, account for the gray bicycle with the straw basket chained to a street sign at the point where the *vicolo* narrowed to a single car width.

"Watch out!" Alec shouted.

Just as he was about to hit it, Jean-Paul clocked the bicycle and veered left. Two seconds later the left front wheel of the limousine connected with the ramp leading to the van, causing the car to roll to the right as it sped forward. For a moment it seemed the black car was trying to mount the white van in some bizarre mating ritual. At the top of the ramp, the terrified courier reeled backward, thrusting the urn forward to protect himself. It seemed to leap from his hands, counterattacking the attacking vehicle.

Inside the limousine, the world flipped onto its side. Jean-Paul screamed. Meg fell on top of Alec. The right side of Alec's head slammed into the car window. The car window cracked.

Outside, the urn hit the cobblestones and shattered.

Inside, Jean-Paul started to cry. Still attached to the rearview mirror, Saint Christopher swung victoriously over his head. Meg pulled herself away from Alec and looked at him. His eyes were closed. He wasn't moving. There was blood on the window near his head. He was unconscious—or dead. Meg slapped him hard. His eyes fluttered open.

"For fuck's sake," he said quietly.

The seventh and final king of Rome, Lucius Tarquinius Superbus, reigned from 535 B.C.E. until the revolution in 509 B.C.E. In the process of maneuvering himself to power, he had arranged the murder of his predecessor, his brother, and his wife. He was a tyrant so despised by his people that they established the Roman Republic, intending never to be ruled by his like again (ha!). Historians will tell you that the king fled Rome and lived comfortably in exile in the court of Aristodemus at Cumae, where he died in 495 B.C.E. I will tell you what really happened.

Tarquinius tripped down the steps of the Temple of Jupiter Optimus Maximus fleeing a mob of angry Romans and broke his neck. Despite the fact that he was already dead, they gave his body a thorough beating, dragged it across the city, and hurled it into the Tiber. In time, debris and silt accumulated around His Dead Highness and formed the foundation of what would become the Isola Tiberina. As it grew, the story of Tarquinius slipped into the mist, merging with myth and legend, but because of the darkness associated with its founding events, Romans avoided the island.

When a plague ravaged Rome in 293 B.C.E., the authorities used the island to isolate the contagiously ill, but it quickly overflowed with the sick and dying. Running out of room, the Roman senators consulted the Tiburtine Sibyl, who suggested they enlist the help of Aesculapius, the Greek god of healing and medicine, by building a temple in his honor. All agreed that this was the most practicable solution.

The plague passed, the temple was constructed, and the island began to forge a new identity as a place of healing. In 998, the emperor Otto III built a basilica on the ruins of Aesculapius's Temple, and in 1584, Pope Gregory XIII called the Hospitaller Order of St. John of God to Rome and asked them to run the Hospital of St. John Calybita there, upstream from the basilica. More than half a millennium's service later, it is still known as the Ospidale Fatebenefratelli. This cracks me up. It's not so funny in Italian, but when you translate it into English, it's the hospital of the Do-Good Brothers.

"The do-good brothers?" spluttered Meg Schack, when she was informed they were taking Alec there. "Sounds like a boy band!"

The ambulance driver exchanged a raised eyebrow with his white-uniformed companion and focused on the road ahead. They wailed down the Lungotevere and across the Ponte Cestio, the bridge connecting the south bank with Tiber Island and the hospital. Pale-skinned tourists and dark-skinned hawkers of knockoff designer handbags scattered from their path. The ambulance screeched to a halt. Meg shot out of its rear doors and raced through the swinging doors of the emergency ward.

Wild-eyed, she shouted, *"Dottore! Dottore! Pronto! Pronto!"*

A large male nurse wearing white scrubs and a navy-blue cardigan grabbed her immediately and tried to force her into a wheelchair.

"Not me, you idiot!" she hissed.

SIX

Piazza della Madonna dei Monti

IF WE WANT THINGS TO STAY AS THEY ARE,
THINGS WILL HAVE TO CHANGE.

—Giuseppe Tomasi de Lampedusa, *The Leopard*

The gleaming white Mercedes taxi drove into the gently sloping piazza, scattering a group of lively schoolchildren, who retreated to the pale octagonal steps of the Fontana di Piazza della Madonna dei Monti, a simple, three-tiered travertine fountain installed to provide water for the locals in 1595. Outside the Hotel Montini, Constance paid and tipped the driver, Gianni. Having endured a vivid and gruesome description of the birth of his third son, they were now on first-name terms. Blasted by the Roman heat, Lizzie wrangled the luggage, while Gianni protested from the air-conditioned comfort of the driver's seat, shouting at his credit card machine to hurry up so he could help the lovely signora with her bags.

It was early afternoon, siesta time, and the two wooden doors of the crumbling hotel were firmly shut. Gianni fretted about this, but the two women ushered him off, as he was already late picking up his elderly mother for her podiatrist appointment.

Lizzie pushed the brass buzzer and banged on the door for good measure. A young waiter appeared from the vine-encrusted trattoria next door but decided there was little here to hold his interest and retreated. Constance looked around. It had been *such a long time* since her last visit.

Nothing much has changed, she thought. *Except you're not here.*

Ah, but I am, her husband chuckled.

And he is, too, she remembered. *In a box.*

The piazza felt as intimate as it always had, bordered on one side by the small white church of Madonna del Pascolo and Saints Sergius and Bacchus, and the yellow-walled palazzo Casa Santa Sofia. On the other side, two villas huddled next to each other, one deep yellow, one pale pink, both with pale-gray shutters. Locals sat at tables outside the piazza's restaurants under stained white market umbrellas, fanning the hot air with menus.

On the far side of the piazza, more sunny yellow buildings were overshadowed by the looming sidewall of Santa Maria ai Monti. A little girl in a pale-blue dress waved to the old ladies from a doorway. Constance waved back and turned to find Lizzie peering up at the bust of the strange goat-lion creature that supported a small Juliet balcony, directly above the front door.

"Is that thing new?" said Lizzie.

Constance turned. "What?"

"That, the goat thing."

"I don't think so. Why?"

"I don't like it."

"I shall have them remove it immediately."

Lizzie smiled. "When is Charles coming?"

Constance sat down on the largest of her bags. "Remind me not to complain about the heat," she said. "It's so *English*." And then she added breezily, "He's not."

"Not what?"

"Coming," said Constance. "Charles isn't coming."

Charles and Marina were Constance and Henry's two adult children. Marina, an oenologist based in Bordeaux, was married to a dull equestrian who had sired three children, now all in their teens. Charles, a consultant with the IMF, had adopted two children from the slums of Buenos Aires with his Argentinean polo-playing partner, Alfonso. Henry had made no specific requests about their presence in Rome, but Lizzie had *assumed* they would be here for such an important event. She was on the brink of registering her dismay when a man finally answered the door. He introduced himself rather mournfully as Bronco and carried their bags inside as if someone had threatened to beat him if he did not.

Constance stood in the foyer and looked around. She could not remember precisely how many years it was since she had been here, but it was all exactly as it had been. The lift was only large enough for two. Bronco said he would take the bags up first and then come back down and get them. Constance said they would take the stairs and meet him up there. Bronco shrugged, closed the mesh doors of the elevator, and rose skyward.

Lizzie could contain herself no longer. "Charles isn't *coming?*"

Constance started to climb the stairs. "Some conference in Berlin," she said, "and before you go making a scene, he can't get out of it."

Lizzie started to follow. "Not coming! To his own father's—"

Constance cut Lizzie short. "He's done enough, Lizzie. It's time he moves on. It's time we all moved on."

They clomped up the stairs in silence for one flight.

"Well, that's a very odd thing to say," Lizzie said finally. "Your husband, my brother, his father has—"

Constance swirled on Lizzie with greater ferocity than she'd intended. "Stop right there, girlie. I will not spend this trip regurgitating our misery. I need to press on. I need you to press on with me."

She turned and resumed her ascent.

Lizzie followed, flummoxed. "What about Marina?" she asked.

"She's flying in from Paris this afternoon."

"Good. Because Aunt Lizzie would have quite a lot to say on the matter if she wasn't."

"I'll bet she would," said Constance.

Lizzie had always felt at ease criticizing Constance's children because she loved them as if they were her own. She had never made a conscious decision not to have children; she simply got busy elsewhere. In an attempt to prolong the Swinging Sixties for as long as she possibly could, Lizzie had left the London hospital where she was nursing and moved to a commune in Provence. She remained there through a series of unhappy love affairs until the midseventies, when she developed an interest in wine making and, supported financially by Henry and Constance, had restored a derelict vineyard in Pomerol. To everyone's surprise it was a success. It was only when Charles and Marina began visiting regularly on school breaks that Lizzie began to ache for children of her own, but an appropriate co-parent never showed up, and besides, she was completely occupied with her business. It had nevertheless thrilled Lizzie that Marina had chosen to follow her into wine making, and she took every opportunity to dote on her niece and nephew, and her great-nephews and nieces as well.

They reached the top floor to find Bronco waiting for them, smiling. With a shock, Constance realized that he might be attempting to look seductive. It wasn't that she was too old to be seduced; even at her great age, men flirted with her. It was more that Bronco, with the exception of his luxuriant moustache, looked so worn out. She bustled past him and into the room. Their bags were sitting there waiting for them, but she knew at once that she was in the wrong place.

"No, no, this isn't it," said Constance.

"But, signora," said Bronco, "this is the room you asked for."

"It may be the room we asked for," said Constance, "but it's not the room we want."

"Constance, does it matter?" said Lizzie. "We're in the right hotel."

The room looked perfectly lovely to Lizzie. A little faded, perhaps, but large and light with an enormous fireplace and two sets of tall french doors (did one call them french doors in Italy?) opening to a verdant roof garden. Outside she glimpsed potted lemons laden with fruit and a riotous collection of geraniums. *Lovely.*

"It mattered to Henry," said Constance. "He wanted us to stay in room 34."

"This is room 34," said Bronco.

"No, it's not," said Constance.

"Perhaps you just don't recognize it," said Lizzie.

"I'll recognize the floor."

"The floor? You'll recognize the floor from thirty-eight years ago?"

"How did you remember that?"

"What?"

"That it was thirty-eight years ago."

Lizzie shrugged. She had no idea how or why she remembered. She just did. She was more concerned about Constance, who stood transfixed, staring at the blue-green tiles of the floor. *What on earth is going on?*

"There was a small tile, loose. I took it for luck," said Constance. "I carried it around with me for years." She offered a smile to Bronco. "This is the wrong room."

Bronco took a long breath and muttered something quietly, but not quietly enough. He had no idea that both the old ladies standing in front of him spoke Italian and therefore had understood that he had just said, "Probably got the wrong hotel, crazy old lady."

Lizzie and Constance exchanged the smallest of smiles and entered an unspoken agreement not to let Bronco know that they there were both fluent in his native tongue. Not yet, anyway. They were scary old ladies, and scary old ladies conserved such information for the moment when it would wreak the most havoc.

Bronco slapped his forehead in a lavishly Latin gesture of forgetfulness and said, "There is an e-mail for you," adding unnecessarily, "I forget."

As part of his elaborate plans for their Roman sojourn, Henry had banned smartphones and laptops, insisting they travel old-school. Constance asked Bronco, not very hopefully, if the room had any means by which she could access the e-mail. She imagined herself struggling to use an old clunker at one of those dreadful Internet cafés and made a mental note to disinfect the keyboard first. Bronco proudly led Constance to the dresser, where it was already printed out, waiting for her. She scanned the e-mail and related its substance to Lizzie.

Marina had fallen from one of her horses. Nothing too serious, but she had sprained her ankle. The long and the short of it was she wasn't coming.

"I'm so glad I didn't have children," said Lizzie. "They're so disappointing."

Constance felt something tugging at her sleeve. She turned to see a boy of ten or eleven, his shining white smile and flashing dark eyes embodying mischievousness itself. He stepped toward the door and motioned for her to follow. The moment Bronco saw the boy, he let fly with an invective of *Italiano* so fast and furious that, despite their excellent comprehension, Constance and Lizzie failed to follow. Whatever he said, though, was clearly of little consequence, as the boy took no notice of him at all.

The boy led Constance into the hall and opened the door

of the next room. He swept his hand in a gracious arc, inviting her to enter, which she did. Lizzie followed. Once again, Constance studied the floor. The room was almost a clone of the first one, but the tiles were different here, a purer, brighter blue. She looked up at Lizzie, smiling.

Lizzie was about to say *Oh thank God,* but Constance suddenly frowned and started scanning the tiles again. Bronco joined the boy at the doorway, and they all watched as Constance appeared to hunt around the floor. She stopped at an old Persian rug and bent down. Using the bed to steady herself with one hand, she flipped back the corner with the other. One of the blue tiles was missing.

"Oh," said Constance.

"What?" said Lizzie.

"The tile," said Constance. "It's gone."

"You just said you took it," said Lizzie.

"Yes, the first time we came, but then I put it back," said Constance, "on our last visit. Of course, that was thirty-eight years ago. Lord knows what's happened to it."

She looked around, satisfied she was in the right place. "Anyway, the point is, this is the room," she said.

"But it's room 36," said Lizzie, peering at the door, inwardly berating herself for throwing a pointless wrench in the works.

"They change the numbers," said the little boy, "a few years ago."

Once again Bronco smacked his forehead. "They change the numbers!"

Constance bent to the boy's height and asked his name.

"Marco," he said.

She thanked him in impeccable Italian and asked if they could have this room, please. Marco said yes. Lizzie watched Bronco realize that Constance could speak Italian. Then to assure Bronco that both of them had heard and comprehended his earlier insult, she also addressed Marco in Italian, asking about room service and breakfast. Bronco began to rub his forehead and shuffle his feet.

"I get your bags," he said, backing out of the room.

When he had gone, Marco said, "I'm sorry about my cousin. He lacks charm."

"Well put, Marco," said Constance.

Marco was very pleased. He was learning English as part of a master plan to become a guide for American tourists, who, everyone knew, tipped large amounts of money. With the money, he would buy his family out of this hotel and then open more hotels and become rich and drive a red Ferrari 365 GTC coupe. Possibly he would become famous as well. But the first step, he knew, was mastering the language of international commerce. English.

"Are you famous, Contessa?" said Marco, lining Constance up for a five-euro tip.

"No, I'm not," said Constance, seeing right through the charm but enchanted anyway.

"I think you should be," said Marco.

He took Constance's hand and kissed it.

Lizzie put her hand over her mouth to stifle a laugh.

"Don't you just love Roma?" said Constance.

SEVEN

Via dei Coronari

BUT HE THAT DARES NOT GRASP THE THORN
SHOULD NEVER CRAVE THE ROSE.
—Anne Brontë, *The Narrow Way*

At regular intervals along the irregular avenue, elaborate iron brackets reached into the air, each limb bearing a glass-paned coach light. Rick parked his *motorino*, but Alice remained seated for a moment, watching the lights flicker on, lost in the rich egg-yolky haze of their illumination. The sky was fading but still bright, which made the lamps seem an unnecessary but delightfully theatrical touch.

The other boys dismounted their *motorini* and peeled their backpacks from sweat-stained shirts. Pea Green tapped Alice on the shoulder and said, "I'll go see if they have a room for you." He scooted into a tiny dead-end street rendered with such an infinite variety of autumnal patinas that Alice began to search for her cell phone so she could take some photographs. As she was doing this, New Alice told Old Alice that she was not to spend her precious time documenting the experience; she was to experience the experience. *Look,* she told herself. *Look properly.*

Alice stopped and looked. The Via di San Simone was something to behold. Ten paces wide by thirty paces deep, it opened behind her to the Via dei Coronari, the Piazza San Salvatore in Lauro, and, beyond, the beige brick monolith of San Salvatore church; to her left and right, the little square was bounded by two four-story villas with cracked and crumbling walls. A combination of arched and square iron-grilled windows, some with dusty shutters, punctuated the opposing façades. Below, a smattering of patrons sat in curved iron chairs outside a gelateria and a pizzeria, chatting animatedly around iron tables with tiled tops.

Fifteen paces into the little square, a large stone staircase, edged with travertine and pitted with age, hugged the exterior of the right-hand villa, climbing toward a set of four bottle-green timber doors, each inset at head-height with an iron lace panel. At street level, the stairs extended halfway across the street, but by the time they made their way to the green doors, shifting slightly and changing angles, they retracted to a few paces width.

How, Alice wondered, without symmetry or apparent planning, did it all manage to achieve such glorious composition? She felt light-headed. Heat beat at her temples. She peeled off her cotton vest and turned toward the sound of running water. Flanked by pots of variegated glossy-leaved shrubs, a small gray iron fountain the size of a New York fire hydrant burbled water from a thin, curved spout. Alice lowered her hand and filled her palm; the water was cooler than she'd expected. She splashed her face, shuddering involuntarily, then, without thinking, squatted, formed a cup with her joined hands, and began to gulp.

"I wouldn't do that if I were you!" said Blue Backpack.

Alice paused and turned to make sure he was talking to her. He was.

Standing next to him, Rick nodded authoritatively. "You could get dysentery."

Alice knew, of course, that there were many cities in the world where it was essential to boil the water before drinking. She was pretty sure that Rome was not one of them. Already on their brief journey through the city she had noted a number of small fountains like this, running freely. If they were not for drinking, what would be their purpose other than to waste water? She turned and resumed drinking.

"No, really," said Rick with some force, "I wouldn't."

Pushing his round John Lennon glasses up his nose, Blue Backpack decided it might be more constructive to outline the specific physical consequences of Alice's promiscuous gulping. "You'll get really bad stomach cramps, and then your feces will liquefy and erupt in . . . ergh!"

A black-leathered elbow thrust into his ribs suddenly silenced Blue Backpack.

Alice laughed and snorted water into her lungs, coughing and sputtering.

Rubbing his rib, Blue Backpack turned defensively to Rick. "I was only trying to—"

But once again he was interrupted—this time by Signore Giorgio Vincenzino, who lived in an apartment around the corner above the hairdressing salon that he had run before arthritis forced premature retirement. Unlike many Romans,

Signore Giorgio liked tourists; he enjoyed seeing his city swell and almost burst with humanity at certain times of the year. In his working years he had been grateful for the extra customers, but more than that, he simply enjoyed the *otherness* of foreigners. Especially pretty foreigners like the young woman—English or possibly American, he guessed—trying to drink from the street fountain in Via San Simone.

"Signorina! Signorina!"

Alice turned to see an older Italian gentleman with jet-black hair walking toward her. It did not occur to her for a second that he might dye his hair, which he did, every third Thursday after morning Mass, but it did occur to her that it was far too hot for him to be wearing a three-piece suit and tie, however lightweight and impeccably cut it might be. Were they to engage in a conversation on this matter, which they did not, Signore Giorgio would have vehemently disagreed: regardless of the temperature, it was always incumbent upon a gentleman to appear finely attired when dining in public, which he had just done with his cousin Alfreda at the excellent but inexpensive Da Tonino on the Via del Governo Vecchio.

"No, no, you drink it like this, see?" said the signore. He blocked the hole at the end of the spout with his finger, causing a little geyser of water to shoot upward from another hole farther up the neck of the spout.

"Oh, look, it was even designed for drinking." Alice made a great show of drinking down the cool, fresh water.

Signore Giorgio turned to her British backpacking audience. "You want to try?"

"Oh no, *grazie*, signore. Englishmen are very weak," said Alice. "They only drink water from their mommies' houses;

otherwise, it makes them sick." Signore Giorgio didn't catch all the *Inglese* because she spoke too quickly, but he did understand that the pretty girl was enjoying a joke at the expense of the eager boys.

Slick Rick pushed Alice out of the way and drank from the fountain. Then Blue Backpack pushed Rick out of the way and drank, then Pink Polo pushed Blue Backpack out of the way. Alice tried to push her way back in, but Pink Polo flicked water at her, and Blue Backpack elbowed her out of the way. At this point, Pea Green appeared at the top of the stairs. "Come on up!" he called down to them.

That evening, Florentina, who ran her little guesthouse like clockwork, an aberration that many credited to her German grandmother, served pasta early at 8:15 P.M. Normally she was a stickler for 9:00 P.M., the traditional time for the evening meal in Rome, but seeing some of the boys rubbing their stomachs, she could tell that they were starving. Also, truth be told, she was meeting her Web designer later in preparation for relaunching Villa Florentina as Florentina B&B and wanted to get dinner over and done with as soon as possible.

Florentina held back on the garlic and chili in the ragù for the pasta because she knew that English boys had bland tastes. She was glad for the presence of the pretty American girl at her table, as it had put the boys on their best behavior. Sometimes she had the most appallingly mannered guests, especially groups of students. It was not uncommon for her to wrangle food fights. She hated to see her handmade fettuccine flying about the table. But these boys were not like that. They were pleasantly subdued. Strangely subdued, now she came to think about it.

Alice sat at the dinner table feeling awkward. A pall of restraint had descended over the boys, and she knew it was her fault; this was not the rowdy, gregarious gang that she had encountered at the airport. They were modifying themselves on her behalf, and she did not want it. Even the obnoxious one in pink was quiet. She wished she had stuck to her original plans and gone to her hostel near Termini.

Halfway through the meal, Rick looked around the dinner table, feeling a little . . . *wonky* was the best word for it. He could see that his friends were not in the best shape either. Perhaps it was the change in weather. It had been quite cool when they left Sheffield, and Rome, by contrast, felt like an oven.

Pink Polo put down his fork and announced that he was full. Next to him, Blue Backpack wrapped both his arms around his abdomen and doubled in two, almost planting his face in his pasta. With a slightly panicked look on his face, he asked whether there was a toilet downstairs and immediately absented himself. Pink Polo asked if there was a toilet upstairs and also left. They could hear his urgent footfalls thumping up the stairs when Pea Green asked to be excused as well.

Florentina knew this was not food poisoning—not from her kitchen anyway, praise Jesus—because it was all happening too fast. Alice, on the other hand, knew exactly whose fault this was. She felt sick. Not as sick as the boys, or a least a different kind of sick. Listening to the sounds of flushing toilets, opening and closing doors, and moans of misery, she waited for retribution to strike.

EIGHT

The Do-Good Sister of Via Margutta

WE ALWAYS DECEIVE OURSELVES TWICE ABOUT THE
PEOPLE WE LOVE——FIRST TO THEIR ADVANTAGE,
THEN TO THEIR DISADVANTAGE.
—Albert Camus, *A Happy Death*

In a blue-curtained cubicle, the doctor flicked her glossy chest-nut hair over her shoulder like a model in a television commercial. She applied a third and final stitch to the cut on Alec's forehead while he studied the amber flecks in her hazel eyes, trying not to flinch unmanfully.

"Breathe. You're not breathing," she said, concentrating on tying off the thread.

Alec realized that he had indeed been holding his breath. He let go, surprised by how much better he felt. He became conscious of her breath on his forehead, steady and warm. She stepped back and shifted focus from the wound to the man.

"You'll have a small scar," she said, "but this is a face that can carry a scar."

"You mean so ugly it doesn't matter?" said Alec, secretly alarmed but not wanting to appear vain.

"No, that's not what I mean," she said, looking boldly at him.

Alec felt his body stir and quicken. He smiled and discovered it hurt to smile.

"Where are you staying?" she asked.

"Um, some place off Piazza del Popolo."

"That's just near me. Near my apartment."

Behind the doctor Meg appeared, bearing two espressos in white waxed-paper cups. "Your English is excellent!" she said with an edge intended to communicate that she had intercepted the doctor's attempted flirtation with her husband.

"Thank you," said the doctor, rounding her vowels crisply. "That would be because I am English."

Alec piped up with an introduction. "Meg, this is Dr. Stephanie . . ." he faltered, remembering her first name but not her last.

"Cope," she said. "Stephanie Cope."

"Dr. Cope, this is my wife, Meg."

"You're married," said the doctor.

"To each other, yes!" said Meg merrily.

"Sorry, I didn't realize." Stephanie briefly contemplated stabbing herself with the stitching needle or nearest scalpel. *Will I ever develop a capacity for self-editing?* she despaired.

"Oh, don't be sorry," said Meg. "We're really very happy."

They all laughed, but Meg laughed the hardest because she was the most hilarious. She downed her shot of espresso. Then she downed Alec's shot for good measure.

As Dr. Stephanie put a bandage over Alec's stitches, he took great care not to look at her.

"I'll take the stitches out in a week or so," said the doctor.

"We'll be back home by then," said Meg.

"We're only here for a day," said Alec.

"Only one day in Rome?" said the doctor.

"You know us Americans. Very short attention spans," said Meg, marveling that she had never pursued a career in stand-up. They all laughed again.

Dr. Cope discharged Alec and, as it was the end of her shift and she would be heading home, offered them a lift to their hotel. Alec accepted, and Meg declined, then Meg declined on behalf of both of them. Out in the waiting room, Meg told a triage nurse to order a taxi. The nurse was so taken aback that it did not occur to him to say no.

Outside, the sky had intensified to a deep brilliant blue, electrified by the setting sun. Having absorbed the heat of the day, the stones of Rome were now radiating it back in eddies. They waited with their bags on the small pedestrian island in the parking area until it became clear that no taxi was coming. Meg tried calling one from her cell but could not understand the stream of Italian that poured forth, so she hung up. She called back again and shouted instructions over the top of the person speaking, but this had no effect either. Eventually, Alec persuaded her to cross the small bridge that connected the island to the rest of the city and try their luck on the busy Lungotevere where traffic was passing all the time.

Despite assurances that he was perfectly fine, Meg forced Alec to sit on their luggage while she attempted to wave down a taxi. A powder-blue Fiat Bambino slowed, and Dr. Cope wound down the driver's window. "Come on," she said. "You'll never get a cab at this hour." Meg begged to differ; it had been her experience, with the right dress and shoes, that she could hail a cab in Rome at any time. Nevertheless, she accepted the offer with a smile.

It soon became apparent that the only way to squeeze the three of them and their bags into the silly little car was to wedge Meg in the backseat and feed the bags through the sunroof on top of her. Alec pretended to be concerned for Meg's comfort, but she could tell that he was loving the sight of her with limbs enfolded, face squished against the side window. *You'll keep,* she thought.

As Stephanie negotiated the traffic like a rally driver, it occurred to Meg that she was one of those annoying women who did everything well. In the front seat Alec was thinking exactly the same thing about the pretty doctor, only he didn't find it annoying at all.

"This is very kind," said Alec.

Stephanie flashed him a smile in return. "Actually, you're doing me the favor," she said. "I can't tell you what a relief it is to be able to prattle away in English for a while."

"So what brought you to Rome?" he asked.

Dr. Stephanie sighed. "I spent the last few years in a medical unit in Gaza, and before that I was at an orphanage in Baghdad," she said. "So I guess I'm going through some compassion fatigue. I guess that's what you'd call it. Anyway, Rome seemed like the perfect place to recoup. That sounds very self-indulgent, doesn't it?"

"Not at all," said Alec, delighted that his wife was listening.

With her face pressed against the window, Meg was still able to roll her eyes.

The Fiat swept around the great graceful oval of the Piazza del Popolo, past its ancient central obelisk, and headed down the busy shopping strip of Via del Babuino, brimming with Romans and tourists alike. Meg usually thrived in the evening heat, but she was beginning to melt.

"What brings you to Rome?" Dr. Stephanie asked.

"What brings us to Rome?" Alec said.

Meg had no idea which way he was going to go with this. He might confess the true nature of their—what had he called it?—*vacuous and unimportant* mission, seizing the opportunity to contrast the nobility of the woman in the front seat with the superficiality of the woman in the backseat. *Or.* He may be too embarrassed to confess the pale motivation for their journey and simply make something up.

Both would have been defeats in Meg's eyes, so she leaped in before he could say anything more. "We're here on a secret mission," she said. "We could tell you what it is, but then of course we'd have to kill you." It was a tired line, but it was edgy, Meg thought; not quite war-zone edgy, but it did the job.

"Oh, look, this is my street! And yours now," said Dr. Stephanie. As she turned right from the Vicolo dell'Orto di Napoli into the Via Margutta, she gestured airily to her left. "Fellini used to live down there."

Of course he did, thought Meg. *Of course you live on the most stupidly beautiful street where a famous film director once held court. Of course.* Just then, to add insult to injury, all the way down the Via Margutta, the coach lights flickered on. It was a magical sight.

"And I'm in there," said Stephanie, pointing to a magnificent courtyard draped in Virginia creeper and lanterns of purple wisteria. "It's just a tiny studio."

Meg immediately imagined a vast rococo suite, complete with its own walnut-floored ballroom, but if they had stopped to look in, she would have seen that Stephanie was not exaggerating. The studio was tiny. It was also beautiful. It had been a part of a coach house, built into the boundary wall of the garden of a Renaissance villa. The villa had long been divided into flats and studios, once inhabited by painters and sculptors. On the ground floor a few galleries still displayed art, but this was clearly no longer an area for struggling artists—or anyone who struggled, for that matter.

The owner of Stephanie's building had given her the studio for very low rent in the hope of forging a closer bond with the lovely doctor, preferably every Tuesday and Thursday night, when his wife was at bridge. But Stephanie, oblivious, in her Anglo-Saxon way, to the kind of Latin contract she had unwittingly entered, simply smiled and laughed when her benefactor made the first of several advances. Eventually, he had given up.

Moving slowly now through the press of pedestrians, they approached a wall fountain of two gargoyles mounted on angular stone that gave it an odd, military air. As they passed, Meg saw a girl place a champagne flute under the gargoyle's stream and fill it with water. It occurred to her, not for the first time, that nothing in Rome, not a single gesture, ever seemed ordinary. The car passed antique shops and exclusive boutiques, jewels gleaming enticingly from subtly lit alcoves. A gallery blasted great splashes of color from huge vivid canvases.

"This is you," said Stephanie as she pulled into the entrance of the Hotel San Marco lined with terra-cotta pots of lovingly tended Buxus and azaleas. Alec looked up at the magnificent yellow-washed palazzo draped luxuriously in glossy vines. A doorman dressed in a cool gray silk suit opened the door and extracted the luggage through the sunroof so Meg could unfold her sweaty limbs and clamber out of the backseat.

It was not an elegant entrance, but Meg was well pleased with the destination.

"Actually, I've got the day off tomorrow," Stephanie began to say. "I could—"

Meg cut her off. "We'll be running around like crazy people, but thanks for the offer."

Alec shook Stephanie's hand and added, "And thanks for the brain surgery."

"All part of the service," said Stephanie. "It was great to meet you."

"You, too," said Alec. Without looking at his wife, he added, "Would you like to join us for some supper?"

"Oh, Alec, the poor doctor wants to get home and relax," said Meg brightly. "Besides, we haven't even checked in yet."

Stephanie took the hint and said her good-byes.

"Maybe next time," said Alec.

He watched the doctor execute an awkward five-point turn and head back down the Via Margutta. Then he went inside and joined Meg, who was checking in.

"I think she wanted to stay," he said to his wife.

"I think she wanted to have your babies, though Lord knows how she'd schedule it between immunizing the or-

phans and saving the rebel soldiers," said Meg without paus-
ing from searching in the recesses of her vast vintage Gucci
shoulder bag for their passports.

"I prefer you when you're jealous," said Alec. "You get this
really interesting edge."

Meg excused herself from the desk clerk. She took a breath
and faced her husband. A summation of her adventure thus
far formed in her head: She'd just flown halfway around the
world and been in a car wreck that she was partly if not
wholly responsible for; a car wreck that had caused the de-
struction of an irreplaceable and uninsured Chinese urn as
well as almost killing him (her husband) and an obese father
of eight who worked part-time as a courier. She'd been in an
ambulance, taken to hospital, and accosted by a hairy nurse.
She was tired and hungry and badly in need of a shower, and
she didn't give a flying fig about some British twit rushing
around the world saving everyone.

She was on the brink of sharing all this with Alec when
she suddenly thought better of it. Instead she flashed him one
of her smiles and said, "Let's go have an Aperol Spritz, okay?"

NINE

Ponte Sant'Angelo

THERE IS A LAND OF THE LIVING AND A LAND
OF THE DEAD AND THE BRIDGE IS LOVE,
THE ONLY SURVIVAL, THE ONLY MEANING.
—Thornton Wilder, *The Bridge of San Luis Rey*

During the Middle Ages, huge numbers of pilgrims flocked to Rome from all over Europe. As part of their holy journey to the basilica of Saint Peter, they would make their way down the Via dei Coronari, stopping to buy religious souvenirs from the rosary bead vendors, the *Coronari,* who lined the street. Afterward, they would cross the river over the bridge, Ponte Sant'Angelo, and walk through a maze of streets into the Vatican. Just before they reached the bridge, a Roman arch and a cluster of buildings caused the passage to narrow, and on busy days the crowds would often be funneled to a standstill at this point. Pilgrims would sometimes panic, pushing and shoving in a most unholy manner.

I will never forget one terrible day in 1450. The veil of Saint Veronica was a hugely popular relic back then. It was a cloth, miraculously impregnated with an image of the Savior's face after Veronica had wiped it on the path to Calvary. At the time the relic was so embedded in popular culture that it was referred to simply as "the Veronica," and when displayed at the Vatican, as it regularly was, thousands flocked to see it.

On this particular day, word came from the Vatican that the Veronica was to be taken down. Pilgrims panicked and rushed to the basilica lest they miss one of its main attractions. When they reached the bridge, there was such a crush around the arch that people fell underfoot and were trampled. In desperation the crowd surged over the bridge. The balustrades collapsed, and pilgrims toppled into the Tiber. In the end hundreds died, crushed or drowned, among them a gypsy girl named Angela.

Angela had been one of my charges. Recently widowed, she was supporting a one-year-old boy and an invalid father. I had been in the process of brokering a romance between her and a potter named Melozzo when an extraordinary thing happened. I became enchanted with her. A dazzling truthfulness in the directness of her gaze had somehow enraptured me. I found myself frequenting Melozzo's tile store, where she worked. One day as she was locking up for the night, Angela paused and said to the room, empty except for the piles of tiles, "I go because I know I will return." I decided then that I would make this humble tile shop my base, my home, and wait here for Angela to return. The next day, the balustrades collapsed, and she drowned in the Tiber, one of hundreds.

In response to this terrible loss of life, Pope Sixtus IV ordered the demolition of the arch as well as the buildings at the entrance to the bridge. It was a wise decision; the number of visiting pilgrims continued to grow, but the tragedy never repeated. In time, no one was left to remember a single name from the hundreds who had fallen. No one except me.

Eventually, via circuitous means, I was able to inspire Pope Clement VII to commission statues of the apostles and prophets to guard the bridge and honor the dead. They stood on that bridge for a hundred years in remembrance of Angela, but somehow it was not enough.

When Pope Clement IX commissioned the brilliant Gian Lorenzo Bernini to replace the stucco statues with ten astonishing marble angels, he thought it was his idea. I am aware that this is a grand claim to make, particularly given that Clement is no longer with us to refute it, but the inspiration was actually mine, transmitted to the pope via the newly laid floor tiles in his bedchamber. I do not make this claim to appear clever or powerful but merely to establish the facts. The bridge, with its angels standing sentinel, provides passage for pilgrims six centuries later. But be in no doubt about this: if ever there was a bridge built of love, it is this one. Among the genii of Rome, the Ponte Sant'Angelo is kindly referred to as the *Ponte d'Angela*.

Heading down the Via di Panico, Constance and Lizzie glimpsed a mighty set of wings and knew they were near. A breeze from the river brought blessed relief from the dusky heat, cooling their sweat-dampened clothes. Lizzie offered for the third or fourth time to share the load of the Henry box that Constance was carrying inside a Harrods bag. Once again her sister-in-law refused.

Outside the Ponte Sant'Angelo Methodist Church, the two

women paused to listen to a spinto soprano singing Puccini from within. Constance put down the Harrods bag and rested. Then they crossed the Lungotevere Tor di Nona and paused, briefly this time, to take in the bridge. A diminutive elderly man, bent almost in two, shuffled toward them, one hand working a cane, the other holding an empty cap. He reached toward Constance with this cap, smiling a toothless grin.

"He's a gypsy," said Lizzie, sotto voce, looking everywhere but at him.

"I know that," said Constance, gripping her Harrods bag.

"Don't give him any money. He'll follow us."

Constance uncharacteristically obeyed her sister-in-law. "*Mi dispiace. Buonasera,*" she said to the man.

The man bowed low, twisted his face up toward Constance, offered another smile, and returned her greeting without malice or disappointment. Lizzie immediately felt mean. Why did she stop Constance like that? What harm would it have done to hand him a couple of euros? For a moment she contemplated rushing after him, but then she remembered there were more pressing matters at hand.

Henry had requested that his ashes be scattered by the Ponte Sant'Angelo, and finally they were here. The old ladies walked to the middle of the bridge. Constance rested the Harrods bag on the balustrade and removed the Henry box. The sun hung low in the sky; the air was thick with heat and honey-colored light. The cooling breeze rippled the surface of the Tiber and caressed the world.

The moment was perfect. Lizzie rested her hand on Constance's hand.

"I'll never forget scattering Angus Millington into the sea

at Dover," said Constance. "Perfectly fine day. Not a cloud in the sky, hardly the mention of a breeze, until Daphne tipped the ashes out of the urn. Then—*whoosh*—there was this enormous gust of wind, and suddenly we were all covered in bits of Angus. Up our noses. In the ears. Daphne was mortified, of course. We all were. But we did laugh afterward."

This was not the sacred moment Lizzie had imagined for the scattering of her brother's ashes. She looked at Constance, wondering what was going on.

"Possibly not the best timing for that story," said Constance, "but do let's make sure we're upwind of Henry." She turned to Lizzie and observed a couple of stray hairs, escaped from a bobby pin, trailing in front of her face. "Oh no, we're fine; the breeze is on our backs."

"Constance?"

"Yes, girlie?"

"Are you all right?"

"I'm a bit nervy."

"Of course you are, sweetheart."

Lizzie put her hand on Constance's back and gave her a supportive pat.

Constance twisted away. The Henry box rested on the balustrade of the bridge, but Constance made no move to open it.

"Would you like me to help you?" said Lizzie.

"No, no. Here we go."

Clutching the Henry box, Constance bent as far as she could to look down into the water. Lizzie wondered for a moment whether she was going to throw the whole kit and caboodle into the river. "You still have the lid on," she said gently.

Constance nodded. Lizzie looked around. While they did have official permission to bring Henry's ashes to Italy, they had not actually asked permission to release him into the Tiber. And she certainly didn't want to be negotiating now with the Polizia di Stato or the Carabinieri, or the Guardia di Finanza, or the Polizia Penitenziaria, or the Corpo Forestale dello Stato, or the Polizia Provinciale, or the Polizia Municipale.

"Are we waiting for something in particular, darling?" said Lizzie.

"In a moment, when the sun is a little lower—oh, here we go—the angels will turn red."

Lizzie turned to look at the ten white Bernini angels hovering around them. They had already turned sunset pink, and now, as the sun bled into the horizon, they turned red, a deep fiery red. Lizzie held her breath, witnessing a miracle. This would be the moment.

But nothing happened. Lizzie did not look at her sister-in-law but could tell that she was not moving. Soon the statues began to fade. She looked to the horizon as the sun melted into it. Finally, Constance started to remove the lid of the box. Then she paused.

"I'll help," said Lizzie. "We'll do it together."

"Not yet," said Constance.

Lizzie gently put her hands on the lid of the Henry box. Constance tried to move the box away from her, but Lizzie gripped the box.

"I can't," said Constance plainly.

"It's getting dark," said Lizzie firmly.

Lizzie started to draw the box away from Constance. She could feel Constance yield. Then without explanation

Constance gripped the box and tried to pull it back toward her. Lizzie, however, was determined and did not loosen her grip. It hovered between them, marooned by equal and opposite forces. To break the impasse, Lizzie yanked the box. Startled, Constance stumbled back, wrenching it from Lizzie's grip.

"Stop it!" said Constance.

Feeling as if she had suddenly reentered the earth's atmosphere, Lizzie said, "I'm sorry, darling. I'm so sorry."

"Tomorrow. Can we come back tomorrow?" said Constance. "In the day? In the light?"

"Of course we can," said Lizzie. "We'll come back tomorrow."

Back on the Lungotevere, the old ladies hailed a taxi and crossed the city to the Hotel Montini. The reception desk was unmanned, so they could not order any dinner. This did not matter; they were too tired to eat anyway. Lizzie made them cups of Irish breakfast tea using the kettle and complimentary tea bags on the credenza while Constance opened the doors to the roof garden to admit some of the cooler night air. They drank their tea in silence, and Constance retired with barely a word.

Lizzie lay in bed watching Constance sleep, or pretend to sleep, feeling hurt and confused but knowing that above all it was her duty to extend kindness to her sister-in-law, who had, after all, suffered the greater bereavement. Lizzie had never had a relationship with someone who she could claim to be "the love of her life," but Constance had. Lizzie had often envied Henry and Constance's grand passion but, of course, there was a price for everything. And now Constance was paying it.

. . .

Sunrise seemed to herald a slightly cooler day than the previous one, although in Rome it was always hard to tell. Lizzie, who had barely slept, showered quickly and busied herself decapitating dying geraniums on the terrace while Constance seemed to take an age in their shared bathroom. When she finally emerged, Constance was bustling with efficiency. "I've found the most wonderful spot to dry our delicates," she said.

"Oh, marvelous," said Lizzie.

"Oh, God," said Constance.

"What?"

"I'm talking like an old lady."

"We *are* old ladies," said Lizzie.

Constance laughed, and then Lizzie laughed, surprised by the extent of her relief that equilibrium had been restored.

Bronco knocked on the door bearing a breakfast tray. He knew it was foolish to feel resentful—this was, after all, his job—but he felt it anyway. They ate like birds, these old ladies. It was hardly worth bringing it up in the elevator. On Lizzie's instruction, he loped across the room and set the breakfast on the terrace.

When he had gone, Constance sat at the breakfast table, bracing herself for the inevitable conversation that was to follow. She knew she owed Lizzie an explanation, and probably an apology, and was contemplating how to begin when Lizzie dove straight into the deep end.

"Last night, at the bridge," said Lizzie, "what happened?"

"Coffee?" said Constance, feeling her back stiffen.

Lizzie nodded, and Constance poured. Her arm was sore, too, from lugging Henry around in the Harrods bag.

"Last night . . . last night . . ." said Constance, sounding like the ingénue she never was.

"You were quite peculiar, you know," said Lizzie, not letting her get away with anything.

"I know," said Constance. Then she stopped and decided on a different tack. "Last night on the bridge something occurred to me. It occurred to me that possibly Henry's motives for being scattered into the river weren't . . . how shall I put this?"

"I have no idea, but you certainly have my complete and undivided attention," Lizzie said, dry as a bone. *Have we suddenly been transported to an Agatha Christie novel?* she wondered.

"I think Henry may have had a reason for wanting to be scattered from the bridge," said Constance.

"It's where you met," Lizzie reminded her.

"I think there is another reason. I think before we take Henry to the bridge today we make a visit to a little church, just off the Campo. I think this is the best place to begin to . . . one sugar?"

"Yes, please," said Lizzie, on the edge of her seat. "To begin to . . . ?"

"*Explain,*" said Constance, clasping a sugar cube with a pair of silver tongs.

TEN

Via di San Simone

Florentina had returned to her guesthouse, soon to be relaunched as Florentina B&B, with a glorious sunshine-yellow-and-burnt-orange logo, in the early hours of the morning. Her session with the Web designer had become amorous, and they ended up making violent love on the floor in the space between his mother's sofa bed and his grandmother's coffee table. She had thoroughly enjoyed the interlude, although during part of it, her lover's discarded boot had been pressing into her spine, which had resulted in an aching back.

In the morning Florentina woke to discover her back had seized. She managed to roll sideways out of bed, shuffle to the kitchen, and place a few help-yourself items on the table. She scribbled a note saying, *Help yoursef* (minus the *l* in *self*) and shuffled back to bed, unintentionally slamming the door behind her.

Alice woke to the door slam and went to the communal bathroom for a shower. It was empty but filled with the lingering and unmistakable smell of diarrhea. *Serves me right,* she thought. She opened the window as wide as she could and took the shortest shower she had ever taken.

Rick woke to the sounds of clinking in the kitchen directly below him. He was dimly aware that his friends had been up and down all night, but with the exception of one horrendous explosion he seemed to have been spared. He dressed quickly and went downstairs, delighted to find Alice alone in the kitchen, squeezing a halved orange on something that looked like a metal rocket. The table was set with rough-sawn bread, a great block of pale-yellow cheese, cabanossi or salami, he wasn't sure which, and a pile of glazed pastry.

He noticed something at his feet. It was a note saying *Help yoursef.* He thought, *Don't mind if I do,* announcing his arrival with an "Aha."

Alice turned and saw him. "Morning. How are the boys? Would you like some orange juice? Is it dysentery?"

"Looks like you and I are the only survivors. Yes, please."

"Oh, God, I feel so bad," said Alice, holding up two empty glasses. "Big or small?"

"Don't feel bad. Small. Look upon it as an opportunity."

"To . . . ?" said Alice, squeezing him an orange juice.

They both paused to register the sound of the front door opening and closing.

"For you and I to get to know each other," Rick said. "Does a turn of the Colosseum tickle your fancy?"

Pea Green T-shirt, whose real name was August Clutterbuck, appeared holding a twelve-pack of toilet paper. August had been born in October and didn't see the point of his fore-name. When he complained about it at a family dinner once, his grandfather had squinted in consternation and said, "But October would be a *ridiculous* name for a boy." After that, August gave up. For a brief time when he started his A levels, he tried to get his friends to call him "Gus," but the moniker never seemed to stick.

Standing in front of Alice, he was suddenly conscious of holding a great stack of paper used for wiping people's bottoms. He thought about putting it behind his back but decided that would only draw attention and possibly ridicule. He also regretted that he was wearing a green T-shirt almost identical to the one he was wearing yesterday; it would appear that he was one of those boys who never washed or changed their clothes.

He did not and could not know that Alice's keen eye had already assessed that this green shirt was a shade darker with a hue bluer than the previous green T-shirt.

"Mind if I tag along?" he said.

"Hey," said Rick, disappointed. "I thought you were—"

"Nope," said August. "Just went out to get some supplies for the lads."

Alice gave Rick his orange juice and offered to make one for August. He declined but added "kind" and "generous" to his growing list of attributes for this beautiful girl. August ducked upstairs to deliver his cargo and rejoined them in the kitchen.

Alice was not normally a breakfast person but was suddenly ravenous, eating a slab of white bread topped with some delicious pale European butter and a hunk of cheese and salami. She imagined her mother's disapproval at the load of carbs and fat she was ingesting and felt quite pleased with herself.

Rick pressed her about an excursion to the Colosseum again. She demurred. He changed seats, moving from the head of the table to sit right next to her. He did not touch her, but his presence commanded attention. "Come on," he said.

"I have to catch a train at two," she said.

"No point sitting in the station for half the day," he said.

Rick looked to August for support. Alice looked at August too. He looked back at her and felt himself blush. He hoped against hope it didn't appear as intense as it felt. But Alice being Alice had registered the precise tone, depth, and hue of the red in his cheeks. To her horror she felt her own cheeks responding. She quickly got to her feet and turned to the sink, gathering plates and cups to wash up. Why had New Alice abandoned her this morning? Where had she gone?

Florentina staggered through the door clutching her back and told Alice what a good girl she was for washing up. She dropped into a chair with a groan and asked if she would be so kind as to make her a cup of coffee, instructing Alice on the process of unscrewing her aluminum moka pot, loading it with freshly ground coffee and water, rescrewing the pot, and placing it on the burner. During Florentina's long and sometimes confusing instructions, the boys negotiated with Alice to meet her outside in fifteen minutes.

When they went upstairs to check on Pink and Blue, Florentina said to Alice, "Be careful of that one."

"Who? Rick?" said Alice. "I think he's pretty harmless."

"No, not the Casanova one," said Florentina. "The other one. The real one."

Alice didn't need to ask Florentina to explain "real" one; she knew what she meant. "Why would I need to be careful of him?"

"Be careful not to break his heart."

"Why would I . . ." Alice stopped, genuinely flummoxed. "How would I break his heart?"

Florentina smiled and rolled her eyes. The moka pot began to gurgle and splutter with freshly brewed coffee.

Outside, the day was heating up beneath a cloudless sky. Rick and August drove their *motorini* to the foot of the stairs and sat in companionable silence waiting for Alice.

After a few minutes, August cleared his throat and trying to sound casual said, "I thought she might want to ride with me this time, you know, for a change."

"I saw her first," said Rick, cutting straight to the truth of the competition between them.

Alice appeared at the top of the stairs. "Should I bring my backpack?" she called over the puttering of the two small engines.

"We can get it later," Rick called back.

Alice shrugged agreement. She looked up for a moment and took in the cerulean sky. The light was clearer this morning, turning the softer autumnal tones of the buildings into the vivid ochre and orange.

As she pattered down the steps, August said quietly to Rick, "Let her choose."

"Choose what?" she said, overhearing.

"My compadre here wants you to ride with him," said Rick, already grinning like a winner.

"Oh," said Alice.

"No, I meant—" August began to elaborate, but Rick cut him off.

"Who do you want ride with?" he said.

New Alice, who had been dormant all morning, suddenly awoke. She looked from August to Rick from Rick to August and back to Rick. Then she turned to August, who thought in that instant that she was the most magnificent thing he had ever seen. *Take a picture of this in your head,* he told himself.

"His is bigger," she said.

Indeed, Rick's motorino was slightly larger than August's. August felt himself blush again. Fortunately, it was only a split second before Rick revved his engine a couple of times and signaled for Alice to hop on, which she did. Once again she had registered August's blush but this time mustered the bravado not to return it.

August watched as Alice wrapped her arms around Rick. Rick doubled up in pain. This was not the reaction he had expected. Rick groaned and switched off his *motorino.* Alice put a concerned hand on his shoulder, but Rick was too occupied to notice.

"Oh, poor Rick," August said with little conviction as Rick scampered up the steps, almost bent in two.

"Do you think we should . . . ?" began Alice.

"I'll just . . ." answered August.

He dismounted and followed Rick inside. Alice sat there for a beat before deciding to head up the stairs, too. By the time she had reached the front door, August reappeared. "I think he'd like to be alone right now," he said. "In fact I'm absolutely certain of it."

Alice nodded. They looked at each other, suddenly awkward. New Alice felt irritated with Old Alice for being so pathetic. She knew perfectly well how to handle the other boys. What was the problem with this one? Why had Florentina said that about him? And anyway what did it matter? In a few hours, she'd be gone and would never see him again.

"So what do you want to do?" she said briskly.

"Oh, you don't want to . . . ?"

"Do the Colosseum?" said Alice. "No. Yes. Yeah, let's do that."

August pointed to Rick's abandoned motorino. "I'm sure Rick wouldn't mind if you . . ."

"Oh. I don't know how to," said Alice. "Drive one," she added.

"Oh, well, hop on."

Alice hated this. Who was in charge here? Old Alice or New Alice? Why was she behaving like this? She leaped on the scooter behind him and put her arms around his waist, half expecting to get an electric shock.

As soon as her hands took grip of his torso, August felt his whole body jolt. His crotch stirred, and once again he blushed. Alice did not register his blush this time, but she did feel the heat of his body. She wondered for a moment if he were running a temperature and whether he might also double in pain at any moment. He revved the engine a little more obviously than he intended, and they lurched into the Via dei Coronari.

ELEVEN

Hotel San Marco

COULD A GREATER MIRACLE TAKE PLACE THAN
FOR US TO LOOK THROUGH EACH OTHER'S
EYES FOR AN INSTANT?
—Henry David Thoreau, *Walden*

Meg woke and blinked at the fractured reflection of their room in the chrome domes of the seven-pendant light that hung over her bedside table as an extravagant reading lamp. She was extremely satisfied with the orange flock wallpaper and strange mix of Swedish modern with late Baroque furniture. When it came to decorating she had a natural inclination toward the less-is-more approach, although she had to admit more-is-more was definitely working for this room. But that was the great thing about Rome. Nobody bothered with restraint.

Meg listened to the shower running in the Versailles Hall of Mirrors bathroom and knew that Alec would soon emerge in a regulation white fluffy robe emblazoned with the Hotel San Marco crest, wanting sex. Well, she didn't mind if he did. She briefly thought of having a shower herself but remembered she had taken one the previous evening before bed and did not wish to spoil the moment.

When Alec appeared wearing his white fluffy robe, he discovered his wife arranged just so on the bed, also wearing a white fluffy robe. He grinned the grin of the soon-to-be-fornicating and slipped on the bed next to her. She shifted slightly as he rolled toward her and her gown fell open. She watched his pupils dilate as he scanned her body. It aroused her to see the primal pleasure she incited in him. He kissed the side of her neck, and his minty breath washed over her.

"My breath," she said, suddenly realizing that she had not cleaned her teeth.

"Doesn't matter," he said hoarsely.

Alec pulled Meg on top of him. He knew she would enjoy it more if she felt she was in control. Each knew precisely how to please the other. She rocked back and forth on top of him, making love with easy and familiar expertise. For a moment, she caught her own reflection in the gilded mirror above the bed. She noted the slightly demented arrangement of her features when she moaned and decided to look beyond herself, through the window and across the rooftops of Rome.

"I've got the strangest feeling that funny old hotel is around here somewhere," she said.

He knew she was thinking of the hotel they had stayed in on their honeymoon. The one with the kissing concierge. He recalled that it was, in fact, miles away, toward the Colosseum, but all he said was, "Can you not talk?"

"What? Oh, sure," she said. "Sorry."

Meg focused on a spot on the wall, just to the left of the mirror, and soundlessly rocked on top of him.

"You can make *some* noise," he said.

She began to groan, for him at first, but then lost herself in pleasure until she remembered the odd look on her face when she made those noises. As she checked the mirror, her eye caught a brief glimpse of an Agrodiaetus butterfly fluttering past the window. It's shimmering blue wings reprised the exact blue of the—

Meg stopped and sat rigidly upright. She could not recall whether she had packed the sample tile in their luggage or whether it was in her shoulder bag. The sample tile was the Rosetta stone of the whole project. It was the one perfect tile that they would use as a template to create all the others. Surely she would not have been so cavalier as to assign it to their larger bags where it could get lost or stolen. Their bags that were, indeed, still missing.

"What?" said her husband, alarmed.

Meg leaped off Alec and scrambled from the bed. She seized her shoulder bag and upended its contents on the hot-pink Arne Jacobsen egg chair.

"What are you doing?" said Alec.

"The tile. The sample tile. I think it's in the luggage."

"*What?*"

"*The sample tile!*" screeched Meg as if it were the answer to all questions that had ever been asked.

"They said the luggage would be here this morning!" yelled Alec.

"Don't yell at me!" yelled Meg.

Alec wanted to do more than yell at her. He wanted to slam her stupid face into the wall. Meg suddenly seized upon a small package wrapped in tissue paper.

"Oh, thank God!" she exclaimed. "It's here! I've got it," she said to Alec as if he gave a hoot. She put the package on the crystal-topped coffee table and took a deep breath. Then she turned and looked at her husband, propped up on his elbows, his penis still erect despite the waves of fury emanating from the rest of him. Instantly she was filled with the complete comprehension of what a fool she was. *This man puts up with so much crap from me,* she thought. Remorse flooded her, but she swept it aside and instead of beating herself up, determined to make good.

Meg smiled seductively at him and unpeeled her dressing gown, letting it drop to the floor. Then, climbing on the bed, she crawled on all fours toward him. Alec swung his feet to the floor and sat upright with his back to her. She put her hands on his shoulders and began to kiss the back of his neck. He picked up the phone, and her hands roamed over his chest to his nipples. Alec shrugged her off and started to dial.

"What are you doing?" she said.

"Calling a taxi," he said, businesslike. "Let's get this tile business out of the way so we can get on with our lives."

"Don't you want to . . . ?" she purred into his ear.

Alec stood up, still on the phone, and faced her. She noted, despondently, that his penis was losing interest. "I did want to," he said. "I've wanted to for the last ten days. But I don't want to now."

Meg reached out for the corner of his dressing gown.

"Megan," he snapped, stepping from her reach. She hated when he called her that. He only ever called her "Megan" when she was in serious trouble. She slumped back on the bed, defeated.

He hung up and started to dial again. "No answer," he said by way of explanation.

"I'm going to have a shower," she said.

"Okay."

"I know I'm obsessing about this renovation thing, but I promise when it's all over—"

Alec cut her short. He was not going to listen to this drivel. "There'll be a summerhouse or a theme party for Adelaide's sixteenth. Something to have us all running around following your orders."

Meg felt tears welling, but she beat them back. "Why are you doing this?" she said.

"Ah," he said. "Here we go."

"Here we go where?"

Alec shook the receiver violently and shouted into it at the top of his lungs. "Oh, for Christ's sake! Would somebody answer the fucking phone!"

There was a knock at the door. Meg put on her robe, and Alec retreated to the bathroom. A man from the airline had arrived with their luggage.

The taxi crawled down the street, negotiating tourists in flip-flops and Romans in haute couture. It was ridiculous to attempt such a journey at this time of day, but it would have been even more ridiculous to attempt the Via dei Condotti, as the *Americana* had requested. The Via dei Condotti was even more crowded because it was home to all the major names of European fashion. The Via della Croce, being the off-Broadway version of Condotti, with lesser-known designers, was slightly less crowded but tricky to navigate nonetheless.

Italo, the taxi driver, had a cousin, Italo (named after an evidently beloved grandfather Italo), who had a small boutique that sold well-made and competitively priced gentlemen's apparel just up ahead on the left. Italo (the taxi driver) received a 10 percent commission for every customer he sent Italo (the tailor). Occasionally he was even presented with a handsome end-of-season coat.

Indeed, one such coat, with which Italo (the taxi driver) had fallen hopelessly in love, was currently featured in the window. It made a bold statement, this coat, and although it caught the eye of many a passerby, it was, as their grandfather Italo would have said, *molto particulare,* meaning that a grass-green cashmere three-quarter-length coat, with sky-blue silk trim, was not for everybody.

It was, however, Italo had decided, for him. Which is why he was making a slight detour with the rich Americans in the backseat. The gentleman was clearly one of those types with no real interest in shopping, but his wife was a whole different boccie game. Italo knew that if he could get her inside she would be hurling clothes at her hapless husband and buying up big on his behalf.

Italo let his passengers stare out the window, soaking up the magic of Rome, and waited for the right moment to regale them with stories about his grandfather Italo's legendary love of quality fabric, which led him to open a boutique, which now his cousin, etcetera, etcetera, etcetera. Unfortunately, the plan collapsed when the American gentleman turned to his wife and said, "I'm not happy."

"How many happy people do you know?" she said.

Alec looked out the window.

"We have fun together," she said.

"Is it fun?" he asked, thinking it was more some kind of *routine* they did; their own silly sketch show.

Meg sighed. "What would make you happy?"

"I dunno. A move to Rome."

She nodded, humoring him.

"I mean it," he said. "Why not?"

They both knew he didn't mean it, that he had just pulled it unimaginatively out of the air in front of him, but she pretended he was offering a serious suggestion.

"Because we have friends, children," she said. "Things you just can't leave behind."

"You can make it work if you want to."

She wanted to hit him, but instead she turned the other way and looked out the window. "That's just some vacation fantasy," she said. "People the world over go somewhere exotic or exciting or relaxing and think, *Oh, if I just stay here, everything will be different.* Trouble is, wherever you go, there you are. And sooner or later you're leading the same old dreary life. Only now you're in Rome, not California."

"Jesus, you should listen to yourself," he said.

She kept looking out the window and told herself to let it go, that she had ruined the morning and this was his way of punishing her for it, that she had, in effect, *asked for it,* but she heard herself saying, "Don't lay this shit on me now, okay? Let's just enjoy being in Rome without turning it into a big production about moving here."

He turned to her. "You never look at me."

"What?" she said, not looking at him.

"Even when we're making love, you never look at me."

She offered up a silent prayer: *Make him shut up shut up shut up.*

He saw her body stiffen. She was forever at him to *talk to her.* Well, now he was talking. "You're always looking out the window," he said, "or over my shoulder like we're at a Hollywood party and you're hoping someone more interesting will walk through the door."

"You're determined to spoil this, aren't you?"

He knew he had wounded her because now she was picking a fight. Well, he'd said his piece, and he wasn't going to allow this to disintegrate into an argument. He said no more.

In the front, Italo was kicking himself. He should have taken the bull by the horns as soon as they got in his taxi. Now the train had left the station, the ship had sailed, the horse had bolted, and they had passed his cousin's boutique. Eighteen years of driving taxis had taught him a thing or two about the kind of silence you could interrupt and the kind you could not. And this new silence in the backseat was definitely the kind you could not.

Meg opened her shoulder bag and unzipped a silk-lined compartment from which she removed the small parcel wrapped in tissue paper. She put her bag back on the seat and placed the little parcel in her lap. With a reverence that irritated her husband enormously, she lovingly unwrapped it layer by layer until they were both staring at a small, shimmering tile, with the kind of illusive blue glaze that recalled an electrical spark, a flash of lightning, or a lost lagoon.

Meg wondered for a moment whether she might dive into it. Alec knew that he should just snatch the wretched thing and toss it out the window. But he couldn't. He couldn't put his finger on it, but there was something about this tile. There was just something about it.

TWELVE

Colosseo

A THOUSAND WILD FLOWERS BLOOM
FROM EVERY CHINK, AND THE BIRDS BUILD THEIR NESTS
AMONG THE RUINED ARCHES, AND SUGGEST
NEW THOUGHTS OF BEAUTY TO THE ARCHITECT.
—Longfellow, *Michael Angelo*

Lizzie and Constance were back in the dusty white Mercedes, turning into the Via Cavour. Gianni had collected them after he had dropped his niece's piano teacher for a manicure and shellac at Nice Nails in the Piazzale Montesquieu. It was across town, but he didn't mind; he was fond of these old English ducks, and besides, they tipped like Americans.

Directly ahead, looking down the Via degli Annibaldi, Constance glimpsed the Colosseum framed by the dusky stone-and-render buildings. "Magnificent, isn't it?" she said.

"What?" said Lizzie.

Constance could hear the irritation in her sister-in-law's voice. She didn't blame her. She knew she was behaving strangely. They had always been frank with each other; it was part of the rules of their engagement, rules strictly adhered to over decades of friendship, and suddenly she was behaving like a fractious diva.

"Roma," answered Constance.

"Well, yes, I suppose so," said Lizzie, "although it's difficult to find anything magnificent when your companion drops a bombshell at breakfast and refuses to elaborate until you get to some chapel halfway across the city."

Quite. Constance searched for something funny and modern to say. "Build a bridge and get over it, girlie," was the best she could come up with.

"If I die of curiosity before we get there," said Lizzie, "be it on your head."

Constance smiled and took Lizzie's hand, a gesture that startled Lizzie with its intimacy. She looked down at the veined fingers clasping hers and then looked out the window. As they turned in the Via dei Fori Imperiale, there it was again, the Colosseum, ancient and full of stories.

Inside the sunlit arches of the Colosseum, Alice lifted her phone to take a photo. She knew that she would never show these snapshots to anyone, not even Daniel. They were just for her, to remind herself of a time that suddenly, inexplicably, she, who was always so concerned about what others thought of her, felt miraculously free of the burden to please anyone but herself. Even New Alice, with her mandate to live in the moment rather than document it, approved. She felt so light and happy she thought she might float.

Alice framed her shot, and August seized the moment to examine her. He felt an impulse to bury his face in the titian hair that cascaded from her perfect head and tumbled onto her shoulders. It would smell of sunshine, he knew. He felt his crotch stir again and, begging it not to make a spectacle of itself, tried to remember when his dog died. God, she was Life and Beauty. Her breasts, round and splendid with two ripe, eager nipples, suddenly flashed before him. What if he just took her and ravaged her mouth with his tongue? What would she do? *Call the police, that's what she'd do.* He tried to recall his dying dog again.

A cloud moved across the sun and swept Alice with it; she was suddenly taken by the true antiquity of the space, transported back two millennia. She looked down into the network of underground cells where the wild animals and gladiators were once incarcerated; she looked up and saw the crowds of spectators waiting for the free show. First, the animals doing circus tricks then the gladiators fighting until one is killed or horribly wounded. A thumbs-up from the emperor, the wounded man is spared; thumbs-down, he dies.

"Unimaginably cruel," she said. And then realizing that he had not made the detour with her, she elaborated, "The men killing each other and animals. And all of Rome showing up to watch like it was . . . okay."

The semester before last, August had completed a major project on the Colosseum for ARC 235 Architecture in History. So had his compatriots, and he now realized that this was why Rick wanted to bring her here. *So he could show off.* But of course Rick was occupied elsewhere, and August had hit Rick's jackpot. He smiled. She frowned, and he realized that his was not an appropriate response to her comment. He went mining for an interesting fact with which to redeem himself.

"It was horrible," he said. "They had other stuff, too, like women gladiators fighting dwarf gladiators."

"Women gladiators?" she said. "You're making that up."

"But you have no problem with the dwarves?"

"I was getting to that," she said, "but I've never heard of women gladiators."

"It's true!" he said. "They were, like, Ethiopian, I think."

That was probably enough. It would be foolish to prattle on like a know-it-all, but she was looking at him like he knew what he was talking about, and while she kept looking, he kept saying stuff to make her look.

"It's the largest amphitheatre the Romans ever built. Well, they didn't build it; Jewish slaves did."

"Jewish slaves. Wow," she said, looking around.

Was she being ironic, or was she genuinely impressed? The girl he met yesterday at the airport would definitely be going for ironic, but this girl he was with now seemed softer somehow. A cultural divide suddenly opened before August. If she had been British, he would have known in an instant whether she was toying with him. He knew Americans weren't strong on irony, so he decided to carry on as if she were interested.

"They used to flood the arena as well and hold full-scale naval battles," he continued, "with real ships." Somewhere in the back of his mind he remembered reading that this was incorrect and that the mock battles were actually held in another part of Rome. But he could see her staring into midair, imagining, so he decided not to correct himself and continued with his naval narrative.

Alice could listen to him all day, she decided. Was it the timbre of his voice that was so mesmerizing? Was it the British accent, almost upper class but a trace of something else—a place maybe, or a city, like Liverpool or Manchester? Whatever it was, she liked it. And while she was at it, she liked his forearms, too, the meaty way they met his wrists. And his mouth; lips a little too thin but such a clever smile. If she licked him on the neck, he would taste salty and musky. She imagined his hand resting on her belly, pushing downward, pressing against her. A liquid swoon between her legs jolted her back to reality.

"I'm getting married," said Old Alice.

"What?" he said.

"I'm getting married," said New Alice. It was true. He had to hear it sometime.

"No, you're not," he said.

"I am," she said. "That's who I'm meeting in Florence. My . . . him."

Both Old and New Alice felt it was important to declare this before . . . before what? Nothing had happened. Absolutely nothing. Sometimes at home, in an attempt to bond with her brilliant but short-tempered older brother, Alice would watch football matches with him in their father's plaid-wallpapered study. Once she watched a player shoot across the field and tackle another who was seconds from a touchdown. The camera was in a close-up at the moment of the tackle. Clearly the player had not seen his opponent coming. His expression was one part devastation, one part astonishment. She could now see this look on Pea Green's face. *Pea Green.* She didn't even know his name.

August had no idea why he was so upset. What did it matter what this girl did? Yes, he loved her, but he wasn't deluded about it. Or rather, he knew he was deluded and that she would never love him back. And besides, she was getting on a train soon, and he would never see her again. Still, he felt like someone had squeezed his heart, or punched it. He wanted to sit down and put his head in his hands.

"You don't have to make up some mythical guy," he said, trying not to sound hurt or bewildered, both of which he unaccountably was.

"I'm not," she said. "It's true."

"How old are you?"

It was a reasonable question, but Alice found it infuriating. "Nine-year-old girls in Africa get married every day," she said. New Alice stepped up, front and center. "I've been menstruating since I was eleven years old. Old enough to reproduce, old enough to get married." She liked the shocked look on his face when she said "menstruating," although she was a little disconcerted by the surge of anger she was feeling.

August found his wry smile and pasted it on his face. He decided to leap over the issues of eligibility and menstruation, returning to her announcement of impending nuptials. "You don't exactly have a lot of credibility after the whole '*Scusi,* I gotta getta my bagga' routine at the airport yesterday," he said.

"I was in a hurry."

"And nowa you needa to get rid of me."

"If I was trying to get rid of you, I'd just do this." She raised her middle finger at him, turned, and started to walk away across the giant paving stones, horrifying Old Alice by what she was doing but compelled by New Alice to do it anyway.

He followed her, confused. "Sorry, I just don't see you as

the kind of . . ." No, this was heading in the wrong direction. "I just don't see you being *engaged* with a *fiancé* and all."

"He's not a fiancé, he's a guy," she said, "and we're getting married. No big deal."

But of course it was a very big deal. It had been ten days since she had announced to Daniel that she was going to spend the summer in Italy. It was a last-minute thing, she explained, a kind of challenge laid down to her by one of her professors.

Alice had always suspected that she was much more into Daniel than he was into her, and she guarded her heart accordingly. Part of her had sensed that he was as much attracted to her mother's power to advance his career as he was to anything else she had to offer. So, when she tentatively outlined her travel plans, it surprised her that he was quite put out, or rather, how put out he was.

She didn't want to disappoint him; she liked Daniel enormously. He was much more sensible than other boys she had dated, because he was older, she supposed. Not just sensible, sensitive; interested and therefore interesting. And he genuinely tried to help her with her assignments. Sometimes he could be patronizing, but it was just his way of expressing frustration with her, which was as much her fault as his because she allowed him to treat her like that. Aside from the issue with his ears, he was certainly "eye candy," as her mother had somewhat creepily observed, and he was a nice lover. No, not nice; he was considerate. A good lover.

He was also ambitious. Not in a ruthless way, but he was clear about what he wanted, and he was set on achieving it.

It was well known that he was right on track to being the youngest senior partner in her mother's firm. So it came as quite a surprise that Daniel suggested he come to Rome, too.

"You can't," said Alice. "Mom would flip."

"Not if there was a special reason," said Daniel. "I could get away for a week or so if there was a special reason."

"What kind of special reason?"

"We could be getting engaged, for example," he said.

The example lay on the black granite bench between them while Alice buttered toast. Daniel smiled and put his hand on hers. "If you wanted to," he said very quietly.

This lovely man is asking me to marry him, thought Alice. She had never given it serious consideration; it was something she might like to do when she was older, when she was about thirty, say. She was not one of those little girls who hijacked her tutu for a veil and playacted her big day. She did appreciate, however, that she was being asked now, that the opportunity may not come again, and that if she accepted his offer, her life would be imbued with purpose and direction. Her mother would be pleased. He would be pleased. She would no longer be a disappointment.

"Are you sure?" she asked.

Daniel looked her in the eye. "Very," he said. "Completely."

She loved his certainty most of all. She, who had little or no certainty about anything, who had developed such a phobia about disappointing people that she could only make decisions after writing extensive lists of pros and cons, felt herself falling into him. Into his certainty. It was such a relief.

Strangely, it was also a relief that Daniel could not get himself on the same flight to Rome as she had. The best he could manage was a flight into Florence the day after, and the most he could get was three days off. Alice couldn't work out why she felt relieved, but she told herself, for once, not to over-think it and not to make lists.

As they exited the Colosseum, a morbidly obese gladiator waved his plastic shield at August and Alice, shouting excitedly in a mix of *Italiano* and English, inviting them to pose for a photo with him. They both smiled, declining with grateful gestures, both of them feeling sick to the stomach. It was awful. Something had broken between them; they each felt it and each knew the other felt it. *Not that there was anything to break in the first place,* Alice reminded herself. She decided she should get herself to the station and wait for her train.

A raggedy boy with dark skin and cheeky grin approached them. In a gravelly little voice, he said, "*Scusi,* photo? Photo? With both, you and you."

August shook his head and smiled. Alice reached into her pocket and produced a couple of euros. The boy looked most offended; he wanted to earn his money.

"Photo. Photo," he said.

Surrendering, August and Alice stood next each other.

"Camera?" said the boy.

It occurred to Alice that he might try to run off with it, but she handed over her phone anyway. The boy put the phone into camera mode and framed a shot. Almost immediately he lowered the phone from his expert eye and looked disapprovingly at his wooden subjects. "*Baci. Baci.*"

"What?" August squinted.

"It means *kiss*," she said to August and then loudly and firmly responded to the boy, "Just take the photo."

The boy took the photo. Alice handed him the two euros, and this time he accepted them. Without a word he scooted off. (He was, of course, acting on my behalf. If ever you encounter a scruffy boy in Roma who wants to take your photo, do be kind to him. He's more than likely engaged in very important work.)

August and Alice looked at the photo on the screen of the phone. Their heads pressed together for a moment before they simultaneously became conscious of touching each other and pulled away.

"I'll send it to you. What's your number?" she said.

August could see that she was withdrawing, preparing to leave. He knew he should let her go, that even "letting her go" was a delusional notion; he never had her in the first place. While one voice shouted at him to not let this pass, to take this moment, to seize her somehow, another voice laid out two major obstacles: firstly, she was engaged to someone else; secondly, she was out of his league.

He realized that if he gave her his phone number, it would not be the beginning but the end; she would use it to message him their photo, and having bookended their brief encounter, she would not contact him again. He could, of course, contact her, but his romantic history told him that he would hear the reluctance in her voice, feel foolish, say something stupid, and end up wishing he hadn't.

It was now or never. So instead of giving her his phone number, he gave her an idea. "You know when you have a big night out and you end up completely legless, exchanging life stories with some stranger? You get their number and vice versa, but when you wake up the next day you realize that what you thought was a life-changing mind-orgasm was actually two piss-heads rambling shit." He could feel the wind behind him, suddenly inspired just when he needed to be. "You feel obliged to call, but you don't want to. And you end up ruining what would have been an enjoyable moment, if you'd just let it be."

Alice hadn't really ever had a night like that, but she got the point of what he was saying. And she enjoyed his funny way of saying it. He could see that he had hooked her, and the feigned boredom of her tone confirmed it.

"Is there a point to this story?" she said dryly.

It was an invitation to dance.

"Let's not do numbers or swap e-mails," said August. "I've got two hours in this amazing city with this gorgeous American girl who has already broken my heart by running off to marry some tosser—"

"He's not a tosser, whatever that is," she interrupted, grinning.

"How do you know he's not a tosser if you don't know what a tosser is?"

Alice rolled her eyes.

"Anyway, in two hours you are getting on a train to Florence, and I will return to my farting, fouling companions—"

"Erck. Thanks for the visual."

"You're welcome. So what do you say we really enjoy this? Really live it and all that. Then we go our separate ways, and *phht,* that's it." He suspected it sounded a little lame. But he hoped she would see that it also made sense.

"Do you always go on like this?" Alice said.

"Yeah, sorry. Second-child syndrome. Brilliant but silent older brother. I'm the talky one. Dysentery of the mouth." The last quip was one bridge too far, he knew, but he didn't care. He was feeling light-headed, heady, victorious, happy, and glorious.

Alice decided she liked this guy. They could be friends. Men and women could be friends. She had other male friends. Just because he was a man didn't mean it had to be sexual, proclaimed New Alice. What harm could happen in two hours with a fun stranger in a magical city? She felt herself letting go.

He could feel it too. She smiled at him.

"Oh, really? Great!" he said.

They walked along in silence, oblivious to the bustle of tourists, pleased with their new resolution, smiling uncertainly. Eventually, they stopped below the ruins of the temple of Venus and Roma at the Forum.

"So what do we do now?" she asked.

"I have absolutely no clue," he answered.

Alice laughed a long, musical laugh, up and down the scale. If he did one thing before he died, August decided, he wanted to hear those notes again.

Alice settled in the happy haze of her after-laugh. She could not remember laughing so freely since she was quite small; she vaguely remembered someone tickling her—her father, perhaps?—and giggling until she was limp. She had felt safe and happy in the most uncomplicated way. In a flash the memory faded.

THIRTEEN

Arco di Santa Margherita

THE SOUL BECOMES DYED WITH THE
COLOR OF ITS THOUGHTS.
—Marcus Aurelius, *Meditations*

Italo drove the taxi down the Via del Pellegrino, watching the Americans in his rearview mirror. The *Americano* kept to the side of the narrow street while the *Americana* strode straight down the middle of the cobblestones, daring someone to run her over. He was kindly disposed to the couple, as they had just given him a twenty-euro tip, but he did not hold much hope for them.

Meg had been given fairly precise instructions from the tile maker on how to find his shop, but she had left the printout at the hotel. She had tried to find the tile maker's e-mail on her phone, but it had vanished. Alec said that e-mails didn't disappear—that it must have been somewhere—so they had another spat about that. All she could remember was that his shop was in a small street off the Via del Pellegrino, opposite a door with a sign that said *The Conspiracy Club*.

They decided to solve the problem scientifically, walking the length of the Via del Pellegrino, banking that Meg would recognize the name of the street when they came across it. Passing a hardware store, a tomato-red wheelbarrow attracted Alec's attention. It was solidly made with thick pneumatic tires, precisely the kind of barrow he had been wanting for his vegetable patch at Silver Lake. Its hardwood handles were leaning against the wall of the store, below a worn marble plaque inscribed in Latin. The two opening words immediately stopped Alec in his tracks: *I, Claudius . . .*

Alec studied the plaque, mustering enough of his schoolboy Latin to work out that it said something along the lines of *I, Claudius, declare this to be the outermost limit of the city of Rome.* He could not dredge enough of his ancient history class to recall exactly when Claudius was emperor, but he knew he was reading something that had been there for about two thousand years. A shiver ran up his spine.

Meg strode on without noticing he had stopped. Alec was about to call out to her to share the small thrill of his discovery but changed his mind, choosing to protect the moment by keeping it to himself. He trotted to catch up with her until he was a few paces behind his wife. Meg marched ahead, broadcasting over her shoulder; *Like a loud American,* he thought. Alec wished that he was carrying a sign saying, *Actually she's Australian.* Meg, oblivious, resurrected a conversation that he thought they had killed off ten minutes ago in the taxi.

"I don't know why you're making such a big deal out of this," she said. "It's never been smooth sailing for us. It's always a battle. That's how we relate."

Alec decided not to engage with her.

Receiving no reply, Meg assumed that he had not heard her and began to repeat herself. "I said—"

"I heard you," he interrupted.

They walked along in silence for a while.

"Well, then," she said, "what is your reply?"

Alec studied the new Mephisto walking shoes that he had not broken in yet. They were hurting. "I'm tired of being at war," he said quietly.

"I'm tired of being at war," she mocked over her shoulder.

It occurred to Alec that he could kill her, dispose of her body, and be back in California before anyone had even noticed she was missing.

Meg was sure she could feel waves of hatred emanating toward her back. She stopped and turned to her husband without looking directly at him. "Okay, let's call a truce," she said and added, genuinely meaning it, "I'm sorry."

Alec remained unmoved by his wife's sudden and sincere declaration of repentance because he knew it was unlikely to be supported by any change in her behavior. "I don't want a truce," he said. "I don't want to make happy families. I don't want to pretend."

The thing Meg disliked most about her husband was the way he cast himself as the perpetual victim of her capricious whimsy. He was *such a boy.* "Oh, grow up," she said, sidestepping an oncoming *motorino.* She pointed to a girl clinging precariously to the *motorino*'s driver. "That girl is pretending she's not scared to death." The *motorino* swerved around a thick-middled man patting the yapping poodle of a girl in a floral miniskirt. "That man is pretending to like that dog." The girl in the miniskirt teetered on her striped fluorescent stilettos. "That girl is pretending those shoes go with that dress," said Meg, pointing directly at the girl without a moment's concern that she may be able to understand English. "That's how we operate as adults in the world without killing each other. We pretend!"

She swiveled on her heel and marched boldly forth.

"You are scary," Alec called after her.

"So?" she said. "Nothing's changed. I haven't changed."

Meg almost missed it. But swirling back to look in his general direction, she noticed an archway with a street sign inset on a crumbling render and brick wall. The sign had a slash of bloodred graffiti across it, which made it hard to read, but on closer inspection she could see it said *Arco degli Agetari* or *Acetari*. That was it! *Arco degli Acetari*.

Meg passed through the archway into an enchanted medieval courtyard. Here and there, external staircases clambered up the outside of buildings accompanied by the thick trunks of old vines. A rich terra-cotta dominated render colors ranging from dusty yellow to plum purple. Some of the render had disintegrated and fallen in places, exposing the brickwork underneath, but the effect, far from being chaotic, created visual unity among the eclectic styles. Alec absorbed the harmony in wonder.

Meg knew she had arrived. She spotted a battered door with a small glass window and a security camera mounted on it. A very small sign read *The Conspiracy Club*. She remembered now what she must do. Turning around, she walked twenty paces across the courtyard to a set of unmarked double doors that were flaking and bubbling with a myriad of colors layered down over the centuries. She knocked, and the door fell open.

Alec joined her, and they looked in, not daring to enter without an invitation. Vaulted brick ceilings crouched over a vast storage room brimming with pallets that were piled high with tiles. There was no sign of any life or movement.

"Hello," Meg called out.

"*Buongiorno,*" Alec called out.

Meg threw a barbed look in Alec's direction.

"What?" he said.

"Like he's not going to answer because I say *hello* in English," she said.

Alec sucked his teeth and held his tongue.

They waited. Craning her neck, Meg could see doorways beyond the dim cellar. She glimpsed what might have been a kiln through one and possibly a staircase through another. She called out again, but there was no answer. Then she recalled that the tile maker had e-mailed her times that he would or would not be there. She decided not to share this fresh recollection with her husband, lest he use it against her. Besides, if the shop was open, the tile maker could not be far away.

Standing at the threshold, waiting in silence, Alec began to feel an enormous irritation once again for this silly project. What did she call it? *A mission.* They could be exploring the Pantheon or having an espresso in the Piazza Navona. What a ridiculous waste of time this was.

"I don't want to fight anymore," he said, resurrecting their discussion. "I don't think it's cute. I don't enjoy it."

So let me get this straight, thought Meg, *he doesn't want to fight, and he doesn't want to pretend.* "Isn't fighting a way of not pretending there are differences between us?" she said. "Isn't fighting a way of working things out?"

At that moment, a man appeared, not from the shop but in the cobblestoned courtyard behind them. "You are looking for the tile maker?" he said in heavily accented English.

They both turned to find a cross-eyed man with one blue eye and one brown eye, standing behind them. He was wearing a thick, greasy green coat at odds with the heat of the day. His dark hair and skin appeared to be unwashed, and he smelled strongly of cologne.

"Yes," said Alec. "We are looking for the tile maker."

The man nodded, almost to himself, and said nothing.

"Do you know where he is?" asked Alec. "We have an appointment."

Strictly speaking, they did not have an appointment. The tile maker had simply said that he would be in the shop at certain times. Meg knew this, but Alec did not. The cross-eyed man studied them, evidently assessing whether they were worthy of assistance. Meg flashed what she hoped was an endearing smile.

"He is not far from here," the man said. "I can take you to him if it pleasures you."

"*Si, grazie,*" said Alec.

The man turned and headed across the cobblestones. Meg and Alec watched him vanish in the shadow of the archway and reappear in the bright light of the Via del Pellegrino. He turned and motioned toward them, and they hurried after him.

. . .

A block away, in the Via dei Cappellari, named for the *cappellari,* hatmakers whose shops once lined the narrow lane, Lizzie and Constance each clasped a handle of the Harrods bag, sharing the load of the Henry box. They were trying to find the tiny church of Santa Barbara dei Librai. Constance knew that it was in a small square near the bustling food markets of Campo de' Fiori but was not aware that they were, unfortunately, headed diametrically in the wrong direction.

The taxi had dropped the pair in Piazza Farnese outside the symmetrical monolith of a Renaissance palazzo designed by some of the most prominent architects of the sixteenth century, including Michelangelo. An enormous blue, white, and red flag hung in the hot air above the massive central entry, indicating its current function as the French embassy. It was an architectural and geographical marker that Constance had been using for the last fifty years to negotiate her way around this quarter of the city.

Constance had led Lizzie to a corner of the Campo de' Fiori, hoping to avoid the madness of the marketplace teeming with humanity. They had peeled into the laneway next to the famous Forno that smelled deliciously of freshly baked bread and walked on for a while, but the small square with the church failed to appear.

"We're lost, aren't we?" said Lizzie. She was wearing sensible walking shoes, as was Constance, but the cobblestones were murder on her feet.

"No, it's just up here," said Constance, trying to sound convincing.

"The taxi driver said right at the Campo."

"He was wrong."

"Yes, what would a Roman know about getting around Rome?"

"I lived and worked here," said Constance.

"Yes, fifty-three years ago," said Lizzie. "You must know these streets like the back of your liver-spotted hand," she added.

Constance stopped and laughed a loud and hearty pirate laugh. It felt good. It was also good to be reminded of their long and deep friendship, based on the capacity of one to shock the other, just *enough*. Once or twice over the years their exchanges had toppled into nastiness and feelings had been hurt. But silences were soon broken and bridges quickly mended.

"Nasty old lady," Constance said to Lizzie.

They put down the Harrods bag to rest. Lizzie flexed her palm, which was red and indented from the strap. Constance looked back down the lane from whence they had come and inwardly conceded defeat. They were going the wrong way.

Suddenly Henry appeared before her. As a man, not a box of ashes. "Giordano Bruno," he said. "It's over his right shoulder."

Constance looked around. Lizzie had not noticed. But her husband had been standing there in front of her. She knew he was not, of course, that she had imagined him, but he was *so real*. More than half a century before, she had complained to Henry once about losing her way to Santa Barbara. He had told her that if she got lost, she should go back to the markets and stand in front of the statue. The road to Santa Barbara was behind it, to the right.

"Come," said Constance. She picked up the Harrods bag and headed back toward the Campo. Lizzie caught up with her and after a small squabble wrested back her share of the Henry load.

"Do you think we should ask directions?" said Lizzie.

"What fun would that be?" said Constance, deciding to keep the strange apparition to herself.

This time, they braved the cut and thrust of the markets and consulted the great bronze statue of Giordano Bruno, which stood in the center of the Campo de' Fiori where he'd been burned at the stake four hundred years before. Giordano had been a Dominican friar, philosopher, scientist, and poet. I never met him, but he was well known for his radical ideas, among them the notion that the sun was just one of many scattered across the universe and that these other suns had life-sustaining planets revolving around them. The prevailing theology of the day held that God had placed the earth at the center of the universe and appointed man the boss of everything (still cracks me up, that one). When Giordano refused to recant his outlandish ideas, he was executed.

Had Constance and Lizzie not consulted Giordano Bruno and remained on their path down the Via dei Cappellari, they would have encountered an American couple following a cross-eyed man in a greasy green coat. There would have been an astonished recognition and some *what-are-you-doing-heres*. This would have been genuine coincidence and not a meeting of my design. There was no need for them to meet. Indeed, a meeting may have altered their trajectories. So they did not meet.

. . .

The American man was beginning to feel apprehensive. It's never easy to keep one's bearings in the laneways of Rome, but he had a sense that he and his wife were doubling back on themselves, following the cross-eyed man in a large circle.

"I thought he said it was close by," said Alec quietly.

"Maybe this is the Roman version of close by," whispered Meg, adding, "Let's go back to the shop."

"I hope you left a trail of bread crumbs, Gretel," said Alec, "because I have no idea how to get back there."

"I've got a very strange feeling something bad is about to happen," said Meg.

Just then a door opened. Wrangling the stethoscope that was unfurling from her bag, Dr. Stephanie stepped into the Via dei Cappellari and literally bumped into Alec. She got such a surprise that she stumbled backward, and Alec had to put both his arms around her to stop her from falling.

"Alec!" said Stephanie and, immediately clocking his wife, added, "and . . ."

Nothing.

She had drawn a blank on Meg's name. Meg could see she had genuinely forgotten, which somehow made it more annoying; because it meant that she was genuinely forgettable, she supposed.

"Meg," said Meg.

"Meg, yes, sorry," said Stephanie.

Alec let Stephanie go, and she smiled her gratitude to him. "What on earth are you doing here?" she said.

"What on earth are *you* doing here?" said Meg very quickly before her husband could answer.

"Me? Oh, I run a free clinic for the gypsy children," said Stephanie, tossing away her good work as if it were the least consequential thing in the world. "I was just going to—"

"A free clinic?" Alec interrupted.

"Yes," said Stephanie. "I was just going to grab a pasta if you'd like to—"

"Yes, we'd love to," said Meg, sounding completely thrilled. "Only that gentleman up there," she added, pointing to the cross-eyed man who was waiting about ten paces ahead of them, "is taking us to see a tile maker, and we mustn't keep him waiting. But great to see you again!"

Stephanie looked past them to the cross-eyed man. She frowned slightly and said something very quickly to him in Italian. He said something quickly in return. Meg took Alec's arm, and they hurried up the road, saying their good-byes over their shoulders. Stephanie watched them go for a while and then headed around the corner for some fresh pasta.

Alec and Meg followed the man through an archway into an alley. Alec noted the name of the alley, just in case. *Arco di S. Margherita.* He presumed the *S* stood for *Santa,* meaning "Saint." They passed an abandoned wooden cart, moving into an area where every inch of the brick-and-render walls were covered with brightly colored graffiti. The place was pungent with the stink of rotting vegetables. Wall-mounted gas meters were attached to each other via a complex arrangement of external lead piping. Mysteriously, the word "fish" was handwritten in black marker on each meter. Along both sides of the alley, large openings about the size of a single garage were sealed shut with old metal roller doors or ancient wooden ones, each brightly painted and then oversprayed with vulgar lettering and obscene motifs.

The cross-eyed man bent and lifted one of the roller doors. It clattered and complained, revealing a yawning darkness. He gestured for them to enter. Meg shot Alec a worried glance, but Alec shrugged. They had come this far . . .

As their eyes adjusted to the darkness, Meg and Alec could see a door at the far end of the space. It was partly ajar, revealing a dimly lit room. The figure of a man appeared and said, "*Buongiorno*."

Alec took his wife's hand, and they walked toward the man. "*Buongiorno* at last," he said, while Meg bristled that he was doing the talking. "We've been e-mailing about the blue tile. I'm Alec, this is my—"

The man raised his hand and put something very sharp against Alec's throat. He realized with a jolt that it was a knife.

"Money," demanded the man in heavily accented English.

Before she could even process what was going on, the cross-eyed man grabbed Meg from behind. She started to scream but stifled it quickly, as she too felt the blade of a knife against her throat.

"Bag," said the cross-eyed man into her ear. This close, he stank of sweet cologne. He pulled the bag from her shoulder. Her whole world was in that bag, but there was only one thing that really mattered.

Alec took the wallet from his back pocket. In the zippered section, there was about five hundred US dollars and in the open section just over a thousand euros, the bulk of it intended as a deposit for the tile maker.

"Please, in the bag," said Meg to the cross-eyed man, "there's a tile, a blue tile wrapped in—" In one motion, the man slapped his hand across Meg's mouth and began to propel her backward. Shock rocketed through her. She had never been handled like this, except maybe in play as a child. A memory triggered of a moment on her parents' outback property. There was a party to send her off to boarding school in Toowoomba. One of the jackaroo's sons pushed her backward toward a bale of hay. He, too, had his hand clamped over her mouth. But underneath it she was laughing.

Adrenaline shot through Alec the moment he saw what was happening to his wife. Despite the blade against his throat, he began to twist in protest toward the cross-eyed man, shouting, "Hey!" He heard Meg stumble and fall in the darkness and felt a blow to the side of his head. He fell, too, landing on the hard concrete. They heard the door bolt behind them and found themselves in pitch-blackness, listening to the sound of footsteps hurrying across the outer room. The roller door beyond rattled shut.

Alec's ear was ringing. He felt Stephanie's bandage on his forehead. It was in place. He wondered if the stitches had burst. They did not appear to be bleeding, but it was hard to tell.

"Are you okay?" he said.

Meg sat up, trying to get her bearings, too stunned to speak. She extended her hand in Alec's direction, but he was out of reach.

FOURTEEN

The Spanish Steps

FORTUNE FAVORS THE BOLD.
—Virgil, *The Aeneid*

Having decided to escape the heat of the city, August and Alice wandered the shady avenues of the Pincio gardens planted with a huge variety of palms and evergreens. August felt his stomach churn but knew he was not ill. It was the kind of churning you felt when, having been awarded the art prize at school, your name was also called out for the physics prize. It was the kind of churning you felt when you could not believe your luck.

Alice looked up at one of the mighty umbrella pines. They were all over Rome, these trees, and she could not help but admire their strong sculptural forms. She imagined teams of winged topiarists shaping their great canopies into compact clouds of green. Patting the rough bark, she asked August what they were called.

"Beverly," he answered authoritatively. "They're all called Beverly."

Alice laughed.

"I have no idea," he added, looking up at the tree. "It's a pine of some sort." By the time he looked back, Alice was walking toward one of the 228 busts of famous Italians that also lined the paths of Pincio.

Alice did not know it, but she was walking toward the Jesuit astrophysicist Angelo Secchi, whose likeness had been placed, not by accident, precisely over the Rome meridian. Angelo had been the director of the astronomy observatory, and fortunately for him, the intellectual mood of Rome had shifted in the 250 years since they had barbecued his fellow scientist Giordano Bruno in the Campo de' Fiori. Indeed, Angelo was so revered for his work in solar physics and stellar spectroscopy that he had been placed here among the other stars of Italian science, art, philosophy, and politics.

"Do you know him?" said August.

Alice almost answered, "Not personally," but decided it was too close to his Beverly quip. She shook her head instead. He observed her studying the bust, captured by something in particular; he couldn't tell what.

"What are you looking at?" he said.

"The colors," she said.

He laughed, thinking she was joking. It was a white stone bust. There were no colors. Until she pointed them out to him. Driftwood, bone, milk, cream, blue-white, warm white, lime white, chalk white. A hitherto undiscovered universe opened before him.

"So is this some idiot savant thing?" he said, trying to get a rise out of her.

Alice had never confessed the full extent of her strange obsession with color. It seemed too mad not to keep private. But since they had agreed to part, never to see each other again, she decided there was nothing to lose by telling him everything. She told him about her childhood spent secretly color-coding closets. She told him about working in the boutique and how they depended upon her exacting eye; how she loved her job and mourned its passing. She told him that she saw the world in color first and form second.

"So when you look at my face, say, you see the green of my eyes first?" he said.

"They're not green," she said, and she proceeded to catalog the seventeen tones she had observed in his iris thus far.

He stood there smiling at her.

"What?" she said. "Don't tell me you don't do something strange. I can tell there's a weirdo in there somewhere."

"I skip," he said.

It was true. August's father produced recyclable packaging for the free-range organic egg market, but before that he had been, for a brief time, a professional boxer. Part of his fitness regime had been skipping rope, an exercise he carried into later life and encouraged his young son to practice as well.

August practiced rope-skipping well into high school and would have been tortured for it were he not so adept with a left hook. One day, after an altercation with a chum, he tried skipping rope to quell his fury but failed to find catharsis. So he dropped the rope and took off across the football field, a small hop with his left foot followed by a bound with his right, a small hop on his right foot followed by a great bound with his left, off he went, alternating left and right, hops and bounds, skipping across the muddy grass. It was a strange, mad, wildly liberating thing to do. And he loved it.

August told Alice how he loved it, how he still skipped regularly although no longer with a rope, and how it helped him think, especially when he was stuck on something like a design assignment.

Now it was Alice's turn to smile. "The scary thing about this," she said, "is I think you may be telling the truth."

"Don't knock it till you've tried it," he said, taking her hand.

She wrested it back. "I am not going skipping with you."

"Oh, come on. What have you got to lose?"

"My dignity."

"Besides that?"

"I am not going skipping with you," she said firmly.

He smiled a disappointed smile.

"Although I may steal the idea," she said.

"What for?"

"My sculpting," she said. "I am a sculptor." This instantly sounded like a pretentious claim to make, and she felt compelled to explain. "I'm at art school, majoring in sculpture." Even that sounded ridiculous. She felt like an impostor.

"What kind of sculptures do you do?"

"B-grade ones, mostly."

"So you're just another narcissistic American who thinks they're brilliant at everything," he said.

She smiled and told him about Professor Stoklinsky, his unfounded belief in her, her mediocre work, Daniel's help, and the professor's command to do something *voosh*. They fell into a broader conversation about what they were studying and why they were studying it. She tried to pin him down on why he had chosen to study architecture.

"I went to one of those posh schools," he said, "where your choices were medicine, dentistry, or law. If you were wildly arty, you did architecture."

"And you were wildly arty?"

"Can't you tell?"

"Do you like it?"

"Better than medicine, dentistry, or law."

"What would you do," she asked, "if you could do anything?"

"Live under the sea with a beautiful fish lady who breathes through her eyelids and has three vaginas."

Alice laughed. Alec shrugged; he never knew what to do with that question. "The truth is," he added, "you can never just do what you want, can you?"

"But say you could?"

"I'd go live in Paris and be a painter," he said, saying something for the sake of saying it and kicking himself for being uninventive.

They walked along in silence for a while. Alice looked at the time on her phone. He didn't ask how much longer they had before she had to catch her train because he didn't want to know.

"Let's do something *voosh*," he said.

She liked that he had remembered *voosh*. "What kind of *voosh*?"

He had no idea what kind of *voosh*. But he knew that, once

again, he had hooked her. And now he needed to come up with something big, something bold, something memorable.

The Spanish Steps tumble downhill from the monumental church of Trinità dei Monti into the busy Piazza di Spagna below where Bernini's pretty boat-shaped Fontana della Barcaccia splashes happily amid the traffic. A network of oddly angled travertine staircases connects 135 steps via a series of grand landings affording panoramic views of the bustling commercial district that spreads in all directions beyond the piazza. At most times of the day or night they are packed with groups of tourists and locals, and on this particular day, the glorious weather had attracted them in droves.

Alice sat on the back of August's rumbling *motorino* mentally listing all the things that could potentially happen to her as a consequence of what she had just agreed to do: death, permanent injury, arrest, deportation; these were just the highlights. New Alice told her to get a grip; if she was genuine about making real changes, now was the time to woman-up and take a walk on the wildly dangerous side. And besides, she knew perfectly well that Old Alice would be too embarrassed to pull out now.

August was so stupidly in love that his brain had turned to gobbledygook. He was certain they were indestructible, and no questions of mortality even entered his head. In another age he would have expressed the enormity of his emotion by challenging someone to a duel or sailing across the Mediterranean in search of lost treasure, but this was all he could come up with at short notice.

He had spent many a summer on his cousin's farm riding cross country, and what they were about to attempt was not much more difficult than that. He revved the tiny engine and lifted the front wheel of the *motorino* onto the sidewalk. There was a moment of rapid acceleration. Pedestrians parted. The bike charged down the white stone staircase.

Alice would have been appalled to learn that she was screaming her head off but fortunately was too preoccupied to notice. As the wheels bounced down the steps, her whole body shuddered so violently that she thought her bones would disconnect, rendering her a jumbled skeleton inside a fleshy sack of skin. She could no longer feel her arms but nevertheless instructed her brain to instruct her limbs to hold on tight. Faces whizzed by. Some alarmed, some smiling, one shouting furiously.

With a thump the bike hit the first landing, and for a merciful few seconds the shuddering stopped as they made their way diagonally across it, speeding from the left-hand side of the steps to the right. Alice relaxed for a moment and almost lost her hold when they hit the second flight of steps. As the *motorino* descended, she gripped tighter. At least, she was pretty sure she did. She gathered she must be holding on because she was not falling off. She closed her eyes, feeling time simultaneously speed up and slow down. This couldn't be happening to her; it had to be happening to someone else. She felt herself rise out of her body, observing events from afar.

As the *motorino* plowed down the stairs, not one conscious thought entered August's head. He did not feel a single bump. He was necessarily completely present in each unfolding moment, his brain absolutely occupied with calculating countless equations and formulating appropriate responses to physical challenges presenting themselves in a relentless second-by-second sequence.

On the second landing, August saw a man in a dark blue uniform with white gloves running toward them, blowing a whistle and waving jazz hands at him. He swerved the bike around the man and continued to descend. Scanning the piazza below for an escape route, he noted two blue flashing lights making their way up the Via dei Condotti. Looking back at the steps, he saw a lady with a trolley of gelati directly in front of him. The woman had just seen him, too, but her face was still blank; she had not yet had the time to register, let alone express, the horror of the potential catastrophe before them. August swung the handlebars quickly to the left.

The sudden turn caused the rear wheel of the *motorino* to slide across the travertine, thrusting Alice sideways. Her eyes sprang open to see the white pavement looming toward her. She felt herself leaving the seat, certain the worst was about to happen. She tried to grip August's torso, but forces were dragging her farther and farther away from him. Color drained from her vision so that she saw the world in fuzzy black and white. Time slowed, and events unstitched themselves from reality. Somewhere in her brain, Alice registered that she was fainting and had, in fact, forgotten to breathe. She commanded her lungs to open and take in air, but they had solidified with fear, rigid as two iron pots.

Then suddenly below her the wheels took purchase, and the *motorino* stopped sliding. There was a bump, and Alice's lungs inflated. Color returned to her vision. She gripped August's T-shirt and with a surge of determination dragged herself upright, against downward momentum. Time resumed its usual speed. Alice shut her eyes again, as if shutting down one sense might help her better manage the others.

Clutching the handlebars, August found equilibrium. With the *motorino* upright and his heart pounding, he steered around the woman and her gelati and made a final descent to the piazza where he drove in an arc around a group of schoolboys. August did not even notice that they were clapping and cheering.

Once the terrible juddering of the descent had ceased, Alice opened her eyes again to see and hear two police sirens wailing toward them. Looking left she saw a third siren approaching from the Via di Propaganda. *This cannot be happening,* she thought.

August turned the *motorino* right and sped toward the Via del Babuino but made a snap decision to turn left down the Via delle Carrozze. They fell into the shade of the buildings, and August registered a drop in temperature. With a sickening lurch, he thought that he had lost Alice somewhere. Removing his left hand from the handlebars, he quickly checked around his waist to discover that she was still holding on.

Still fractured from reality, Alice registered little but the kaleidoscopic blur of pedestrians. She saw a line of market umbrellas with people dining at café tables beneath them, a child in blue-and-white stripes, an amber-brown sign that said *Greco* on an apricot terra-cotta wall.

August noted a change in the pitch and intensity of the sirens: there were more; they were closer. To his right, he clocked a small archway, the width of a doorway with a metal gate, solid to waist height with vertical bars above. It was ajar. He applied the brakes and turned, nudging the gate with the front wheel. It swung open, and he drove the *motorino* into a small alcove. In front of them three marble steps led to a raised porch. On the porch, an exposed brick partition with an off-center doorway revealed what appeared to be some kind of washbasin. The space made little sense, but not much was making sense right now.

Suddenly a blue light flashed around the white rendered walls, growing quickly in intensity. A siren wailed, louder and louder. Pulsating blue filled the alcove. The siren screamed in their ears. Then it raced away. Another blue light came wailing and another and another. Through it all they remained as statues. Eventually, the dim wailing of the last blue light softened into the echo of a distant musical note.

Finally, August unfroze and turned to Alice, forcing her to unlock her arms from his waist. A smile cracked his face. "I reckon that was *voosh,*" he said.

Alice looked at him, blank. Too much data had been entered into her system, and she was experiencing a momentary shutdown.

August leaned in to her. "You okay?" he said.

She could feel his hot breath on her face. He was so close that she thought he might kiss her. Suddenly, she rebooted, wildly, thrillingly, intoxicated. If he was going to kiss her, she was going to kiss him back.

An alarm went off with a piercing, insistent beep. They both jumped. Alice pulled a phone from her pocket. August took it and looked at the screen. It was time to catch her train. He smiled sadly at her and handed back the phone.

The moment when they might have kissed had vanished.

FIFTEEN

The Art of the Cappuccini

OFTEN A MAN ENDURES FOR SEVERAL YEARS, SUBMITS AND SUFFERS
THE CRUELEST PUNISHMENTS, AND THEN SUDDENLY BREAKS OUT
OVER SOME MINUTE TRIFLE, ALMOST NOTHING AT ALL.
—Fyodor Dostoyevsky, *The House of the Dead*

Dr. Stephanie Cope sat at a table outside a small restaurant in the Via del Pellegrino, waiting for her bucatini all'Amatriciana. She was sipping a cappuccino, which scandalized her waiter, Pietro, because, as he explained every time she ordered it, the only occasion anyone in Italy took milk in coffee was at breakfast. But Stephanie had lived too long in war zones not to know the importance of getting what she wanted when she wanted it. She wanted to have a coffee, with milk, before lunch, and so that was what she was having. *For tomorrow we may die.* She had no doubt they were shaking their heads in despair around the espresso machine, but so be it.

In an attempt to drain the last stubborn *splendiferousness*—her word for milk foam—from the bottom of her cup she lifted it high and tipped her head back. Were it not for the strong waft of cologne that made her look, she might have completely missed the cross-eyed man and his furtive companion getting into a clapped-out silver Peugeot, just down the street. She was sure it was the same fellow who had been with the American and his wife. She had asked him earlier if he belonged to the La Barbuta gypsy settlement because one of the little girls from there had not shown up at the clinic for treatment. He had denied any knowledge of the gypsies or the little girl, and even though she had thought he was lying, Stephanie had let the matter drop. She now wondered whether that had been wise.

As the silver car drove past, the doctor saw the passenger rifling through a bag that looked suspiciously similar to the one that the wife—what was her name? *Meg*—had been carrying. By the time Pietro arrived with her perfectly al dente bucatini, Stephanie had left.

Not far away, in the pitch darkness of the cellar where they were imprisoned, Alec had crawled across the floor and found the door. Having established that it was bolted from the outside, he had tried banging on it and calling out, but to no avail. He had also tried to remove the pins from the hinges but had only succeeded in shredding his fingernails.

His next plan of attack was to use brute strength and break the door open with his shoulder.

Meg was also crawling around on the floor, feeling for something useful. *Like a rocket launcher to blow that cross-eyed fucker off the face of the earth.* So far, all she had managed to find were an ashtray, some cigarette butts, and a box of what felt like dried ham bones. She heard the thump of Alec's shoulder hitting the door and a grunt of pain.

"What are you doing?" she asked snippily.

"This may sound like a wacky idea," he answered, "but I thought I might try and get us out of here."

There was another thump and another groan of pain. Meg decided if Alec wanted to dislocate his shoulder, that was up to him.

"You don't happen to have any matches on you, do you?" said Alec.

"As a matter of fact, I do," said Meg. "Just in case my bag gets stolen and I'm locked in a dungeon, I have a candle and matches stuck up my butt."

Her fingers fell on something smooth, and she examined it; a small plastic tube with a metal wheel on top; a cigarette lighter. She flicked it, and a very small flame illuminated the floor around her. Alec turned and saw his wife dimly lit.

"Candles!" he said and scrambled over to her. On the floor next to Meg there was a box of white candles, the kind they light at church offertories. The flame went out. Meg swore in the darkness. Alec found a candle and put it in her hand. Meg flicked the lighter again and produced a tiny flame. The wick seemed reluctant to light but eventually ignited. Alec took a second candle and lit it from the first.

Meg slowly swept her candle in an arc around her. In the small pool of light she saw what she had thought were ham bones. They were not ham bones. They appeared to be human bones. Alec got to his feet and lifted his candle to establish whether there were any other doors or means of escape. Light flickered onto the closest wall. He got such a shock he dropped his candle. In the split second before his candle extinguished, Meg saw what her husband had seen. She screamed.

. . .

Across Rome, just off the Piazza Barberini, underneath the church of Santa Maria della Concezione dei Cappuccini, Father Bernadino Bassi was inspecting the damp-proofing work on one of the crypts. There were six crypts in all, five of which were lined floor to ceiling with the bones and skulls of 3,700 of Father Bernardino's fellow Capuchin friars who had shuffled off this mortal coil sometime between 1528 and 1870. The bones were arranged in elaborate decorative patterns and scenes to remind the living of the brevity of their passage on earth. And just in case the living missed the point, a sign translated into several languages was there to guide them: *What you are now we used to be; what we are now you will be. . . .*

The five skeletal chapels were divided into various themes: the Crypt of the Resurrection, the Crypt of the Skulls, the Crypt of the Pelvises, the Crypt of the Leg Bones and Thigh Bones, and the Crypt of the Three Skeletons. Father Bernadino had reluctantly closed the Crypt of Leg Bones and Thigh Bones because damp was leaching through its walls and corrupting the bones.

In order for the repairs to be carried out, the leg bones and thigh bones had been carefully removed from the walls of the crypt and painstakingly reassembled on portable wooden frames. A kind parishioner had offered Father Bernardino the use of a storage facility near the Campo de' Fiori. The room was now empty but had been used for years by a stall-owner at the markets. It was cool and dry, ideal for storing vegetables and keeping them fresh. Also ideal for storing bones.

And so it was that the Crypt of Leg Bones and Thigh Bones had been temporarily re-created in a dark, quiet room off the Arco di Santa Margherita, where Meg and Alec were currently held captive.

Dr. Stephanie was on her second lap of the Arco di Santa Margherita when she thought she heard a woman screaming. The sound seemed to be coming from a shuttered brown door. The doctor hurried toward the door and noticed a broken padlock on the cobblestones. She rolled up to the door, and the screaming grew louder. It was clearly coming from behind a door on the far wall of the empty space. Stephanie hurried to the door and banged on it. The screaming stopped.

"Hello?" said Stephanie.

A man's voice replied. It was Alec. Meg began to bang on the door and in a strange wail begged Stephanie to open it as if she had some other plan in mind. As she grappled with the large bolt, the doctor could hear Alec's voice trying to calm Meg, but he was having little effect. Stephanie pushed and pulled but was unable to move the bolt. She called out that she was going to look for some instrument with which to dislodge it. On the other side of the door Meg begged her not to leave. Stephanie assured her she would not be long. As she searched the floor for something to bash the bolt with, she could hear what she was pretty sure was a tirade of hysterical abuse directed at her, followed by the low rumble of Alec's voice, urging restraint.

In less than a minute, Stephanie had located a broken concrete brick and was bashing at the bolt. Eventually, it slid across, and she pushed open the door. Meg shot out past her, through the open shutter and out into the air of the *arco*. Alec followed, equally alarmed and grateful. When he had soothed his wife, Alec returned and explained what had happened, thanking Stephanie for coming to the rescue.

While Meg sat crumpled in a doorway, Alec and the doctor went back to explore the mysterious and astonishing sight of what she confirmed were human bones. Stephanie took out her phone and was in the process of dialing the police when Father Bernadino arrived. A neighbor had reported a fracas at his storage facility, and he had come to investigate.

As Alec explained and Stephanie translated, the eighty-six-year-old neighbor, Teresa, timidly appeared with shots of grappa to calm everyone's nerves. She had heard the screaming, she apologized, but was too frightened to respond directly. Father Bernadino assured her that she had done the right thing. Together they all waited for the police to arrive.

As they waited, Meg fell strangely quiet. Alec expressed concern about her to Stephanie, who took Meg's pulse, which was running a little fast but not alarmingly so, given the ordeal she had just endured. She assured Meg that the culprits would be tracked down, that she was almost certain they belonged to a band of gypsies camped on the outskirts of the city at a well-known settlement called La Barbuta. The police would have her bag back to her in no time.

At the mention of her bag, Meg returned to life. "I don't care about the bag," she said. "I just want the tile." Drawing her knees toward her, she repeated, "I just want the tile."

Sensing that she was spinning off into some strange new world, Alec said steadily, "It's best to leave these things to the police."

Ignoring him, Meg asked Stephanie to repeat where she

thought she might find the gypsies. Reluctantly, Stephanie told her. Meg asked her to write it down. She knew that Stephanie, good Girl Scout that she was, would have a pen and paper in her bag, precisely for occasions like these. As the doctor jotted the details of La Barbuta, Alec said, very firmly, "We are not going on a wild-goose chase across Rome. We're going to wait for the police."

"You can wait for the cops," said Meg, getting to her feet. "I'm going to get my tile."

"You don't know where it is," he said.

"No, but I know where to start looking."

"Maybe the tile maker has one just like it."

"Maybe he does. That will be my second port of call after La Barbuta."

"Meg, this is nuts."

Ignoring this, Meg said, "Meet you at the tile place at three. Unless you're coming with me."

"I'm not coming with you. You're not going anywhere."

Meg started to walk away.

"Where are you going?" he called after her.

She did not answer because he knew where she was going.

"How are you going to get there?" he said.

"Taxi," she called over her shoulder.

"You don't have any money."

Meg stopped and walked back.

"Could you lend me some euros?" she said to Stephanie.

Stephanie shot a glance at Alec, who almost imperceptibly shook his head.

"Do you need a man to give you approval?" said Meg, knowing exactly where to aim her arrow. "I'll pay you back, double." She added, "I'm good for it."

Stephanie hated being trapped like this. She knew that she should not enable this reckless behavior. She knew she was being bullied into showing solidarity to the sisterhood when it wasn't really appropriate. But she handed over the money anyway, almost eighty euros. "I wish you wouldn't," she said to Meg. "It's not safe."

"I'm just going to ask for the tile," said Meg. "They can keep the rest of the stuff."

When he hated his wife, which he did, not irregularly, this is what Alec hated the most: her capacity to sound rational and act irrationally. She would drag him into some crisis that he would never have entered of his own volition and then blame him for not being able to resolve it. He could see this happening right now, and he was not going to tolerate it. He stood in front of her.

"You are not going," he said.

Meg snorted derision and stepped around him. He grabbed her arm to try to stop her leaving. She pulled away. What followed was a brief but embarrassing wrestling cha-cha, which ended in victory for Meg when she stamped on Alec's foot. For good measure, she threw a knowing look at the priest and the doctor—a look laden with the implication that this was a regular occurrence. This infuriated Alec for a whole bunch of reasons but mostly because in eighteen years of marriage he had never once resorted to physical violence.

He had, however, regularly resorted to imaginary violence.

Indeed, he was doing this right now as he limped around the *arco*. He hoped with all his heart that Meg would be able to locate the gypsies. He hoped that she would be her usual obnoxious self. He hoped that the gypsies would take offense and slit her throat and cut her up into little pieces and put her through a mincer and feed her to the rats.

SIXTEEN

Santa Barbara dei Librai

I HAD TO TOUCH YOU WITH MY HANDS, I HAD TO TASTE YOU
WITH MY TONGUE; ONE CAN'T LOVE AND DO NOTHING.
—Graham Greene, *The End of the Affair*

Having braved the crowds of the markets and consulted the
great Giordano Bruno, Constance finally set herself and Lizzie
on the right track, and they jostled through the throngs of
shoppers on the Via dei Giubbonari, toward the Jewish Ghetto.
In the cold light of the hot day, Constance began to feel foolish about the fuss she was making. She suddenly regretted
dragging her sister-in-law though the heat and the crowds to
make a point about she-was-no-longer-sure-what exactly.

At the first turn on their left, they came to the Largo dei
Librari, a funnel-shaped courtyard, three buildings deep. At
the very end of the courtyard, there it was, the little church of
Santa Barbara, wedged between two large, old secular buildings. The neighboring apartment building had been extended
so that it sat in the airspace right on top of the left-hand nave

chapel. It looked as if the big bully building was trying to nudge the diminutive church out of the way.

"Funny-looking little thing, isn't it?" said Constance.

Lizzie was tired, thirsty, hungry, hot, and not in the mood to find anything particularly funny. She suggested they stop for a drink and something to eat, sinking into an aluminum chair set outside the small bar at the entrance to the Largo.

As they waited in the shade for their *acqua frizzante* and panini, Constance prattled on about a series of name changes that the church had undergone in the thousand years of its existence.

Lizzie marveled at Constance's capacity to recall all this minutiae, although it was becoming clear to her that she was using it to delay arriving at some large central piece of information.

"Constance, why are we here," blurted Lizzie impatiently, "sitting outside this church?"

"Bear with me," said her sister-in-law. "I'm almost there."

She went on to explain that although the church was currently a place of worship, for a good part of the twentieth century, it had been deconsecrated and used for storage. Sometime in the early 1960s a stack of church pews collapsed, damaging one of the altars. "I was part of a small restoration team bought in to repair the damage," she said, finally placing herself in the picture.

"Oh, this is what you were doing when you met Henry," said Lizzie. "You were fixing the mosaic, I remember now."

"It wasn't a mosaic; it was a pietr*rra* dur*rra*," said Constance, rolling her *r*'s beautifully. "The altar was the most extraordinary example. The artist cuts and fits highly polished stones around each other to create an image. Ivory, mother of pearl, agate—"

"Yes, yes, yes," interrupted Lizzie, "all very fascinating, but please get to the point before I lose the will to live."

"Okay."

"Okay."

"Okay. So," said Constance. "There were two other members of the restoration team, a brother and sister, both born and bred here in Roma. The girl, Gina, and I were great chums until one day she took me to meet her boyfriend."

A warm breeze scooted down the Via dei Giubbonari and twirled in little eddies around the Largo, dancing here and there with paper bags and other detritus. The wind lifted Constance up, transporting her over half a century to the Ponte Sant'Angelo.

She remembered walking toward the bridge, arm in arm with Gina, feeling slightly intimidated by her sultry radiance, by the ease with which she traveled in her body, and by her impeccably cut dress. Constance knew she was no slouch herself. She was well aware that the pair of them turned heads wherever they went, but she thought of herself as a paler, less exotic version of her knockout pal.

Gina suddenly waved at a man on the bridge. She uncurled her arm from Constance's and ran ahead, into the man's embrace. Constance registered that he was pale, probably a northerner from Venice or Milan. As he kissed her friend, she also noticed that he was very handsome, with thick, wavy hair and a drooping moustache, reminding her for all the world of the *Dying Gaul,* a classical statue of a naked man that she visited with unseemly regularity in the Capitoline

Museum. She hovered, waiting a respectful distance for them to finish kissing.

Gina saw her friend from the corner of her eye and waved her over to make the introductions. The first surprise was that she spoke in English, not Italian.

"Henry, this is my friend Constance," said Gina in her lusciously accented *Inglese*.

Henry offered his hand. "How do you do?" he said with a very proper English accent, which was the second surprise. When Gina had told her that she had met someone special, Constance had gone mining for details, but her friend had refused to yield. "Come and meet him," she had simply said.

Constance took Henry's hand. "How do you do?" she said.

"You're British," said Henry. He wanted to add, *And you talk like a pirate. How wonderful.* But he did not. Constance had wanted to reply, *And you're British, too!* But that seemed a very dull response to this very interesting man. So she did not.

"Finely observed," said Constance instead.

"Thank you," said Henry. "I'm a whiz at the bleeding obvious."

They stood there grinning inanely at each other.

Through a wormhole in the space-time continuum, Lizzie shouted at her sister-in-law, dragging her back to the Largo dei Librari. "You stole him! You stole Henry from that poor Italian girl! I never knew! Oh, my dear, how appallingly sluttish of you."

"Before you go choking on your glee," said Constance, "there's more."

Lizzie turned to the Harrods bag sitting on the aluminum chair between them. She pulled open the handles and spoke directly to the Henry box. "And you never told me either, you dog. You dirty old dog." She took a gulp of her water and added, "Well, this is remarkable. I find myself perking up enormously."

"Yes, I can see that," said Constance.

"Do go on," said Lizzie, taking a great chomp out of her panino and bracing herself for the next installment.

"Well, Henry and I get married, blah, blah," said Constance, "and twenty years later we return to Roma for a kind of second honeymoon thing, and who should we bump into?"

The Pantheon had always been Henry's favorite building in Rome. He especially loved to go there during a storm and stand inside the great domed rotunda, watching the rain sheet through the central oculus and vanish into the drains concealed in the marble floor. He loved that this building invited the rain in rather than struggled to keep it out. He loved that it had been doing this for two thousand years. In these divine moments it was impossible, he claimed, not to believe in God, or gods.

Constance had spent much of their twentieth wedding anniversary shopping for a gown for their daughter, Marina, to wear to her graduation ball. Henry had been content to tag along, but one afternoon when the storm clouds gathered and lightning sliced the sky, he grabbed his wife by the hand and started running. She knew where they were headed and started to complain; she was dressed for shopping, not sprinting, but Henry would not be dissuaded.

Rounding a corner onto the Via del Corso, a royal-purple velvet dress caught Constance's eye, and she stopped to look at it, forgetting to let go of her husband's hand. Coming to an unexpected halt, Henry bounced back and bumped into a woman who had also stopped to admire the dress. He was halfway through an apology when he recognized her.

"Gina?" he said.

Gina had weathered the intermittent twenty years better than any of them and now in her early forties was enjoying the prime of her exceptional beauty. She looked at him quizzically for a beat and said, "Henry?" and then scanning the panting woman next to him added, noticeably cooler, "And Constance."

Constance had known this meeting was a possibility from the moment that Henry had announced he was taking her to Rome for their anniversary. She should have been prepared for it but was not. All she could think to do was tell the truth.

"Gina," she said, "you look marvelous."

"You do!" exclaimed Henry with unbridled enthusiasm. "You look absolutely marvelous!"

Later in the day, they returned to their room in the hotel, the same room where they had first made rapturous love on the blue-tiled floor twenty years before. Henry had booked it as a surprise, and Constance had done her best to look pleased but in truth had been hoping for more opulent digs, befitting the significance of the marital milestone they just reached together.

As Henry began to undress her, she could tell from the goony look on his face that he was not undressing her, but Gina, and she turned to ice. Sensing the sudden change in temperature, Henry asked what was wrong. Constance said that nothing was wrong, but he insisted on dragging it out of her. As soon as she outlined her observation, Henry denied it with such ferocity that it was immediately apparent to Constance she had been correct. An argument erupted. The pretense of Henry's indignation enraged her. Constance was not a violent woman. She had never struck her husband. But there was something about being in Rome that lent permission to unleash her passion. Objects were thrown. Ornaments, too. A plate narrowly missed Henry's head and smashed on the wall behind him.

Henry left and wandered the streets of Rome for some hours until he found himself outside Gina's family palazzo. He rang the buzzer, and soon Gina was standing before him, wrapped in a red silk dressing gown. He had no idea what to say to her.

"Henry," said Gina, "what do you want?"

"May I come in?" he said.

Lizzie's cry of disbelief sucked Constance back down the space-time wormhole, and once again she was back in the Largo dei Librari.

"It wasn't a very long affair," said Constance. "We'd been going through a rough patch. Henry was"—she paused, searching for a word—"lost. And there was Gina, full of womanly compassion, ready to show him the way." Constance smiled and shrugged.

Lizzie sat mute, reeling. Constance took a deep breath and sighed.

"Yesterday at the bridge," said Constance, "it occurred to me that maybe the affair went on for longer than I knew. That maybe all these years—"

"Oh, girlie!" Lizzie interrupted. "He loved you. He married you."

"That he wanted to be in Rome," Constance plowed on, "so he could be near her."

There. She had said it. She had said it out loud. It did sound foolish and small as she thought it would, but nonetheless she was glad to admit it. Tears of relief welled in her eyes.

In all their years, Lizzie had never seen Constance cry. She found a handkerchief in the sleeve of her blouse and handed it to her sister-in-law. Constance took it and blew her nose. "Ignore me," she said. "I'm a silly old lady."

"No, darling," said Lizzie, "this is your head doing you in. This isn't real. This is—"

"I know, I know," Constance interrupted. She went to return Lizzie's handkerchief and realized it was damp. "Oh, sorry. And the point is, there is nothing I can do about it. I will never know the truth. Henry is not here to illuminate us." She tucked the handkerchief in her pocket.

Lizzie reached over the table and took her hand. "I'm here to illuminate you," she said, "and I can tell you that my brother loved you with all his heart and soul and every fiber of his being." She knew she was being sentimental and that under normal circumstances Constance would have been repelled by sentimentality, but these were not normal circumstances.

"Come on," said Lizzie. "Let's go look at that mosaic of yours."

"*Pietra dura,*" corrected Constance.

"Whatever," said Lizzie, unfolding herself from the chair. Constance called for the bill and staggered to her feet. They were both stiff and sore from sitting for so long. Lizzie paid the bill, and together they gathered up the Harrods bag and headed across the Largo to the steps of Santa Barbara dei Librai. Constance noted with irritation that they were ambulating with far less grace and vigor than they had been previously.

SEVENTEEN

Stazione di Roma Termini —Giovanni Paolo II

I AM NOT A THING—A NOUN. I SEEM TO BE
A VERB, AN EVOLUTIONARY PROCESS—AN
INTEGRAL FUNCTION OF THE UNIVERSE.
—R. Buckminster Fuller, *I Seem to Be a Verb*

Alice and August returned to the guesthouse to collect her avocado-and-lime backpack. While August checked on the lads, discovering that they were all still indisposed, Alice went looking for Florentina, who eventually appeared in the kitchen, flushed and breathless.

"I can see I was wrong about that boy," said Florentina.

"What boy?" said Alice.

"You do not break his heart," said Florentina. "He breaks yours."

As Florentina swept her into a farewell embrace, it occurred to Alice that her landlady smelled distinctly of sex. Indeed, had Alice walked six paces to her right and opened the pantry door, she would have discovered Florentina's Web designer waiting in priapic splendor to conclude another extremely creative consultation with his client.

Outside, August swapped his *motorino* for Rick's. They were both the same ubiquitous beige color, but as Alice had earlier pointed out, Rick's was bigger and, more important, it had a different license plate. August felt a little uneasy about driving Alice across Rome with her distinctive flaming hair waving behind them, but she solved the problem by tucking her red locks into a helmet. Traversing the Centro Storico, they made it to Roma Termini without incident and pulled up outside the monumental wall of glass that fronted the long lobby of the station. August watched their reflections as Alice alighted, took off her helmet, and handed it back to him.

"Thanks," she said.

Not knowing what else to do, he extended his hand. As she took it, he said, suddenly feeling like he was appearing in some old black-and-white movie, "I'll never forget you."

"Me neither," said Alice. "Whatever your name is." She let go of his hand and asked, "What *is* your name?"

August had given her his heart. It suddenly seemed strangely important to him that he not give her his name as well.

"Let's do this right," he said. "You head off through those doors now, and you don't look back."

Alice nodded. She hitched up her backpack so that it rested more comfortably on her frame. "Just do one thing for me," she said.

"Sure."

"Go to Paris and paint."

"That's two things," he said, "but sure."

Alice smiled, and he smiled back. She turned and walked

away. As he watched her disappear into the anonymous stream of commuters, it occurred to August that she was the one who should go to Paris and paint; she was the one who saw seventeen colors in the green of his eyes; she was the one who could see the kaleidoscopic universe around her; she was the one with the gift. He hoped that she would realize that one day.

Alice walked under the cantilevered concrete canopy that extended over the entrance, through the crowds in the great hall, to the ticketing office where she waited in line and collected her prepaid ticket to Florence. In a daze, she found her way to platform twenty-two and boarded the silver bullet-shaped train with its dashing red-and-dark-gray stripes. In carriage number four, she hoisted her backpack into the overhead locker and slumped into her maroon leather seat, wishing she'd never met Pea Green and cursing the broken certainty that lay like Humpty Dumpty at her feet. *All the king's horses and all the king's men . . .*

Looking out the window, she was caught between studying her own dull reflection and watching the world that was bustling by with complete disregard for her ennui. A young man passed the window. He looked just like Pea Green. Alice sat up, suddenly alert. The young man returned, looking in the windows. It was Pea Green.

He waved. She waved back. She waited as he boarded the train and made his way to her. Her heart was pounding so loudly she thought the other passengers would hear. Pea Green dropped into the empty seat opposite her.

"Okay, so here's the thing," said August. "Imagine it's ten, fifteen years from now, and you're happily married to the tosser—"

"He's not a tosser."

August pressed on. "Okay, so let's call him the Not-Tosser. And you're married, and you're a famous artist because *you* went to Paris and painted, by the way, not me, but you're blocked and you can't work. So you try skipping and it helps, but it doesn't really do the trick. But the skipping does remind you of that English guy you met in Rome all those years ago, and suddenly—wham—it hits you, that's why you're blocked. Unconsciously, you're wondering what would have happened if you'd got off the train and spent one more day in Rome with him."

Alice swallowed, and August could see he was making inroads. He kept going. "Wouldn't it be nice to know for certain that I'm the wrong person and he's the right person? To be sitting in your studio in fifteen years' time painting your head off without a doubt in the world about the decisions you made?"

"I'm meeting him in Florence in two hours," she said.

August shrugged. He kept staring at her.

"We're supposed to be choosing our engagement ring," she added.

"I happen to know of an excellent invention called the cell phone," he said.

Outside, the conductor blew a whistle. There was a garbled announcement in Italian over the intercom. Departure was clearly imminent.

August gave it one last shot. "In the grand scheme of things . . ."

For a split second, Alice glimpsed what he would have looked like as a little boy.

"Meet me out the front," said New Alice, "where you dropped me off."

August ran to the parking lot. He forgot where he had left the *motorino*, abandoning it, as he had, in a moment of sudden resolve. He had no doubt he was a comical sight, his plight evident to anyone who saw him darting about the sea of cars and bikes like a headless chicken. He told himself to calm down. She wasn't going to get on a bus or something just because he wasn't there immediately. Finally, he spotted the *motorino*, right where he had left it, parked haphazardly in a line of other illegally parked *motorini*. He slipped his hand into his jeans' pocket, but there was no key. He put his hand in the other pocket, but there was nothing there either, just a few English pence and an empty chewing-gum wrapper. He checked the ignition of the *motorino*, but the key was not there. Had he dropped it at the station somewhere or left it on the train? He started to run back to the station when he realized that there was something in his hand. It was the key. *You really must calm the fuck down,* he told himself.

August returned to the *motorino* and drove it back to the place where Alice had disembarked. He could not park on the exact spot because a great caterpillar of a tourist bus, with side mirrors protruding like antennae, had stopped there. So he pulled in behind it; it was close enough. Alice was not there yet. He looked beyond his own reflection in the wall of glass to the mass of commuters inside. He knew the first thing he would see would be the top of the green backpack bobbing through the crowd.

He waited. He waited for the bus to disgorge its passengers, for the passengers to collect their baggage from the underbelly of the bus, and for the bus to drive away. He shuttled forward; now he was in the exact spot. It did not occur to him that Alice may have changed her mind, that she may have heaved her backpack from the luggage rack and dragged it down the aisle as far as the door before suddenly realizing the mistake she was making. He did not imagine for an instant that she might, in fact, have returned to her seat and could now be watching the outer suburbs of Rome sweeping past the window, that she could well be on her way to Florence into the arms of her fiancé.

Alice returned to platform twenty-two. She had tried to call Daniel from the main hall and had actually connected, but the din of the other commuters and the almost constant stream of announcements made it impossible to hear anything. Now that the train for Florence had departed, the platform was comparatively quiet, although the announcements continued to blare forth. Old Alice was determined not to begin this new episode without speaking to Daniel. New Alice counseled her to let the wild rumpus start and warned that her Englishman would not wait forever, but Alice knew this was not true. She was certain that he would be out there waiting for her.

Alice tried to imagine where Daniel would be. Her first call had connected, so he must be off the plane and was probably on his way to the hotel or at the hotel already. Or maybe he had managed to get a flight to Rome and had come here to surprise her. In a hot panic, she spun around, expecting him to appear behind her, arms outstretched in greeting. He was not there. Nor was he, she reminded herself, the type to change his plans without telling her. Then again, neither was she until very recently.

On her sixth attempt, Alice finally connected with Daniel. They were both on US cell phones, so she imagined her *Hi* traveling from Rome to her service provider in New York, to his provider in New York and on to Florence. Then his distant *Hi* making the journey in reverse. She trotted out the bald-faced lie she had prepared with an ease that surprised her. She had missed the train, she said, and because it was tourist season could not get a seat on another until tomorrow morning. She was relieved to hear the irritation in his voice because it meant that he believed her.

Had she forgotten that he could only get three days off? He wondered aloud whether he should try to get a train down to Rome. Alice suggested he go to the hotel and enjoy some me-time instead. She cringed at how silly this sounded, but it seemed to appeal. He even proposed that he spend some time scoping out engagement rings before she got there. "Great idea," said Alice with her shoulders hunched guiltily around her ears.

Finally, August saw the green backpack bobbing through the crowd toward him. Alice appeared, looking serious. He knew what she had been doing even though she had not told him.

"How'd it go?" he asked as she approached.

"Fine."

"What did he say?"

"If this is going to work," she said, "we're not talking about him."

He handed her a helmet. She bent as far forward as she could wearing a backpack, scraping her hair up her neck. She fed a knot of red hair into the helmet and straightened back up again.

"So what *are* we allowed to talk about?" he said.

"Don't do this," she said.

"Do what?"

Alice hoisted her backpack, getting it into a more comfortable position for sitting on the *motorino*. "You wanted more time so you could pick a fight with me?"

"Is this what this is?" he said. "Are we having our first fight?"

Alice punched his left shoulder with her right hand. Hard, just like her brother used to do to her when they were younger. She had never hit anyone like that in her life, not even in retaliation.

"Ow," he said as if it didn't hurt, even though it did.

Alice mounted the *motorino* and put her arms around him. Into his ear she said, "I lied to him. I told him a lie."

This was not a confession, August knew. This was an announcement: *I am the type who lies to the one who loves her; beware.* He knew she was pointing to her capacity for dishonesty, and he knew he should pause to consider this. But the truth was, if she had whispered, "I killed him," he would have found a way to live with it. Right now, she was with him, August Clutterbuck, and the world was filled to overflowing with this astonishing and glorious fact. He kicked the *motorino* into life.

"So where to?" he called over his shoulder.

"I dunno," she said. "I thought you had a plan."

EIGHTEEN

La Barbuta

HE HAD DISCOVERED A GREAT LAW OF HUMAN
ACTION, WITHOUT KNOWING IT——NAMELY, THAT IN ORDER TO
MAKE A MAN OR A BOY COVET A THING, IT IS ONLY NECESSARY
TO MAKE THE THING DIFFICULT TO ATTAIN.

—Mark Twain, *The Adventures of Tom Sawyer*

Meg hailed a taxi in the Campo de' Fiori and, consulting Stephanie's barely legible scrawl, instructed the driver to take her to the Ciampino airport. She decided not to disclose the specific destination of La Barbuta, just in case she spooked the driver. She would simply relay Stephanie's directions until it was too late for him to refuse to drive into the gypsy camp.

The driver, Aldo, who was fluent in six languages and held a master's of philosophy in literatures of the Americas from Trinity College Dublin, detected her American accent and calculated that, with tip, the trip would pay for his date tonight with Rosa, his on-again off-again girlfriend. He was a little surprised that Meg did not have any luggage, not even a purse, but he knew that she would soon be explaining why.

They were very gregarious, these Americans; they loved to natter, especially about themselves.

He was very surprised, therefore, that Meg sat in the back, silent as a stone. To open conversation, Aldo asked Meg who her favorite nineteenth-century American novelist was. Meg answered that she didn't have one. When he asked if she read novels in languages other than English, opening the door for him to reveal the extent of his multilingual accomplishment, Meg said she was having a bad day and would he mind not speaking.

Allora, Aldo did mind, *grazie* for asking. What was the point of acquiring six languages and dedicating seven years to the study of literature if he wasn't allowed to talk about it? He clenched his jaw and made a mental note not to speak unless directly addressed and even then to restrict himself to mono-syllabic responses. He turned off the radio so there was only the rumble of the engine to entertain them. Two could play at this game.

Meg had no idea they were playing a game. She looked out the window, grateful for the quiet. As they traveled toward the outskirts of the city, ancient Rome gave way to modern Rome. Block after block of midcentury apartment buildings passed by. A chilling sameness spoke not of the *grande bellezza* but the daily grind. Laundry flapped from flaking balconies. Pave-ments cracked, and shoulders were infested with weeds and dying plants. All cities had places that were ugly and unloved, but she had never been to these parts of Rome before and was unprepared for this assault on her idealized view of the city.

The landscape morphed into an eerie mix of rural and industrial, typical of so many areas around city-fringe airports the world over. Small commuter planes began to land regularly up ahead. Meg explained to Aldo that they were not going to the airport but somewhere *near the airport.* Following Stephanie's notes, she instructed him to find the Via Giovanni Ciampini. Consulting his GPS, Aldo pulled off the Via Appia Nuova into the Via di Ciampino that ran parallel to one of the airport runways. They passed a burned-out chassis and turned into Via Giovanni Campini, a thin stretch of decaying asphalt, one car wide. On either side of the road, the brown tufted grass was strewn with building waste and plastic bags. To their left, a group of battered caravans had been bookended with conjoined portable toilets, jaunty red cubicles with white curved roofs and gray doors, covered in graffiti. *This can't be it,* thought Meg. A little farther on, the road simply ran out. Aldo turned to her for further instruction.

"We're looking for La Bar-buta," said Meg, unsure whether to put the emphasis on the first or last syllable.

"The gypsy camp?" asked Aldo.

Meg was relieved to hear that there was no alarm in his tone.

Aldo looked around and pointed. Meg followed his finger across a wasteland littered with refuse to a wire-fenced enclosure with row after row of 160 identical red-roofed white-metal huts. Floodlights on tall steel poles towered over the settlement. Some poles supported surveillance cameras as well. Wedged between an eight-lane freeway, an airport runway, and a railway line, it was hardly the jaunty circle of painted wagons that Meg had imagined. It looked more like a prison or a concentration camp.

Aldo turned the taxi around, drove back down Via Giovanni Ciampini, turned left, then left again into another lane also called—*rather promiscuously,* Aldo thought—Via Giovanni Ciampini. They approached the wire fencing and came to a gravel driveway that led up to the settlement. Aldo made it clear that he would go no farther. Meg had hoped that he would drive her right up to the entrance but decided not to push the point because she had bigger fish to fry. Also because she needed him on her side so he would wait for her to return. She handed him all her money—Stephanie's eighty euros—and asked him to wait, promising to double his payment when they got back to the Storico Centro.

Meg got out of the taxi and walked briskly up the gravel driveway. Aldo watched her until she passed through the open wire gates and disappeared behind a small mountain of bursting garbage bags. Then he called Rosa to tell her about the exciting adventure that was unfolding before him.

Operating on his grandfather's edict that the only bad story was a boring one, and drawing on seven years of the study of narrative, Aldo began to confabulate. He was with an Americana, he told Rosa, who, he was pretty sure, could be that mistress of the Mafia boss. She had gone to the gypsy camp to arrange an execution, maybe, of that other Mafia guy who puts toxic waste in the concrete pylons of the highways he builds. Rosa, who was not of a stable disposition at the best of times—hence the on-again, off-again nature of their relationship—accelerated straight from alarm to hysteria. Did Aldo not appreciate the danger he was in?

Meanwhile, the Polizia di Stato finally arrived in the Arco di Santa Margherita. Having listened to a sketchy and somewhat

confused overview of events from the priest, the doctor, and
the American, Assistente Capo Domenico Cilento began to
take statements. During the forty minutes that they had waited
for the police to arrive in their Alfa Romeo with the racy
white stripes, Alec had calmed down. Once his anger had dis-
sipated, he began to worry terribly about the kind of danger
his headstrong wife could be in.

As the CEO of a company employing hundreds of people,
Alec was accustomed to issuing orders and having them acted
upon promptly. He asked Stephanie to translate while he instructed the *assistente capo* to escort him immediately to this
gypsy camp where they would hopefully find his wife in one
piece. As an *assistente capo* of the Polizia di Stato, Domenico
Cilento did not appreciate the tone with which he was being
addressed. The English doctor was doing her utmost to couch
the American's commands in elaborately polite *Italiano,* but
he was a man who knew when he was being bossed, and he
did not like it one bit.

Stephanie translated back to Alec as the *assistente capo* explained, slowly and with precision, the order of events as they
were about to unfold: no one was going anywhere until the
relevant parties had made their statements and the facts of
the case had been established. Once the facts had been established, they would be acted upon. If he believed that the
lady in question was in danger, he would not waste time
driving across the city; a car or cars would be dispatched
from a station close to the Ciampino airport. He did not
know what it was like in America, but in Italy it was not
the custom to endanger civilians by involving them in an
investigation. If the gentleman was truly concerned with the

safety of his wife, the best course of action would be to immediately and fully cooperate, which would allow him to get on with his job.

In the yard at La Barbuta, a dozen or so old cars were parked against the wire fence. Car parts and bits of broken furniture lay on the ground. The occasional whiff of raw sewage wafted through the hot air. Meg stopped and looked around. The sun beat down on a group of dark-haired children crouched on a stained mattress, freeing its fluffy stuffing from the torn cotton casing. Three little girls with braided hair played in a large pile of white gravel, their brown skin powdered pale by the dust. One of the little girls clambered over the pile and ran to Meg. She looked up at her with serious brown eyes, neither friendly nor unfriendly.

"Why you here?" said the little girl, who already knew enough about the world to use English with this woman.

It was a very good question. Meg had spent most of her life pretending that poor people did not exist. She contributed regularly to several charities via a trust fund associated with their lighting business and felt therefore she had done her duty as far as the underprivileged were concerned. If Meg was the sun of her own solar system, the poor were orbiting somewhere out past Pluto. And that's just where she wanted them.

Meg looked over the head of the serious little girl, down the rows of white huts without a single stick of vegetation between them. They looked practical, she supposed, designed with kitchens and bathrooms and places to sleep, but it seemed they had also been designed to suck the hope out of people's souls. Meg felt afraid. Not of the people inside the huts. She felt afraid of something much bigger, something she could not define, which made it all the more frightening.

The little girl reached up and took her hand. Meg started and wrenched it back, frowning at the little girl accusingly. The little girl did not flinch. She held her gaze as Meg stepped backward, away from her.

Meg wanted her blue tile badly. But she wanted something more. She wanted to preserve her uncomplicated sense of entitlement; it would crumble away from her if she stayed in this place for too long, she knew. She did not want to feel bad about being rich. Or wonder about what else she could do with money that she was spending on redecorating her house. Or think about the choices she could make that these people could not. Or ask why me and not them. The questions were as numerous as they were enormous. They came from a yawning bottomless pit from which there was no escape. If she fell in, she would keep falling.

Two swarthy dark-haired men appeared around the corner of a hut. One shouted something at the children, who scattered. The men began to walk toward Meg. Meg felt her veins turn to ice. It suddenly struck her that she was in very real danger and that she had placed herself there because she was spoiled, willful, and foolish. These men might be approaching to ask why she was there. They might be approaching to rape and murder her. She could not know their intentions until they were upon her. When it would be too late. She had been living her life as if it were a game in which she could control every outcome and make up all the rules. Well, she sure wasn't in charge now. Slapped in the face by the sudden acknowledgment of her monumental hubris, Meg turned and ran. A lump rose in her throat as she sprinted down the gravel driveway in time to see her taxi driving away. She shouted after Aldo and waved her arms, but he neither heard nor saw her.

Aldo's Rosa had worked herself into such a state about his misadventures with Mafia mistresses and the great peril in which he had placed himself that she was now standing on the stone balustrade of her grandmother's Juliet balcony overlooking Santa Maria in Trastevere. A crowd had gathered in the piazza, drawn by her wailing. Rosa was threatening to jump. Aldo was racing back to Rome to resolve the crisis.

"No!" screamed Meg at the disappearing taxi. "No!"

On the dirt road, the cab vanished in a cloud of dust. Aldo showed no sign of slowing down, but this did not deter Meg from running after him as fast as she could. Even when she stumbled and almost fell, Meg kept up her pace. She did not look back to see that the men had not pursued her. She just kept sprinting until she left the dirt road and reached the asphalt, where she ran directly into the path of a yellow Citroën truck.

On the other side of the river, Assistente Capo Domenico Cilento had finished taking statements and was now dispatching two vehicles from the Commissariato Romanina to La Barbuta in search of, in no particular order, a vintage Gucci bag, a blue tile, a cross-eyed man in a green coat, and an American woman who actually sounded quite attractive from her description. The *assistente capo* assured the American husband that he would be in contact as soon as he had any information.

"Do you want to come back to my place," Stephanie offered, "to wait for any news?"

Alec checked the time on his phone. "It's almost three," he
said. "I think I'll go back to the tile shop in case she shows up."

"Do you want me to come with you?" asked Stephanie.

"Thank you, no. I'll be fine, thanks."

They parted in the Via del Pellegrino, and the doctor
wished him good luck with a fond hug. Alec liked hugging
this woman; she was soft and compliant, and her body seemed
to fit with his. As soon as he realized that he was thinking this,
he broke the embrace and stepped away, walking backward
and waving awkwardly at the same time, dimly aware that had
his wife been witnessing his unintended parody of a schoolboy, she would have laughed heartily.

Signore Horatio Zamparelli, tile maker, was accustomed to
customers appearing in his cavernous shop in the Arco degli
Acetari with astonishing and dramatic stories to tell. Indeed,
they were the only type of customer who ever appeared. In the
early years, Horatio worried terribly that he was doing something weird to attract them. Some of his predecessors spent
their entire tenancy bewildered by the dramas that seemed to
perpetually engulf them. Some were even driven to madness.
And because I have no mouth with which to speak and no
hands with which to write, I had no means by which to allevi-
ate their confusion.

Here is what I would have told them had I been able: most
individuals develop the capacity to manage their own hearts
well enough. Some, however, do not. Others develop the

capacity but lose it, for an infinite variety of reasons. These people need help and are likely to be *disturbed*. It is my vocation to render them assistance. I cannot help everyone, of course, but those who come often bring chaos as their companion.

Horatio, fortunately, had long sensed my presence in his workshop and intuited that this had something to do with the crazies who were drawn regularly to his door. Although it made little sense, he had decided to simply stop worrying about it. Thus his sanity was saved. And thus, as Alec Schack stood before him, narrating his nutty story of thieving gypsies and dungeons of bones, Horatio was able to listen with a sanguine and steady heart.

Alec attempted to describe the tile that he and his wife were looking to reproduce. Blue. Beautiful. Shimmering. Magical. The words sounded faintly ridiculous spoken by a grown man, but the bonfire in Alec Schack's eyes left Horatio Zamparelli in no doubt the American gentleman had come to the right place.

He suggested Alec wander around his workshop and see if he could find any tiles similar to the sample that had been stolen. Alec thanked the tile maker and started to explore. A particular tile caught his eye. As he picked it up, a shaft of sunlight suddenly penetrated the shop, and the shimmering figure of a tiny woman appeared on its glazed surface. Alec looked to the open door where the silhouette of a woman had materialized. He thought for a moment that Meg had returned.

"I'm feeling awfully guilty," said the silhouette. It was Dr. Stephanie. "It was so stupid of me to pass on those details about La Barbuta."

"She bullied you into it," said Alec.

"You haven't heard anything?" asked Stephanie.

It had been half an hour at least since Assistente Capo Domenico Cilento had left and half an hour since two police cars had been dispatched to the gypsy camp. Alec checked his phone to make sure there was a signal and to check whether he had missed any calls.

"I should have gone with her," he said.

"I can take you there," said Stephanie.

"Thank you," said Alec, "but if you went missing, the health systems of several countries would completely collapse."

"Don't make fun of me," said Stephanie. "I know I come across as some B-grade Mother Teresa, but I'm not that boring, really."

Alec felt terrible. "I don't think you're boring," he said. "In fact, I think you're . . ." He stopped, realizing that string of superlatives for which he was reaching may lead him somewhere inappropriate. "Not boring," he said.

"My car's outside," said Dr. Cope.

NINETEEN

Saint Barbara

SO FULL OF ARTLESS JEALOUSY IS GUILT, IT
SPILLS ITSELF IN FEARING TO BE SPILT.
—William Shakespeare, *Hamlet*

The story goes that the third-century martyr and saint, Barbara, spent much of her life locked in a tower by her overprotective father, Dioscorus. Once, when he was forced to undertake a long journey far from home, her father built a bathhouse where his daughter might be kept away from crusading Christians whose stories of a man called Jesus intrigued and inspired her. Obviously the bathhouse failed, because Barbara not only converted to Christianity but installed a third window in the two-windowed dwelling as an iconological tip-of-the-hat to the Holy Trinity.

Upon his return, Barbara's father, clearly a man of exceptional perspicacity, immediately comprehended the spiritual symbolism of the architecture and concluded his daughter had become a Christian. When he confronted Barbara she confessed that she was indeed a believer, refusing to renounce her faith. This left Dioscorus no choice, of course, but to sentence her to death. Barbara escaped, but her father tracked her down and cut off her head.

Retribution came swiftly and, as a punishment for his act of filicide, Dioscorus was struck dead by a bolt of lightning. It was the bolt of lightning, presumably, that earned Barbara her place as patron saint of military engineers, artillerymen, armorers, miners, and anyone who works with explosives.

The problem with Barbara's story—admittedly there are a few problems with Barbara's story—but the main problem was that her name did not appear in church texts until the seventh century. There was no reference to her in the early Christian writings, and this significant omission cast doubt over the historicity of her story. Which is why, when the church conducted a fresh sweep through its General Roman Calendar in 1969, Barbara, along with other saints who lacked documentation to support their legends, was quietly removed. She was in good company. Saint Christopher was reviewed at the same time, and although it is generally believed that both he and Barbara were stripped of their titles and "de-sainted," this is not the case. Both still appear in the Roman Martyrology, an extensive list of most (but not all) of the saints recognized by the Catholic Church. Their stories cannot be proven, but they are nonetheless acknowledged as legendary saints and martyrs.

As the two old British ladies sat in front of Barbara's *pietra dura* altar, still in fine condition almost half a century since its restoration, Constance had the strangest feeling that Barbara was angry with her. She had followed Barbara's removal from the General Calendar and, as a young mother with two babies running her ragged, had found time to send a letter of protest to her local bishop. "Just because her story sounds unlikely," she said to Henry at the time, "doesn't mean it didn't happen."

Now sitting before the altar she had restored all those years ago, Constance sensed strongly that Barbara had expected more of her. *What on earth could I have done?* Constance wondered. *Who would have listened to me? And what would I have said anyway?*

Lizzie could feel that Constance was getting herself into a state. "Everything okay there, girlie?" she asked. "Shout out when you think it might be time for the bridge."

"I was just thinking of Gina and Barbara."

"Who's Barbara?"

"Saint Barbara," said Constance. "I was wondering if she did anything when she was demoted."

"Who?"

"Gina."

"Why was Gina demoted?"

"No, Barbara was," said Constance.

Lizzie wondered whether she had suffered one of those ministrokes and missed a beat in the conversation.

Constance suddenly froze.

"What?" said Lizzie.

"Gina," said Constance. "I could go and see Gina."

"Whatever for?" said Lizzie, then, as the penny dropped, added, "You're not going to ask her if she was having an affair with Henry?"

"Why not?"

"What?" said Lizzie, warming to her subject. "Hello, have

you been having an affair with my husband for the last thirty years?"

"Not like that."

"You're not seriously considering this?"

"Why not?"

"Because it's bonkers," said Lizzie. "And besides, how do you even know she's alive? How would you even begin to find her?"

Constance paused; they were pertinent questions. "Well, if she's dead, I guess that answers my question," she said. "And if she's alive she probably still lives in the family palazzo. She was there thirty years ago. Romans never move. I won't make a fuss. I'll just ask her."

"And what if she says, 'Yes, I've been having an affair with your husband for the last thirty years'?"

"Then I shall know the truth, and I'll be able to move on."

"Really!" exclaimed Lizzie. "How very evolved of you."

Lizzie could feel her heart racing and could see that Constance's cheeks were coloring. Constance shifted the Henry bag at her feet, moving it slightly left, then right, as if she were placing a vase of flowers, just so. The door to the church opened, and a group entered, speaking quietly in a language with a lot of hard consonants. The old ladies listened to work out where they were from.

"German?" whispered Constance.

"Further north," whispered Lizzie. "One of those smorgen-vorgen languages."

"Smorgen-vorgen?"

"You know, from the IKEA countries."

They returned to the matter at hand.

"I have no doubt it would be unsettling," said Constance.

"*Unsettling*? What's going on? Why are you even thinking this?"

"Why are you getting upset?"

"It's upsetting."

They paused while the Smorgen-Vorgens passed behind them.

"Is there something you're not telling me?" asked Constance so quietly that Lizzie had to ask her to repeat it.

"Not telling you about what?"

"I'd be devastated to learn something from Gina that I might have found out from you," said Constance.

"What are you talking about?"

"Why are you avoiding my question?"

Forgetting herself, Lizzie shot to her feet. "Oh really, Constance, this is too much!" Looking around, she realized all the Smorgen-Vorgens were looking at her.

"Answer me," said Constance icily.

Lizzie sat back down. She understood that grief could strike strangely, but Constance was not the only one suffering bereavement. She did not want to cry but could feel tears welling. Lizzie took a deep breath and managed to speak, quietly but clearly. "Are we going to the bridge or not?"

"No," said Constance, "I'm going to find Gina."

"Fine. I'll see you at the hotel."

"Fine."

Lizzie began to move away but stopped and came back. "You wouldn't go to the bridge without me?" she said.

"Of course not," said Constance as if Lizzie was the one who was behaving outlandishly.

Out in the Largo dei Librari, Lizzie felt the warm air embrace her. She was very, very upset, and she was lost. She had no idea how to get back to the hotel, but then she was not afraid to ask directions either.

Inside the church, Constance tried to think back over half a century to where Gina lived. She had been there a number of times, for lunch, and had once stayed overnight, she recalled. She closed her eyes and thought back to walking with Gina. An emerald dress came to her. Gina, laughing. A man ogling and whistling; in those days they did. Then the Virgin Mary appeared, followed by the face of Harpocrates, the Greek god of silence. That was it! Gina's palazzo was in the same piazza as the ancient basilica of Santa Maria in Trastevere.

Constance picked up the Harrods bag. Its weight had grown exponentially against the time she had been sitting without holding it. She headed toward the Via dei Pettinari and crossed the Ponte Sisto, over the river, into the neighborhood of Trastevere. Twice she got lost in the labyrinth of laneways and was forced to ask directions.

When she finally arrived at the basilica, some kind of fracas had erupted on the other side of the piazza. A crowd had gathered around a young man who was standing on top of a taxi, gesticulating wildly at a young woman who was perched on the stone balustrade of a balcony above him. The young woman was weeping loudly and beating her breast. Constance remained unfazed by the spectacle. This was, after all, Italy. She positioned herself in front of Santa Maria to get her bearings, put Henry down, and looked up at one of her favorite mosaics in Rome.

At the top of the building, the Madonna and Child were

flanked by ten women bearing lamps, all realized in tiny, glittering tessellations, embedded in a sea of golden tiles. She remembered from her studies—God, that all seemed a century ago—that the basilica was much older than this twelfth-century façade and was the very first place where Mass was openly celebrated in the city.

The last time she had been inside, Henry had taken her specifically to see the columns, purloined from the ruins of the Baths of Caracalla and the Temple of Isis. She remembered him telling her that when some bright spark realized that the faces carved in the capitals belonged to the pagan gods Isis, Harpocrates, and Serapis, Pope Pius IX had had them hammered off. A flash came: Henry smiling and shaking his head at the idiocy of this archeological catastrophe.

Constance scanned the piazza, and there it was: Gina's palazzo, she was certain. The walls were painted the same pale brown, although the shutters were a different color. On the roof, she could see the terrace of hardy old potted palms and remembered that she had once admired how they echoed the mosaic palms on the façade of Santa Maria.

A restaurant and bar occupied the ground floor of the palazzo, where it faced the piazza. Constance picked Henry up and walked to the towering double-entry doors at the side of the building. She felt herself overheating, but mercifully the entrance was in the shade. She rang the buzzer. Eventually, a thin, middle-aged woman wearing jeans and a dirty T-shirt answered. Constance inquired about Gina. Gina's family had sold the palazzo almost a decade previously. No, she did not know where they went, sorry, but she could ask. She was only a housekeeper, but perhaps her employers could help. They were away on holidays at the moment, but if Constance cared to leave her details . . .

Constance thanked the woman but, no, she did not want to leave her details. She had come to the end of the road, and she knew it. The woman said good-bye, and the tall door closed in front of her. Constance wavered on her feet for a moment, buffeted by the heat. She noticed a woman standing in the little street, staring at her.

It was Lizzie.

Lizzie approached holding two bottles of *acqua naturale*. She handed one to Constance, who put down the Harrods bag and gulped the cool water gratefully.

"You followed me," said Constance.

Lizzie nodded.

Constance paused. "What am I doing, girlie?"

"You're working very hard to avoid doing what you know you must," said Lizzie.

Lizzie reached down and picked up the Harrods bag. For the first time in their journey, Constance did not try to stop her.

"Come," said Lizzie. "Let's go to the bridge."

TWENTY

Vaticano

I CANNOT FIX ON THE HOUR, OR THE SPOT, OR THE LOOK, OR
THE WORDS, WHICH LAID THE FOUNDATION. IT IS TOO LONG AGO.
I WAS IN THE MIDDLE BEFORE I KNEW THAT I HAD BEGUN.

—Jane Austen, *Pride and Prejudice*

Monsters and despots have ruled Rome, inflicting death and misery upon their people throughout the millennia. The upside of intermittent psychopathic dictators is that they *get things done,* architecturally speaking. Many of the great buildings and monuments around here were initiated by dreadful people—and I mean *dreadful*—seeking to establish some kind of immortality for themselves.

Lorenzo Bernini had originally designed the vast basilica and forecourt of San Pietro in Vaticano to surprise and astonish pilgrims, after they had negotiated the dark maze of narrow lanes that twisted and turned from the Tiber, but thanks to the dictator Mussolini, there were no surprises when August and Alice turned off the Lungotevere and parked the *motorino.* The buildings had been cleared away in the 1930s to create a wide avenue, and they could see Saint Peter's a mile off.

August watched carefully as Alice unfastened her helmet, transfixed by the mighty edifice at the end of the Via della Conciliazione. He had studied the basilica, as well as much of the art within, in ARC 325 Architecture in History. He especially admired Michelangelo's *Pietá* but made no mention of this because he considered it was a little like declaring you liked chocolate. *Who didn't?*

The thing that August wanted to show Alice was not the basilica itself but the piazza in front of it. He had read about a kind of geometrical magic trick that the piazza performs if you stand in just the right spot and had planned to see this for himself. When Alice had left him at the station, for some reason that was not clear to him, he was filled with regret that he had not shown it to her.

"So what's this trick?" said Alice, handing him her helmet.

"You have to wait till we get there," he said. "Can I take your backpack?"

"No, thanks." She wanted to carry it herself, to remind herself that she was on an excursion; that this was not her real life.

Chaining their helmets to the *motorino*, August's certainty swept away like the sea receding before a tsunami. Why had it seemed like such a good idea to bring her here? Was he showing off? *Look what I know about that you don't know about.* He gestured authoritatively toward the Vatican. "This way."

"Really?" she said dryly.

He strode out in front of her, hoping she hadn't noticed the flush blossoming across his cheeks. Had she noticed? *Of course she had noticed.* She trotted a little to catch up and fell in next to him. He could sense her looking at him. Any minute now she would ask why he was blushing or what was wrong.

"So how do you know you're in love with someone enough to want to marry them?" he said.

Alice stopped. August looked back at her, surprised. No internal guidance system had warned him that he had been about to blurt that question.

"I don't want to talk about Daniel," Alice said. As soon she said "Daniel," they simultaneously registered that she had named her fiancé.

"Daniel?" he said.

"We're not discussing him," she said, and she strode off at full-tilt.

August scrambled after her. "Sorry, I don't mean him. I don't mean you and him," he said. "I just mean in general." August had no idea what he meant; he was clawing at the crumbling edges of the hole into which he had inexplicably hurled himself. "I mean, how does anyone know they love someone?" An alien life-form appeared to be forcing August to ask daft questions.

Alice had not agreed to spend the rest of her life with Daniel without carefully considering the whys and wherefores of such a commitment and was perfectly prepared to provide August with an answer. "You don't fall in love," she said. "You choose to love a particular person. Humor, brains, eye-color, smile, there's a huge list of things that click, that tell you this is the match for you."

"It's a list?"

"It's a list," she said, feeling pleased that her answer had surprised him as she had hoped it would. "For most people it's an unconscious list, but if you actually write down a list of all the pros and cons that you can think of, then you have a much better chance of making an informed decision."

"So you write a list?"

"Yes," said Alice plainly.

It had been Daniel himself who had laid the path for her to find a way to him. He had taught her to make lists to conquer her habit of procrastination, and in the end she had used his methodology to make a list and choose him. Alice reminded herself now that the list had been long and gravely considered. She had not come to her decision, or made her commitment, lightly.

"What about the magic?" asked August. "What about the *voosh*?"

"I guess there's the illusion of magic, of *voosh*," she said, "but really it's just common sense."

"Oh, come on!" said August. He reeled around in front of her with his arms out, like a seagull turning the air. "You sound like a . . . *I dunno* . . . very sad person."

"Well, magic and *voosh* are there, but they're on the list," she conceded. "They're part of the things you consider."

"So this guy is magic, but this guy earns more money," said August, weighing the two scenarios in his hands.

"It's not like that," she said. "It's not about comparisons."

"Lists are all about comparisons," he said. "That's exactly what lists are about."

"You're oversimplifying it."

August didn't know what he was doing, but there was something so bleak about Alice's assertion that he suddenly felt very old. He hunched his shoulders and walked along in front of her with his arms swinging in front of him like a gorilla. She laughed.

Both wanted to escape the muddy depths where they now found themselves, but both were unsure how to do it. They walked along for a while and passed an old gypsy woman kneeling with her forehead touching the pavement. She was murmuring a prayer, clutching a paper cup containing a holy card of the Virgin and a few coins. A man in a striped blue tracksuit began taking photos of the old woman with his phone.

"Tell me something stupid," said August.

Alice turned to him, wondering what he meant.

"What's your favorite color?" he said, giving her an idea of how to play this game that he was suddenly making up.

"Fire-engine red," said Alice. "No, Venetian red."

"Huge difference, I'm sure," he said.

"Shut up. You?"

"Um . . . don't have one."

"Sad little man."

"Okay, green."

"Which green?"

"Leprechaun-armpit green."

Alice lifted her shoulders in a question. Were they playing this game or not?

"Okay, English-lawn green on a sunny summer morning," he said, "after a night of rain."

Alice nodded; she could see precisely the color he was describing.

"First pet?" he said.

"Sam the sausage dog," she fired back.

"Alive or dead?"

"Long dead. You?"

"My condolences. Boris the frog."

"Thank you. Alive or dead?"

"Eaten by Arthur the Labrador. Can't talk about it or I'll cry. First, um, house? No, boring. Love. First love?"

"Matthew McMahon. Oh no. Joshua Vogelman," she said, correcting herself. "I loved him first. I was five; he was four."

"An older woman?"

Alice nodded solemnly. "The scandal broke us up. You?"

"Emily Winterbottom. We were eight, I think. She was my first kiss too."

"Where?"

"Behind the girl's bathroom."

Alice groaned. "Where did you kiss her?" she said. "On the cheek? On the lips?"

"Oh. On the lips."

"Slut."

"Me or her?"

"You."

They started to laugh, mostly with relief that they had been able to negotiate their way out of the gloom. Passersby smiled, enjoying the young couple enjoying themselves.

"Don't you love the way, whenever you talk about people from grade school, you always use their full names?" she said. "It's never just 'Matthew' or 'Josh.' It's always 'Matthew McMahon' or 'Joshua Vogelman' or 'Emily Wildbottom.'"

"Winterbottom," he corrected.

"Winterbottom, sorry," she said. "Great name, by the way.

I'm going to call my first child Winterbottom. 'Winterbottom! Come and show Mommy what you did at school today!'"

"What if it's a girl?" he said.

"Winterbottom. I'll call her Winterbottom," she said. "Winterbottom is bisexual as far as I'm concerned. The name, not the child. Although if the child were bisexual, that would be okay too."

"So you're planning on being quite a liberal parent?"

"Of course."

"You're not going to be one of those cool mums who wants to smoke a spliff with her teen kids, are you?"

"Oh, God, no!" she exclaimed vehemently, simultaneously colliding with a young nun in a white habit with blue stripes edging her veil.

Alice apologized, and the nun smiled her forgiveness. August tried not to laugh but could not help himself. When he had chuckled himself out, he asked her why she had reacted so strongly to his question about being a cool mum. They entered a conversation about Alice's mother.

Alice outlined her mother's rise from broken ballerina to super-lawyer. Although she tried her best to portray her mother in positive terms, or perhaps *because* Alice was working so hard to be nice about her, August got the distinct impression that Alice's mother was not nice, that she was, in fact, a bitch on wheels. He refrained from sharing this summary with Alice, but he did feel quite sad that Alice was clearly in painful territory when talking about her family in general and her mother in particular.

Alice was wishing that the conversation had not taken a

turn down this particular cul-de-sac. Once again she had steered them into the gloom and was hoping to find a way out—another silly game perhaps—when the Vatican came to the rescue: They reached the end of the Via della Conciliazione, and there was Saint Peter's and its great square, demanding attention.

The main section of the square was not a square but a huge elliptical circus framed by colossal Tuscan colonnades, four columns deep. The colonnades did not entirely encircle the forecourt but reached out from the basilica in two arcs, "like the enfolding arms of the Mother Church," said August, who registered Alice's bemusement and was therefore compelled to explain that he was paraphrasing Bernini.

Alice accused August of showing off. August admitted he was. Alice asked him about the large obelisk in the middle of the square, and he immediately came unstuck. He couldn't remember anything about the obelisk except that it had been pilfered from Egypt, as many Roman obelisks were.

Had I been able to converse with August and Alice, I would have been able to enlighten them because of my fond connection with the obelisk. For one thing, it is older than I am—by almost a thousand years. It was moved from Heliopolis and reerected in Alexandria, taken down, shipped to Rome, and placed at the Circus of Nero, where it stood witness to the upside-down crucifixion of Saint Peter. This is why it is called *The Witness,* and this is why it was raised in front of the basilica in 1586. The obelisk was relocated by a team of 150 horses and 900 young men, among them one Benedetto Bresca, for whom I had just brokered a match with an enchanting girl named Maria.

Using meters of rope fed through hundreds of pulleys, the men and horses hoisted the 330-ton obelisk skyward. The massive weight caused so much friction that the ropes began to smoke. Benedetto looked up, the first to see that the whole operation was about to end in catastrophe. "Water the ropes! Water the ropes!" he shouted.

Because of Benedetto's keen eye, the obelisk was saved and, as a reward, his hometown of San Remo was granted the honor of supplying the palm fronds that were distributed in the basilica on Palm Sunday. If August and Alice had arrived in the Piazza San Pietro at Easter, they would have come across worshipers holding the palm fronds that are still supplied by San Remo more than four hundred years later.

Inside the grand ellipse of Saint Peter's Square, August led Alice to one of its two foci. He felt sure there would be some kind of marker to guide him to the right spot, and there was. Among the cobblestones, he found a granite disk encircled with white travertine, carved with the words *Centro del Colonnato*.

"Do I stand there?" asked Alice.

"Not yet," said August. "Look around first. Look at the columns. How many do you see?"

Alice looked around. She saw hundreds, maybe more. There were too many to count. Each column on the rim of the piazza had a row of four or five behind it. She couldn't tell exactly how many there were because the front ones were obscuring some of the rear ones.

"I don't know." She shrugged. "Hundreds, I guess. It's too hard to tell."

"Okay, but we're agreed there's a big messy jungle of columns surrounding us?" he said.

"Yes, agreed."

"Okay now close your eyes and stand on the disk," he said.

Alice peeled off her backpack and handed it to him. "Do I need to say abracadabra?" she said with her eyes obediently shut. He positioned her on the spot.

"Nope," he said. "Just open your eyes."

Alice opened her eyes. All the columns surrounding the piazza had suddenly lined up behind each other. She looked around. Wherever she looked, the illusion held. From the jumble of hundreds, eighty-eight single columns stood at the perimeter of the ellipse with every other column in its row tucked in behind it so neatly that they appeared to have vanished completely. Epic order had materialized from apparent chaos. The simple truth of geometry was playing out in front of her. It felt like a trick, like magic, like a miracle.

August looked at the wonder on Alice's face and felt a rush of emotion so potent that he thought he might vaporize. Alice looked at August and felt her throat tighten. *Who is this man,* she thought, *who is showing me these things?*

"Your turn," she said quietly.

Alice stepped off the disk, and August stepped on.

TWENTY-ONE

Arco degli Acetari

O COME, BE BURIED A SECOND TIME
WITHIN THESE ARMS.
—William Shakespeare, *Pericles*

Signore Gambetta felt slightly alarmed by the frantic American lady who was trying to use his mobile telephone. She kept punching in numbers, listening, then sighing in exasperation, punching in numbers, listening, then sighing in exasperation. He had just delivered three fine Cinta Senese pigs to his nephew who lived near the gypsy settlement when the lady had appeared in the middle of the road and slammed her hands on the hood of his yellow Citroën truck. For one terrible moment, he thought he would run her over. Fortunately, he did not.

The lady did not speak any Italian, but she was very good at communicating. She had made it very clear that she needed to get to the center of Rome as a matter of some urgency. Because Signore Gambetta was driving back to his farm in Tuscany and not going anywhere near central Rome, he had agreed to take Meg as far as the junction of the E80 and the A24, which was as close to the capital as he was prepared to get. He hoped she understood.

Meg sat in the stinky cabin of the filthy truck punching numbers into a cell that looked positively prehistoric. Because it was permanently programmed into her own cell, she had forgotten Alec's damn number. She kept getting riffs of numbers, but they weren't, evidently, in the right order. Eventually, it occurred to her that the call would also be routed via the States and would therefore need some kind of code. She was about to ask, or try to ask, how to dial international, when she looked over at the kind, frightened man who had lent her his phone and realized that the cost of such an exercise might bankrupt him. She decided to give up. She also decided that this had to be the shittiest day of her entire life. But at least this charmingly rustic fellow was taking her back to the tile shop where she would try to find a tile to match her stolen one and get the whole mission back on track. It would make one helluva anecdote for the readers of *Megamamma*.

As Dr. Stephanie drove her powder-blue Fiat into the wire enclosure of La Barbuta, they passed a police car driving the other way. Alec shrank into his seat until he realized that these particular officers had never met him, were unlikely to recognize him, or realize that he was defying the wishes of Assistente Capo Domenico Cilento by pursuing his own line of inquiry about the stolen bag and his missing wife. He tried to see if Meg was in the backseat but could not make out how many figures were in the car, let alone who they might be.

A tinny version of Bruce Springsteen's "Born to Run" began to play. It was Alec's phone ringing. He answered it, forced to talk loudly over the chatter of the gypsy children who had recognized Stephanie's car and gathered to greet her. Domenico Cilento was calling. Alec handed the phone over to Stephanie for her to translate. She shushed the children while the *assistente capo* informed her that a thorough search of La Barbuta had been executed and that neither the wife, nor the bag, nor a cross-eyed man had been located. Inquiries would be made promptly at other gypsy settlements around the city.

Stephanie hung up and relayed this to Alec, who wondered aloud whether they should head back to central Rome. "We're here now," she said. "Let's see what we can find out." Over the bobbing dark-haired heads, she instructed him to follow and let her do the talking. Alec noted how, once they were in her territory, she had naturally assumed authority. He could see how she might quietly command a field hospital or an orphanage of rowdy children.

With a line of kids in tow, they crunched across the dusty white gravel to one of the huts. "Do you come here often?" he asked her. She burst out laughing at his unconscious reprisal of the classic pickup line. When he twigged why she was laughing, he laughed too.

"No, not often," said Stephanie. "Mostly I get them to bring the kids into the clinic in town."

A door opened before they reached it. A young mother with hooded hazel eyes and a whimpering child on her hip acknowledged Stephanie. There was little warmth in the greeting, but it was respectful. She invited them inside. Her small front room was furnished with colorful plastic toys and a worn brown leather sofa. On one wall a giant flat-screen television was blaring what appeared to be a weather forecast presented by extremely curvaceous, scantily clad twins. On the opposite wall, a luridly colored 3-D portrait of Saint Thérèse of Lisieux lifted her hands in prayer as Alec passed her. They sat, the three of them and the child, lined up on the sofa.

Stephanie asked the woman a series of questions, making no attempt to translate back to Alec. After five minutes or so, the woman called out, and a man appeared. He was dressed in head-to-toe denim, cowboy boots, and a cream Stetson hat. Without making introductions, the young woman spoke to the cowboy, who avoided eye contact by tapping at the screen of a cell phone. After a while he left, and the conversation with Stephanie resumed. Alec gave up trying to second-guess what was being said and occupied himself by watching a series of frenetically joyful television commercials.

Suddenly Stephanie got to her feet. The session was obviously over. Alec said *grazie* to the young woman and reached out to shake her hand, but the toddler on her hip started to wail, and she retreated. Walking back over the white gravel, he noticed the place was strangely quiet. The playing children had vanished. The hairs on the back of his neck tingled.

"What did she say?" Alec asked Stephanie under his breath.

"Sounds like Meg came," she answered quietly. "She spoke to one of the little girls then left again."

"Why would she do that?"

Stephanie shrugged. "Maybe the girl gave her the tile."

"So the cross-eyed guy does belong here?"

"She wouldn't say," said Stephanie. "She said she couldn't help, but . . ."

"But you think she can help?"

"No, I think she will help."

"How? What do you mean?"

A warm gust blew Stephanie's hair around her face. When she swept it away, Alec saw that Stephanie's hand was shaking slightly.

"I don't know," she said. "I think we should leave now."

They walked around a stinking mountain of garbage bags to the refuse-littered car park. Both immediately registered that Stephanie's Fiat had moved. Had *been* moved. It was now facing the open gates of the driveway, poised for a getaway. Stephanie riffled through her bag for her keys and produced them. She looked across at Alec, who nodded his comprehension that someone had moved her car by unconventional means in order to make some kind of point, or threat.

They hurried to the Fiat and got in. It took two attempts to insert the keys into the ignition, but Stephanie eventually started it and rocketed down the driveway. They were going so fast when they turned into the Via Giovanni Ciampini that the car skidded across the gravel. Stephanie overcorrected the steering, lurching left then right, almost spinning out of control, before Alec reached over, grabbed the wheel, and steadied the vehicle.

"We're okay," he said gently. "It's okay."

"Sorry," said Stephanie. "So sorry."

She glanced into the rearview mirror to make sure they were not being followed. Something on the backseat caught her attention. She looked back at the road ahead and looked in the mirror again. Stephanie slammed on the brakes and turned around. Alec turned to see what had startled her. Sitting on the backseat was Meg's bag.

Alec grabbed the bag and looked through it. "Cash is gone, but everything else is here. My wallet," he said, producing his empty wallet. The tile was there, too, still wrapped in tissue paper. He looked up at Stephanie and smiled. She smiled back. He reached out and held her arm, accidently brushing her breast. "Thank you. You're obviously a very big cheese around here. Thank you."

Stephanie reached out, put her hand at the back of Alec's head. She pulled him to her and kissed him on the lips. Alec was slightly startled but mostly, suddenly, intoxicated.

"Comes from being in war zones," she said. "You take your moments when you can."

He could feel her breath, hot and shallow, on his face. A barb of lust sliced him wide open. He lunged forward and kissed her fiercely. It was a jaw-clanging exchange, lacking sensuality, charged with desire.

They pulled apart.

"Sorry," he said.

"I think we both know that's not true," she said.

He put his hand to the bandaged cut on his forehead that she had stitched together only a day before. She leaned in to kiss him again, but he pulled away.

"Stephanie, I'm not in a position to . . ."

Stephanie knew enough to know that the moment had passed. For him, anyway. There was no point pushing it any further. He was not going to come back to her place and sleep with her. Or fall in love with her. Or leave his wife and marry her instead.

Alec was both disappointed and relieved when Stephanie put the Fiat into gear and drove on. They headed back to Rome in silence punctuated by polite observations about the landscape or the traffic. Stephanie marveled at how quickly things had gone awry and kicked herself for mucking things up. Would she ever learn not to throw herself at men who could not be hers? As they were drawing closer to the center, Alec received a text from Meg. It was a long and rambling message about a Tuscan farmer who had promised her a lift but had abandoned her at the junction of two freeways. Fortunately, a German couple had picked her up in their campervan and lent her a cell phone. They had agreed to drop her near the tile shop. She was texting to see if he was at the shop. Alec texted back that, no, he was not there yet but would be there soon.

Stephanie dropped Alec off in the Via del Pellegrino, and once again he found himself gushing his gratitude like a giddy schoolboy. She drove away in her powder-blue Fiat, and he made his way under the arch, crossing the courtyard to the tile shop. Stephanie turned the corner into the Via Sora, stopped the car, and banged her palms on the steering wheel. "Shit!" she shouted. "Shit bugger fuck!"

Inside the shop, Meg had just finished introducing herself to Signore Horatio Zamparelli, who had nodded and smiled as she described her lost blue tile with a feverish reverence even greater than her husband's. Horatio was about to suggest that she look around the shop to see if she could find a similar tile to the one she had lost when Alec walked in.

"Where have you been?" Meg said in a flat, dry tone that could only ever be used between husbands and wives.

"Getting this," said Alec, lifting her Gucci bag high in front of him. "Where have you been?"

"Oh my God!" she screeched and raced to the bag, snatching it from his hand.

"It's still there," he said as Meg rummaged through her bag for the blue tile. "What happened?" he continued. "Where did you go?"

"Oh, Alec, we can talk about that later," she said as she extracted the tile from her bag and began to unwrap it.

"As long as you're okay. *I'm* okay," he said pointedly.

"I can see that," she said. Exposing her treasure, she took it to show Signore Zamparelli. "This is it, signore."

"The doctor took me out to the gypsy camp," Alec said, pressing on despite her disinterest. "We're lucky she has so much cred out there."

Meg swiveled toward Alec and issued a single command: "Later." Then she swiveled back to Horatio Zamparelli and, in a much gentler tone, asked, "Is it one of yours?"

Horatio recognized it immediately but made a great show of switching on a special lamp and extracting a magnifying glass. He bent over and studied the glaze, running the magnifier back and forth over the surface. He could tell it was not made by him but that it did contain an element of the magical and mysterious ingredient that seemed to emanate from a certain presence in his workshop.

"It is not one of mine," said Horatio.

Meg looked crestfallen.

"But it comes from this workshop," he added. "It is old, but not very old. Early twentieth century would be my guess."

Horatio was correct. It had been made in 1906 by one of his predecessors, Giuseppe Rizzi. Giuseppe had a knack for the unusual, and Horatio recognized his work. The glaze was obviously made from cobalt but with boron or borium as well, he guessed, and possibly even a touch of copper oxide. Turning it over, he was surprised by what he saw. "The base, you see, is most unusual, not red terra-cotta but white mostly, like the sand," he said, "and the glaze is very thick with not much pigment, no color, you know?"

"No color?" said Meg.

"This special blue comes mostly because she is deep," said Horatio, "like the ocean."

When he turned to Meg and Alec, he could see they were not following him. He told them to wait while he disappeared and reappeared with a beaker of water. He presented it for inspection.

"What color is she?"

"No color. It's clear," said Meg.

"But what color is the water in the Mediterranean?" he said.

"Blue, this blue," she said, pointing to the tile.

"It *appears* to be blue," he said, enjoying his role as tutor. "The water herself filters out the other colors, but the blue remains. The blue light travels down and reflects off the white sand. The waves of light dance with the waves of the ocean. They are in a marriage, you see, of light and form."

Alec picked up the tile and looked across the edge of it.

"And here in this humble tile, one of my forebears has re-created this marriage, most magnificently," Horatio continued.

Alec smiled. "You are a poet, signore," he said.

Horatio gestured to the piles of tiles around him. "And these are my poems."

Meg was less concerned with the poetry and more concerned with the practicalities. "But can you reproduce this tile, signore?"

"*Si.*"

Meg whooped and threw her arms around Horatio Zamparelli. He laughed and decided he liked this angry American girl and her quiet husband.

After they had discussed quantities, prices, and delivery dates, Horatio called them a taxi and pressed a couple of hundred euros into Signore Schack's reluctant hand. Alec assured him that he would be paid back promptly. Horatio had no doubt that this was the case, saying that it was the least he could do, given the rocky and precarious path that he and Signora Schack had taken to get here.

As they were getting into the taxi, the American girl paused. "Oh, I forgot," she said. Still holding the sample tile, she handed it back, but the tile maker pushed it away.

"I do not need it," he said.

"But—"

"Is all in here," said Horatio Zamparelli, tapping his forehead. "Every detail, signora. I will not fail you, I promise."

"But just in case—"

"No, you keep," he insisted. "I have a feeling somehow you are not finished with it."

As the taxi drove away, the tile maker realized that this was not strictly true: It was not that the *Americana* was not finished with the tile; rather, the tile was not finished with the *Americana*.

Horatio went back inside and started to close up the shop, looking forward to his journey home in the warm evening air, when something compelled him to take a final turn around the room. I could sense him staring at his tiles, our tiles, my tiles, vexed, trying to make connections. After a while, he sighed, switched off the lights, locked the door, and headed off across the *arco*.

TWENTY-TWO

Lungotevere degli Altoviti

THERE IS NOTHING I WOULD NOT DO FOR THOSE WHO
ARE REALLY MY FRIENDS. I HAVE NO NOTION OF LOVING
PEOPLE BY HALVES; IT IS NOT MY NATURE.

—Jane Austen, *Northanger Abbey*

Bernini's ten giant angels hovered above the two old ladies standing on the bridge. Clouds had gathered in the sky above; there would be no dazzling sunsets and bloody transformations this evening. Constance and Lizzie lowered the Harrods bag to the ground, and Constance extracted the Henry box, reminded again how heavy it was when carried alone. She lifted it onto the stone balustrade. People were milling about, but no one took any notice as Lizzie bent and kissed the box containing the ashes of her dead brother.

"So long, old man," said Lizzie. "What luck to have known you." She looked at the lined face of her sister-in-law and asked, "Do you think he's with us?"

"You mean now, right now?"

Lizzie nodded.

"I'd like to think he was," said Constance.

"Telling us what silly old ladies we are," said Lizzie.

A young woman, laughing and shrieking, clattered past them in high heels, chased by a curly-haired young man. He reminded them both of a young Henry.

"Just before he went, I asked him if he still believed in an afterlife," said Constance. She bowed her head and pulled the box toward her a little. "He said that people left but that love remained."

Constance peeled the seal from the lid of the box and opened it. She looked at the soft gray ashes, all that remained of the life force that had been Henry Alexander George Kingdom Lloyd-James. She tipped the box, pouring the ashes into the river. The two women watched them trail across the surface of the water, glittering for a moment like silver dust before the current swept everything away.

Lizzie wanted to hug her sister-in-law, but she knew it would only make Constance feel vulnerable.

"Well done," she said.

Constance turned to Lizzie. "I was expecting . . ."

"What?"

"I don't know. I don't know what I was expecting." Constance shrugged. "Not this."

They looked back at the water swirling beneath them.

"Let's go back to the hotel," said Lizzie.

"Yes, let's press on. Time to press on," said Constance, rallying. "I know a shortcut."

"Oh, goody," said Lizzie dryly.

Constance looked at the empty Henry box. She did not want to throw it away, but she did not want to keep it either. She decided to deal with the dilemma later and bent down, returning it to the Harrods bag. As she straightened, she could see a man of Henry's vintage walking toward her, looking directly at her. As he drew toward her, the man slowed. It was not Henry, of course, but it was an apparition from the past.

"Con-stance?" he said with a heavy Italian accent.

"Horatio?" said Constance.

"What are you doing here?" he asked in Italian.

Constance did not wish to disclose that she had just been disposing of Henry. She gestured airily toward Lizzie and said that she and her sister-in-law were visiting from London. Horatio said that she looked very well and that it was lovely to see her. Constance returned the compliment, then, remembering her manners, introduced Lizzie. Horatio bowed and kissed Lizzie's hand. He greeted her in Italian, and she returned the greeting elegantly, establishing that she, too, was fluent in Italian.

Lizzie asked how Horatio and Constance knew each other. Horatio explained that he had met Constance many years before when they had worked together on the restoration of an altar in a little church just off the Campo de' Fiori.

"Yes," confirmed Constance, "it was just the three of us. Me, Horatio, and his *sister,*" said Constance, rather too pointedly, thought Lizzie.

At the mention of his sister, Horatio dimly remembered some kind of falling-out over a boy. He was aware that he should be holding some kind of grudge against Constance on Gina's behalf, but it was all so long ago. He couldn't even remember the boy's name. Constance asked if Horatio was still doing restoration work. He said that he was not, that he had inherited a tile-making business from his uncle and that it was keeping him extremely busy.

Constance recalled Horatio's skills as a restorer and thought it was a funny sort of move to be making tiles. She asked, disingenuously because she already knew the answer, whether he was still living in the family palazzo overlooking Santa Maria in Trastevere. Horatio answered that he had moved years ago. His sister had been living abroad, and when she moved back, they decided to sell the palazzo and buy some apartments overlooking the river.

"In fact," he said, "we are there." He pointed to a brown building overlooking the bridge. "The one with the balcony, this is Gina. And I am the one below."

Constance felt the bridge sway beneath her. She tugged absently at Lizzie's sleeve. "I was right," she said.

"You don't know that," said Lizzie.

"Horatio, I need to see Gina," said Constance.

"No, you don't," said Lizzie.

Horatio was confused. He did not like being put on the spot like this. He was not sure that his sister would thank him for suddenly turning up on her doorstep with her old rival and her old rival's sister-in-law.

"I think she is home," he said. "I can call her . . ."

"I need to see her now," said Constance firmly.

Moments later they had crossed the Lungotevere and were standing at the mighty oak doors of Gina and Horatio's apartment building. Rather than use his keys, Horatio had buzzed Gina from the street to give her the opportunity to decline an audience with the English ladies. To his mild surprise she had accepted. The door buzzed open. Constance pushed it and paused, turning to Horatio and Lizzie.

"I'd like to go up alone," she said.

"Oh, I'll wait down here, then," said Lizzie.

"Please don't," said Constance. "I have no idea how long I'll be."

Horatio wondered whether to ask Lizzie up to his apartment, but he could not remember what state it was in, so he invited her to dinner instead. Constance immediately accepted on Lizzie's behalf and thanked Horatio. Lizzie felt slightly put out at the thought of having to make dinner conversation with a complete stranger, especially given the tumultuous day she had just endured. Nevertheless, for the sake of keeping the peace, she agreed to go, arranging to meet Constance back at the hotel later. Lizzie offered to take the Harrods bag and Constance surprised her by accepting. It was, reflected Lizzie, a day of surprises.

Constance took the tiny elevator to the top floor, where Gina was waiting at the open door of her grand apartment. Constance noted, with a touch of disappointment, that Gina had aged very well. She was slightly stooped, her hair was expertly dyed dark brown, and perhaps her eyes were not quite as luminous as they had once been, but she was still, it had to be admitted, a beauty. Gina looked at her old rival and noted with some pleasure that Constance was considerably more lined than she. The two old ladies greeted each other in very formal Italian, expressing no pleasure in their reunion. Gina told Constance that she had read of Henry's passing in *The Times* and offered her condolences. Constance accepted them icily. It was immediately obvious to Gina that Constance wanted something, and the sooner she came out with it, the better. She ushered Constance into her salon and offered her a glass of wine.

While Gina disappeared into her kitchen, Constance assessed the large room into which she had been deposited. The opulent furniture was upholstered in brilliant red and scarlet. The walls were red, too, although mostly covered by gilt-framed paintings. Constance would never have chosen such a vivid scheme but decided that she would report to Lizzie later that it was *arresting*. A large canvas of Mary Magdalene at the feet of Jesus glowered down at her from the wall opposite. It looked very much like a Caravaggio. Constance realized it probably was a Caravaggio. Still, she had not come here to be cowed by Gina's paintings.

Gina appeared bearing two globes of red wine and handed one to Constance.

"What do you want, Constance?" said Gina, surprising her guest, not with her bluntness but her use of English.

"I'll come straight to the point," said Constance, glad that they were in her native tongue, where she would have the upper hand.

"Please do," said Gina.

Constance leaped straight in. "I don't like you, and you don't like me, but we both loved the same man, and that gives us a common bond, whether we like it or not."

Gina laughed, startled. *My. How direct. How un-English.*

"I want to ask you about your affair with Henry," said Constance.

"It wasn't an affair," said Gina. "We were seeing each other for months before you came along with your sparkling repartee and working-class charm."

Constance was taken aback by just how proficient Gina's English had become. "Not then," she said, determining not to be put off course. "After. When we were in our forties. When did it end?"

"What?"

"When did the affair with Henry end?"

"Why are you asking me this?"

"I feel I have a right to know," said Constance, not really feeling she had a right to anything.

"You know perfectly well when it all ended," said Gina. "You were there. Wearing a large hat and weeping behind your sunglasses."

"And you swear that's when it ended?"

Gina bristled. "What's all this about?"

"Henry asked to have his ashes scattered from the Ponte Sant'Angelo."

The room fell silent. Gina put her wine on the twelfth-century porphyry elephant that served as a side table. She stood up and walked to the end of the room where the doors to her balcony framed the bridge beyond.

"And have you done that?" asked Gina, staring through the distortion of the handblown glass panels at the swirling torrent of the Tiber. She turned and looked for an answer.

Constance nodded, her stomach churning. She didn't say that she had *just* done it. She did not say anything at all until the ticking of a clock in another room began to sound like a bomb threatening to explode. Eventually, she said, "Please don't be coy with me. We're both too old to be playing games."

"You want me to tell you that I have had no contact with Henry in the last thirty-five years?" said Gina.

"I want the truth," said Constance. "Whatever it is."

"You want the truth, Constance?"

"Yes."

Gina had been practicing for this moment for many, many years. During her mostly happy marriage to Robbie, a Canadian diplomat, she had lived all over the world, in Africa, in Southeast Asia, and finally in Spain before returning to Rome. She was a skilled linguist fluent in many languages. But she had always rehearsed this particular speech, on all those foreign soils, in English. Over the years she had reshaped her monologue, adding and subtracting adjectives and accusations. She could not count how many times, in the shower or on her long walks, that she had conjured Constance and confronted her.

Eventually, successive floods of emotion had layered sediment over Gina's outrage and buried the driving need to deliver her censure. Nevertheless, she had never forgotten what she had planned to say.

Gina walked back across the room and sat down opposite Constance. "The truth is," she began, "that over fifty years ago you betrayed me and broke my heart, and I am amazed to find myself sitting here bothering to give you the time of day." She was about to add, as she had long rehearsed, that Henry had been the love of her life but that Constance had been the love of his. She did not, however, wish to furnish Constance with the satisfaction of this admission, so she leaped forward. "The truth is," she continued, "that Henry chose the wrong woman, and the proof is that you are sitting here asking me these ridiculous questions."

Constance sat with her heart pounding and words spinning in her head.

"My God, Constance," said Gina, springing to her feet, "that man thought you were the moon and the stars and everything between, but you appear to be too witless, too absorbed in your own melodrama, to grasp it."

Constance looked up at Gina, horrified by the sudden realization that they both might cry.

"Go home, you stupid woman," said Gina. "Go home."

Outside on the streets, a warm drizzle fell, and dark-skinned men selling cheap umbrellas sprang up like mushrooms. Constance purchased an umbrella and pounded across the shining pavement, berating herself for being such an idiot. Her arm was sore from carrying Henry all day. She could feel a blister on her big toe. Every bone in her body ached. The sole of her left shoe slid on the slippery pavement, and she almost fell. What a perfect end to the day that would be—a broken hip. She wanted to scream and weep and howl. But she did not cry because, where she came from, only babies cried.

In her apartment, Gina returned to the doors and watched the water whispering past, carrying the atoms of the only man she had ever truly loved. She did not feel sad, or angry, or triumphant. She did not feel anything at all, except old. She felt very old. She lay on her bed with her shoes on and flicked through the television stations, but there was nothing on.

TWENTY-THREE

Il Piramide and the Dead Protestants

I HAVE BEEN ASTONISHED THAT MEN COULD DIE MARTYRS
FOR RELIGION—I HAVE SHUDDER'D AT IT.—I SHUDDER NO
MORE—I COULD BE MARTYR'D FOR MY RELIGION—LOVE IS MY
RELIGION—I COULD DIE FOR THAT.—I COULD DIE FOR YOU.

—John Keats, *letter to Fanny Brawne*

For many years, legend held that Romulus and Remus were
buried in two large pyramids on opposite sides of the Tiber.
Romans believed that Romulus, who had killed his twin,
Remus, fighting about whether to found their city on the
Aventine or Palatine Hill, was entombed in a pyramid close
to the Vatican, until, in the sixteenth century, someone discovered that the body of their fratricidal founding father was
not actually there. The pyramid was subsequently dismantled
and the marble recycled for the steps of Saint Peter's. Eventually, restoration work on the remaining pyramid uncovered
inscriptions that revealed this was not the tomb of poor mur-
dered Remus either. A Roman magistrate named Gaius
Cestius had been buried there, a decade or so before the birth

of Jesus. Cestius was a bit of a nobody, historically speaking, but, reaching for immortality like so many Romans before and after him, he had built the monumental white pyramid as his mausoleum. As you stroll down the Via Ostiense it's impossible to miss unless you can't take your eyes off a beautiful girl with a dob of chocolate gelato on her nose.

Realizing that they had not eaten since breakfast, Alice and August had stopped for pizza but settled on gelato, which August assured Alice contained all the necessary food groups for complete and everlasting happiness. They were discussing their tastes in music. August reeled off a list of (mostly UK) bands that he liked. Alice had never heard of many of them and confessed to a taste for pop although she quite liked rap as long as the lyrics did not stray into the territory where people's mothers were ordered to bend over and take it like bitches.

August offered to carry Alice's backpack. She declined. Alice offered August the last bite of her gelato cone.

August smiled. "Why do girls always do that?" he said. "Like that last tiny bit is going to make you fat."

Alice immediately shoved the remains of her cone into her mouth and chomped. For good measure, she snatched the remains of August's cone and ate that as well, in a most unladylike manner. August laughed.

Alice pointed at what appeared to be a pyramid, completely out of place, beyond the ruins of the Aurelian Wall. "Do you think they dragged that here from Egypt?" she said, still munching.

August turned and clocked the massive geometrical structure for the first time. He mentally scanned the archives of ARC 235 History of Architecture but drew a blank.

As they came closer they could see that part of the Aurelian Wall had been built into the side of the pyramid. August
studied a brass plaque that offered a brief history of the structure in Italian and English. The English, however, was so elaborate, with so many strange turns of expression, that it was
difficult to understand.

"Some Roman bloke built it as his grave," he said. "He's
buried underneath, I think."

"He must have been very important," said Alice.

"Look at me," said August, finding a voice for the pyramid's
long-deceased occupant, "I've got a really big pointy one."

"Ah, yes, men and their obelisks."

"I believe what we have here," said August in a low, au-
thoritative tone, "is an early example of obelisk enlargement:
*Turn your obelisk into a great big pyramid and really impress the
ladies.*"

"Quite the expert, aren't we?"

"Quite."

A little past the pyramid, an abundant garden spilled enticingly over a high wall. Alice stopped, momentarily mesmerized
by the colors in the wall's render—pink, yellow, ochre, terra-
cotta, red, brown. "Okay expert," she said, "what's in there?"

On the next corner a middle-aged couple wearing backpacks were consulting a guidebook. "Would you mind averting
your eyes," August said, "while I ask these people and then
pretend I already know the answer to that question?"

August scooted ahead to the couple. Alice watched as they
smiled and nodded and handed over their guidebook. There
seemed to be quite a bit of chatting and exchanging of information. Finally, August handed back their book and shook

hands. He pointed back to her, and they waved, and she waved back as if she had met them. Then they headed off toward the river, and August trotted back to her.

"It's the protestant cemetery," said August. "Keats and Shelley are buried there."

They decided to go in and walked down a side street to the great arched entrance, where a sign on the iron doors announced it would not open until 9:00 A.M. the next day. August started to walk away. There was a beat before he realized that Alice had not joined him. He turned and asked what she was doing. Alice said she found it hard to believe that the guy who taken her down the Spanish Steps on the back of a *motorino* was going to let a gate and high wall deter him.

Oh, bloody hell, said August to himself as Alice started to look for a point of ingress. Farther down the street, a car had backed into a *No Parking* sign and bent it toward the wall. A large oleander bush, covered in pink flowers, provided the perfect cover to scramble up the pole without being observed.

Alice unpeeled her backpack and was up in no time. She reached down from castle-like crenellations on the top of the wall. "Backpack," she said, and August hoisted it up to her. "Come on," she said and vanished, leaving him no option but to follow.

The light was fading, and a gentle rain began to fall. August shimmied up the pole and had almost reached the top when he lost his purchase and began to slip, describing a 180-degree arc until he was dangling upside down. August slid slowly to the ground, very glad that Alice could not see him.

After a second failed attempt at climbing the pole, August scaled the wall, tearing a hole in the knee of his jeans on the jagged render. He hoisted himself up and lay panting between two stone-capped merlons until Alice called quietly that someone was coming. Swinging his legs over the other side of the wall, he hovered for a second before plummeting into a thick hedge.

Removing sticks and leaves from his hair and clothing, August scrambled out of the hedge, warning Alice not to laugh. Alice, laughing, confessed that no one was coming; she just wanted him to hurry up. He checked his knee for blood. There was a slight graze. Alice offered to call his mother and report the injury. He gave her his best withering look, but she was already occupied elsewhere, admiring their environs.

A network of pretty pebbled paths, bordered with little hedges, crisscrossed a gentle slope that rose away from them. Tombstones of many different styles and denominations appeared to have been artfully arranged among the pines, pomegranates, and Judas trees. Swirling through their branches, the rain vaporized into a trail of sacred mist.

August and Alice began to move together along a pebbled path. Alice tucked her backpack into a hydrangea near the entry gates. August found a sign pointing to famous grave sites. Goethe and Shelley were straight ahead. John Keats was off to the left. Without discussion they started up the hill, scanning inscriptions, examining urns and crosses, looking for Shelley.

Alice came upon him first. When August saw her standing still, he realized that she had found him and joined her in front of the simple marble slab, lying in the dirt, engraved, *Percy Bysshe Shelley*. There was a Latin inscription, *Cor Cordium*. August thought it had something to do with hearts but could not be sure. The dates of Shelley's birth and death were also inscribed in Latin above an English verse:

Nothing of him that doth fade
But doth suffer a sea change
Into something rich and strange

Alice moved on. August heard her utter a small cry. He walked over and stood next to her, looking down at a small gravestone.

"His son William," she said. "He was four."

According to his gravestone, William Shelley had predeceased his father in 1819. "By three years," calculated August.

"I wonder how he died," said Alice.

She tried to conjure what it would be like to lose a child, the horror and injustice of it, but the scale of the grief was simply beyond her. She looked around. August was gone. She wandered across the hillside of graves and through a square arch in a weathered orange wall. The garden was less formal here, the graves less frequent. It was, she imagined, more like an English park. In the failing light, she could see August standing by a headstone and beyond him, outside the walls, the looming triangle of the Pyramid of Cestius.

August stood in front of John Keats. He had studied him in English, of course, like all good English boys, but had not realized that the celebrated poet was so young when he died, leaving a significant body of work behind him at just twenty-five years old. Michelangelo had been the same age when he sculpted his masterpiece *The Pietá*. August wondered what he might achieve by twenty-five. He had three years to pull a rabbit out of the hat; the clock was ticking. Alice materialized next to him.

"Keats," he said. "I'm not sure why, but I always felt like I actually got him."

"He was a second child, you know," she said, "just like you."

"Really?"

"Yeah. And he had this really brilliant older brother who never said a word."

"Oh, shut up," said August.

Alice started to chuckle.

"Do you want me to recite something?" he said.

"No."

August decided to press on regardless. "Fill for me a brimming bowl, And in it let me drown my soul; But put therein some drug, designed To banish—" Alice silenced him with her finger on his lips.

"Shh," she said gently, smiling up at him. It was the first time she had touched his face. He thought he might lie down next to Keats and die there and then.

"We're in the poem," she whispered. "Now, this, all around us, is a poem."

They looked around. The rain had stopped, and the world was glistening. The sun had not yet set, but the moon was rising.

August flooded with adoration. Feeling slightly dizzy, he sat on the damp grass. "We should probably be heading back," he said, reaching for something normal to say and think. "Find somewhere to stay."

"Let's stay here," she said.

"It's wet," he said.

"I'll get my backpack. We can lie on my stuff."

"What if it rains?"

"We'll get wet."

Alice ran off down the path toward the bush where she had secreted her belongings. August remained on the grass, unable to move. Something was happening to him, something from which he would never recover, he was certain.

While August was out of earshot, Alice called Daniel to say good night. Daniel was on his way back to the hotel after a satisfactory but not brilliant spaghetti marinara. He asked Alice if she realized that you weren't supposed to put cheese on seafood pasta. Alice replied that her phone was running out of charge. Fortuitously, her phone then ran out of charge, and she was saved from having to respond to his farewell *Love you* with the lie of *Love you, too.*

Alice grabbed her backpack and started off. In the half-light two squirrels scurried across the path on front of her. The truth was, she realized, that she would tell any lie necessary to spend time with the young Englishman sitting in the damp grass next to John Keats. She would do anything for this time with him. She stopped and dropped her backpack on the gravel, circling it to gather herself.

August was still sitting on the grass when Alice appeared through the darkness. They greeted each other with a look. No words formed in the thick, warm air around them. Alice started to search through her backpack. An orchestra of crickets and other insects serenaded them with crunchy, familiar notes. She produced a raincoat and laid it on the grass next to August. He lifted himself onto it. Shyly, Alice sat down next to him. August rested his head on the backpack and cleared his throat. Alice turned and saw that he had positioned his arm so that she could use it as a pillow. She lay back. He smelled exactly as she imagined he would. She nestled into him and closed her eyes. He measured the weight of her next to him. She breathed out. He breathed her in.

He would not close his eyes tonight. He was not going to miss a moment, the only living man in a shimmering garden of the dead, cradling majesty in his arms.

≈≈≈≈

TWENTY-FOUR

Ending in the Via Margutta

THERE WAS A TIME WHEN I THOUGHT I LOVED MY FIRST
WIFE MORE THAN LIFE ITSELF. BUT NOW I HATE HER GUTS. I DO.
HOW DO YOU EXPLAIN THAT? WHAT HAPPENED TO THAT LOVE?
—Raymond Carver, *What We Talk About When We Talk About Love*

Alec stood at the large window of their Rococo-meets-Swedish-Modern room in the Hotel San Marco, overlooking a stretch of twinkling lights on the Roman horizon. A jubilant pop tune blasted from Meg's phone on the orange-and-pink silk bedspread. He had showered and shaved and was solemnly dredging a bottle of birra, when Meg danced out of the dressing room in a little black dress and presented its gaping back for him to zip.

"I ordered some champagne," she said, oblivious to his somber mood. "I know it should have been prosecco, this being Roma and all, but champers just feels more celebratory somehow."

Alec zipped her dress.

"I can't believe we did it," she continued. "We did it! I said we'd do it in a day, and we did." She swept a pair of diamond hoop earrings from the crystal coffee table and began to insert them in her ears.

"So if Horatio can give us the tiles by the end of the month, I guess that means they should be installed—what?—two weeks after that?"

Alec made no attempt to reply.

"I don't think we should use a local company to deliver them," she said. "You know how hopeless the Italians are at moving things from A to B." She inspected her earrings in the mirror. "Do American couriers come here? Of course they do. I'm so thrilled." She slipped her left foot into a black stiletto and her right foot into a red pump, turning left and right to decide on the best shoe for the dress.

"Megan," said Alec, still looking out the window.

She swiveled toward him. "Don't call me that," she said. "I always feel like I'm in trouble when you call me that."

Alec turned to look at her.

"I am in trouble," she said.

"I'm sorry. I don't think I can . . ." He paused, trying to find a way to say what he had decided to say. "I'm not going to . . ."

"What?"

"I'm not coming home."

"What do you mean?"

"I'm staying in Rome."

Meg kicked off her shoes, stormed into the Versailles Hall-of-Mirrors bathroom, and slammed the door. Alec walked to the bathroom and tried to open the door, but it was locked. He knocked. "Open the door," he said. He waited for a while, but when Meg did not appear he sat on the bed.

Suddenly the bathroom door flew open, and Meg barreled out. "It's that slut doctor," she said, "isn't it?"

Alec looked up at Meg.

"Oh. My. God. Are you in love with her?"

He did not answer.

"You can't fall in love with someone in a day!" she spluttered.

"I fell in love with you in a day," he said.

Meg lashed out to strike him, but he grabbed her wrist.

"This isn't about Stephanie," he said, trying to sound calm.

Meg pulled her hand away. "So you're not in love with her?"

"I'm not in love with you anymore. I'm sorry."

He watched a childlike look of shock and hurt move across her face.

"How can you say that?" she said. "Why didn't you tell me?"

"I am telling you now," he said.

Meg looked around, hoping to discover that she had somehow stepped into the wrong room.

"What about the kids?"

"Frankly, I think they'll be relieved," he said.

Why was he doing this? She could not understand why he was doing this. She slapped herself hard across the face. She slapped herself again, bringing release, an instant exorcism. She went to slap herself a third time, but Alec stood and grabbed her wrist again. She had self-harmed in the past, mostly clawing her thighs or pinching her wrists, but only after arguments with her father, with whom she had a particularly combative relationship. Alec had never seen her hit herself before.

"Stop it," he said gently. "Please stop it."

Suddenly realizing that he was restraining her, she wrenched herself from his grip and began to pace up and down in a kind of panic. "So that's it!" she said. "Just like that. No, no, I don't accept it! I do not accept it."

Meg threw her arms around Alec and buried her face in his chest. "Please don't leave me," she said. "I know I'm nuts, but I can change. Please give me another chance. Please, please just say yes."

"Meg. Look at me," he said. "Look at me."

But she would not look. Slowly she melted away from him.

"What a giant cliché you turned out to be," she said. "Successful guy with too much time and money on his hands hits a bump in the road with this wife so bails out with a more exotic model. How predictable!"

"I'm not leaving you for Stephanie," he said. "I'm just leaving."

"Bullshit!" she screeched. "Have the *guts* to admit what you're doing!"

In the mulatto of her Australo-American accent, the word "guts" spewed at him with a peculiarly Australian ferocity. He remembered meeting her father and brother for the first time on their vast outback cattle station. Direct and uncompromising, they were a breed not to be messed with.

"I don't know what I'm doing," he said, trying to be direct and uncompromising himself. "I don't have a clean, strong purpose. I'm not in love with Stephanie, but I do have feelings for her. Which makes me realize I no longer have feelings for—"

"Get out!" screamed Meg.

"If you insist on steamrolling over the top of me," he said, "what hope is there of—"

Once again she screamed, "Get out! Now! Go on. I can't bear to be with you a moment longer!" A fury of spittle sprayed into the air with her words. Alec felt some of it settle on his face. He reached out for his wife, but she recoiled.

"Go!" she shouted.

Alec walked to the door. He turned to say something, but there was nothing he could say that could excuse any of this as far as she was concerned.

"Leave me alone!" she shouted, her voice hoarse with effort and anger.

He opened the door to see the retreating figure of a room service waiter, trotting as fast as he could without actually running. It would have been funny if things weren't so damn sad. At Alec's feet, there was a platinum tray and ice bucket with a bottle of Bollinger Vieilles Vignes Françaises Blanc de Noirs and two crystal flutes.

Alec pushed the tinkling tray into the room with his foot and walked down the hall toward the elevators. He was reaching for the down button when a meticulously engineered hermetic *whoosh* and *click* announced that the door to their room had closed behind him.

Meg lay on the bed. She sat up. She lay down. She sat up. She lay down. The infinite number of things that could happen next began to occur to her in little flash-frame scenarios. There was nothing to do but kill herself. No, she would remarry; a handsome European with a title. No, she would do good works and become famous, and he would come crawling back, and she would make him grovel. She sat up and looked at the very expensive champagne she had ordered less than half an hour ago when she lived in a different universe.

She imagined smashing one of the crystal champagne flutes and carving it up her thigh. She pulled her black dress up her pale legs and conjured the release. She could see the beautiful red blood flowing forth and pooling on the carpet. She could feel blobs of liquid falling on her thighs. It wasn't blood. The liquid was clear; she was crying. *Why am I crying?* she wondered. She fell back on the bed as her diaphragm contracted and she shocked herself with a sob. She sobbed for so long and so loudly that the people in the next room thought she was having a prolonged orgasm and called reception to complain.

Alec burst into the night air and walked toward the Spanish Steps. It had been raining, but the rain had stopped, leaving the air fresh and the city glittering with reflected light. The streets were brimming with tourists on their way home from dinner and Romans on their way to dinner. Half of them were pounding the pavement in sensible nylon-and-spandex-blend travel pants and the other half were teetering in haute couture.

Alec slipped into a noisy bar without noting its name and ordered a double vodka. He sat in a dark corner, filled with the momentousness of what he had just done. Surrounded by jovial chatter, he could hardly think, but this was just as well; he did not want to think. He took a long swig of his vodka, enjoying the burning sensation in his throat. Returning the glass to its cardboard coaster, Alec could feel the muscles of his neck and upper back relax. He was free, *free at last.*

Alec noticed a blond woman across the bar, watching him. He lifted the vodka to his mouth, using the tilted glass as camouflage, while he examined her. She was older than he was but in good shape, with raccoon mascara eyes and at least one bottle of prosecco sloshing around inside her. He put his glass down and looked directly at her. She wasn't just looking back. She was eye-fucking him. Suddenly he was peeling her red-lace underwear down her thighs. After a little trouble extricating them from her shiny stilettos, her vulva lay exposed before him. "What a cliché you turned out to be," the vulva said to him in his wife's distinctive voice.

Alec chugged the rest of his vodka and jostled his way out of the busy bar. As he passed the raccoon blonde, she was greeting someone else and did not notice him leaving. Nevertheless, he paced quickly down the Via del Babuino in case she followed. His head buzzed with adrenaline and vodka, and he kept seeing flashes of the hurt on Meg's face. Not just the hurt, the hurt little girl. That's what made it worse. He didn't want to hurt her, but he could not live with the lie any longer. She would see that, too, that they were both living a lie. She would thank him one day for calling it.

He reached the Piazza del Popolo and sat on a bench, watching a gaggle of rambunctious teenagers gathered around the central obelisk. They would be friends again, too, he thought, if for no other reason than the kids. They would do a good job of raising their children together, even though they would be living separate lives. Meg could be enormously practical when she needed to be. She would see sense and help him make this work. Eventually.

He decided to find another bar. Trouble was, they were all brimming with exuberance. Instead, he bought a bottle of Peroni from a *mercato* and wandered up the Via del Corso, drinking discreetly. He was not going to be one of those ass-holes who was mean with money, either. He fully acknowl-edged that Meg had contributed to the success of Lighting Schack as much as he had. It had been her drive, her vision, her creativity as much as his. She had emboldened him to take risks. Risks that had paid off big-time. And she would be compensated accordingly. He drained his Peroni and bought another.

Alec decided to stop thinking about Meg and think about his future without Meg. He thought he would like to have a lot of sex. He might move down to Santa Monica, near the beach. The kids would like that, too. He entertained the idea of buying a convertible Bentley but decided that was too pre-dictable. After some apparently aimless wandering Alec found himself back in the Via Margutta, outside the palazzo with the lanterns of purple wisteria and the tiny coach-house built into its garden wall. Alec had imbibed just enough alcohol not to confront himself with the fact that he had been headed here all along.

He clambered over a metal gate, climbed a flight of stone steps, and knocked on the purple door. Dr. Stephanie Cope answered wearing a long T-shirt and nothing else. She looked pleased to see him and not really that surprised.

"Alec!" she said. "What a lovely surprise."

Alec did not answer. He stood, swaying slightly, looking at her.

"What's wrong?" she said, suddenly subdued.

Alec stepped inside and wrapped his arms around Stepha-nie's waist. He put his mouth on hers. He kissed her. She kissed him. He slid his leg between hers. He could feel the hardness of her pubic bone on his thigh. He pushed into her. She pushed back.

Meg had sobbed herself to sleep in the enormous bed and was now overheating under the covers. Her arms swept over the sheets, searching for a cool spot. Her right hand slid under the pillow where Alec's head should have been resting and found something cold and hard. Meg opened her red swollen eyes and blinked; the lights were blaring. She felt the object under the pillow. It was square and thin. She removed it and squinted at it, remembering now that she had placed her beautiful blue tile there earlier. She put it back under the pillow and rolled over, deciding she was too tired to deal with the lights. She drifted for a moment and then her eyes snapped open.

Meg took the tile out from under the pillow again. She ran her fingers over the blue glaze, feeling some strange sensation. Starting in her fingertips, the sensation moved up her arm and into her whole body. She would never admit this to another living soul, but she felt as if the tile was telling her something. And then she remembered. She remembered exactly where she had gotten this tile and how she had come to get it. She had not collected it when she was gathering samples for her renovation. She had, in fact, been carrying it around with her for a very long time.

TWENTY-FIVE

Un Colpo d'Aria

GIVE SORROW WORDS; THE GRIEF THAT DOES
NOT SPEAK WHISPERS THE O'ER-FRAUGHT
HEART, AND BIDS IT BREAK.
—William Shakespeare, *Macbeth*

As Bronco descended the stairs of the Hotel Montini, doom
leached into the marrow of his bones. Someone had rung
the buzzer at 11:30 P.M., an hour after lockout, wanting to be
let in. By the time he had crossed the cold tiles of the drafty
reception area in his bare feet, he was certain: He had been
taken by *un colpo d'aria.*

Of the many dangerous things in Rome, there are few
more dangerous than *un colpo d'aria,* the potentially life-
threatening phenomenon of being hit by a gust of cool air. As
any Italian mother will tell you, those unfortunate enough to
experience *un colpo d'aria* are likely to suffer a myriad of health
problems, ranging from a headache to a stiff neck, a sore liver,
influenza, or even death. Prevention is better than cure, and
during the winter months this can be achieved by wearing a
wool vest called a *maglia della salute,* literally a "shirt of health,"

with a warm scarf to protect the very vulnerable neck area. In all seasons, one must never stand on cold tiles. In summer, one must avoid air-conditioning and fans. Fans are lethal. Once a person has been afflicted by *un colpo d'aria,* he or she must absent himself or herself from school or work immediately, go to bed, keep warm, and, most important, keep away from drafts.

So it was extremely unfortunate that, as Bronco opened the door to one of the old British dames and an elderly gentleman, he was assaulted by a gust of cool night air. The lady apologized for rousing him and explained that she had left her room key with her companion. She began to ask what time her companion had returned, but Bronco could already feel that he was slightly feverish. He interrupted and explained that he needed to get back to bed because he was suffering from *un colpo d'aria.*

Instantly appreciating the gravity of the situation, the elderly gentleman apologized sympathetically and sincerely. He asked where Bronco was afflicted. Bronco thought it might be his liver. The gentleman offered his condolences, pressed his lips to the lady's hand, and kissed her once on each cheek. They were still saying farewell when Bronco closed the door between them, but he knew the gentleman would understand. Once inside Bronco explained to the lady that, as they were in the midst of an unfolding medical emergency, he would need to take the elevator first.

Lizzie climbed the stairs, grateful for a moment to collect her thoughts before she returned to the room, and Constance. It had been a remarkable evening. Horatio had taken her to his favorite restaurant. It was not grand by any means but

simple and elegant with excellent food and fine wine. Lizzie
had been dreading the idea of dinner with some fellow she
did not know, so it had come as a surprise that conversation
had flowed and topics were batted back and forth between
them as if they were old friends.

Horatio was a quiet, serious sort of man, but he laughed
easily and often at Lizzie's dry observations, which pleased her
immensely. He sat squarely in the world as if he had seen a lot
of life and not much surprised him. Before she knew it, she
had put aside her worries about Constance and was completely
absorbed in conversation. They chatted about things, silly and
profound. Neither had children, both regretted it. He preferred Venice, she preferred Florence. Together they made up
a story about the couple at the next table having an affair, creating imaginary biographies for the pair and composing ex-
posé headlines for tomorrow morning's papers. They waded
through music and art, more often than not disagreeing with
each other, but they clicked, they just clicked.

When the dessert menu arrived, Lizzie felt herself drawn
to the highly irregular asparagus gelato, but Horatio insisted
she try the tiramisu, which was, he promised, *buonissimo*. By
way of compromise, he offered to bring her back the following evening for the asparagus gelato. She laughed and accepted
his offer, but a small contraction in her heart warned her not
to see him again. She was an old lady. She had long ago given up
any hope at all of finding a life's love. This evening's flirtation
was surprising enough; she should be grateful and move on.
One last hurrah before the curtains closed. To make anything
more of this unexpected delight would be ridiculous. And
foolish. And potentially humiliating. Thank God Bronco had

closed the door between them. She had been on the brink of embarrassing herself with inappropriate gushing.

By the time she reached her room, Lizzie had remembered herself, her advanced age, her necessary lack of ambition. She was quite herself once more, except perhaps for the flush of pink across her cheeks. She turned the handle, hoping it was not locked. The door opened. She crept into the room and closed it behind her very quietly.

A voice in the darkness said, "Did you have a nice evening?"

Lizzie could tell from the direction of the voice that Constance was not in bed.

"Do you mind if I turn a light on?"

"Go ahead," said Constance.

Lizzie turned the night-light on. Constance was sitting in a chair, looking out through an open door onto the terrace. She turned toward Lizzie, squinting in the light.

"Sorry. Is that a bit bright?" said Lizzie.

"How was your evening?" said Constance.

"Oh, it was fine, but more importantly, how was yours? I've been so worried about you. How did it go?"

"Unlike you to stay out so late."

"I'm sorry, girlie. The time just got away. How did it go with Gina?"

"Fine. I was just about to go to bed. Do you mind if we save it for the morning?"

"Don't be angry with me," said Lizzie, suddenly exhausted.

"I'm not."

"Yes, you are."

A mighty pirate voice boomed across the room. It took a

moment for Lizzie to register that Constance was shouting at her.

"Jesus H. Christ!" Constance exploded. "You stay out half the night when I could well have been here, a quivering heap in the corner, and then you come home and start picking fights!" She leaped from her chair, stormed into the bathroom, and slammed the door.

Lizzie walked to the door and studied her aching feet as she talked through the solid wood. "I should have been here with you. I'm sorry. But I'm not the one picking fights."

Constance did not answer. After a while, Lizzie turned the door handle, and it clicked open. She walked into the bathroom.

"You're the one picking fights," Lizzie continued. "You're the one embroidering affairs. You're creating distractions and diversions and anything else you can think of to stop yourself from seeing, from feeling, what's really going on."

Constance layered toothpaste across her toothbrush. "Get out," she said to Lizzie.

"What happened?" said Lizzie, holding her ground. "Was Henry having an affair with Gina?"

"No," said Constance. She started brushing her teeth.

Lizzie watched Constance brush in the mirror. They both looked ancient and furious in the fluorescent light.

"You do this grande dame routine like you're the original Merry Widow," said Lizzie. "*Let's all press on, darlings.* Well, you can't press on from something unless you go there first. Don't you see what you're doing? Making all this drama so that you don't have to face the fact that he's dead, girlie. He's dead and gone and never coming back."

Constance spat toothpaste into the sink and rinsed her toothbrush, flicking tiny white dots onto the mirror. "I'm going to bed," she said, quivering with suppressed rage. "Turn off the lights when you come." She pushed past Lizzie and closed the door behind her.

By the time Lizzie reappeared in the bedroom, Constance was asleep, or pretending to be. Lizzie crawled into bed with every bone and most organs aching. *What an awful end to this strange day,* she thought. As her eyes began to adjust to the dark, she realized that the doors to the balcony were open, but she was too tired to do anything about them. Despite her exhaustion, she lay awake for a long time watching patterns of reflected moonlight play across the ceiling.

In the middle of the night, the pale silk curtains of Lizzie and Constance's room began to dance in the slightest of zephyrs. Constance woke and watched them. She could hear music playing softly on the terrace, a tune from her girlhood. She slipped her feet onto the cold tiles and padded out to the terrace.

A man was standing at the balustrade, looking down into the piazza. He turned, and Constance saw at once that it was Henry. "I thought you were dead," she said. "Everyone said you were dead." She fell into his arms. Henry held her tight and purred an explanation into the top of her head. It was his work, he explained, kissing her hair. He was working for the country on something so important that he was unable to tell her without risking her security. They had faked his death, and he could not tell her about it. He was so sorry for the pain he had caused her.

Constance clung to Henry. Tears of relief tumbled down her face. She could not believe how happy she felt. He was not dead after all! She knew it in her heart all along. Henry wiped away a tear with his familiar hands.

"I've missed you so much," said Constance.

"Shhh," he whispered, and he bent down to kiss her. Constance closed her eyes, and their lips met. When she opened them again, Henry had gone.

Lizzie woke to the sound of a woman sobbing. At first she thought it was Constance but dismissed this idea because it was not coming from the bed next to her. The weeping was horribly forlorn and seemed to be originating from outside, possibly from someone down in the piazza.

As she hoisted herself into an upright position, Lizzie saw that Constance's bed was empty. She hurried outside and discovered her sister-in-law slumped on a stone bench. *What on earth had happened?* She ran across the terrace and gathered Constance in her arms. Constance clung to Lizzie, weeping and wretched. Tears and mucus streamed down her cheeks. Lizzie wiped them with her sleeve. Constance's beautiful face twisted with brutal grief. Lizzie had no idea what to do, except hold her. So she held her, watching the sky lighten.

Lizzie lost all sense of time. Eventually, she led Constance back inside. Constance curled on the bed with her head in Lizzie's lap. Lizzie stroked Constance's gray-flecked golden hair. Constance had long since stopped crying but lay there, helpless as a child. Her body shuddered involuntarily in the aftershock of her sobs. The sun rose over Rome. The sky turned brilliant blue. Turrets and domes began to shimmer in the heat.

"Lizzie?" said Constance quietly.

Lizzie looked down at Constance. Her red–lidded eyes had swollen shut. Lizzie made a mental note to hunt down some ice. "Yes, darling?"

"Let's go home."

TWENTY-SIX

The Angel of Grief

ONLY IN THE AGONY OF PARTING DO WE LOOK
INTO THE DEPTHS OF LOVE.
—George Eliot, *Felix Holt, The Radical*

August woke, lying on his back. His eyes opened to the under-carriage of an umbrella pine, all its limbs collaborating to raise the needled canopy into a brilliant sky. He stretched and registered the assuring presence of someone next to him. He felt the plastic of Alice's raincoat crinkle and yield underneath him. Gently he reached out to touch Alice. She was soft, but cold and lifeless. He turned quickly. It was not Alice but her green backpack. He propped himself up on an elbow and looked around, blinking. Alice had gone. Reasoning that she would not have left without her things, he sat up and waited for her to return.

As the minutes passed he grew more anxious until he could contain himself no longer. He was about to call out her name but stopped, realizing he might be discovered and evicted. He took a quick piss behind a tree, debating whether to leave a note, but decided his time was best spent executing a search. He darted off through the garden and gravestones, one eye open for Alice, the other open for early-morning gravediggers or gardeners. He told himself not to panic, but the more time passed, the harder he found it to heed his own counsel.

August found Alice sitting on a rise at one of the highest points of the cemetery, next to the *Angel of Grief,* an 1894 sculpture by William Wetmore Story that serves as the gravestone of his wife, Emelyn. The large white angel, with her wings outspread, has collapsed in grief over a funereal pedestal. Her head is buried on one folded arm while her other arm drapes in resignation over the pedestal. Otherworldly in form and scale, she is all too human in her despair, captured in a moment when she has been utterly defeated by her loss. It is William Story's last work. After he completed this tribute to his wife, he died, too. It may not be one of Rome's greatest works of art, but it is a great work of love.

"It's not lists," said Alice, drawing in the dirt with a stick.

"What?"

"Love isn't lists," she said. Her face crumpled for a second, but instead of succumbing to tears, she gathered herself and looked up at him. "Sorry."

"Hey."

"I should get going. I've got a train to catch."

Alice got to her feet and bounded down the hill. August stood there massaging his temple as if she had elbowed him in the head as she passed. He felt sick, bad sick, spew-all-over-everything sick. So that was it. She had delivered her verdict. She was going back to what's-his-face. Daniel. He wanted to run after her and shout, or shake her.

He caught up with her at the bottom of the hill, but there was no opportunity to argue because a man opened the front gates and discovered them. He directed an invective of Italian at them but quickly established they were foreigners. In English he demanded to know what they were doing there and how they got in.

Together they tag-teamed a story about another man who had arrived earlier. The fictitious man had said that he was a gardener and let them in. Normally, or in the "normal" that they had established during the two days of their acquaintance, August would have taken a wicked pleasure in the ease with which they were able to fabricate details together, but this just felt tired, another deception he had dragged Alice into.

They collected her backpack and returned to the *motorino* to discover that some joker had left a melting gelato on the seat. Alice went into a shop, bought some water and tissues, and cleaned it. August tried to help, but she insisted on doing it herself, so he watched her, fuming silently.

At the Termini station, Alice collected the ticket that she had booked the day before, and August carried her backpack down the long station to her train carriage. Their conversation was perfunctory, concerned solely with the business of her departure. Which station, which carriage, which seat. Alice climbed into the silver carriage and turned to take her backpack from August. She reached down, but he did not hand it up.

"You know how you said love isn't lists?" he said.

She nodded.

"Then why are you going back to him?"

Because you didn't ask me not to, she wanted to say. *Because when I said, "Love isn't lists," all you said was, "Hey."*

"We agreed that I would stay for another day, and I did. Well, almost a day," she said, acknowledging that it was only 10:00 A.M. "I've had a really cool time."

A really cool time? August thought, wounded and bewildered.

"Yeah, me, too," he said breezily.

Alice thought she might faint. She took hold of a guardrail, without urgency, so as not to draw attention to her state.

"Well, ciao," she said.

"Yeah, ciao," he said, and he handed her backpack over. Alice disguised the effort required to take it with a sunny smile.

"Okay, I'm going to sit down now," she said.

"Safe travels," he said as if she were an elderly aunt on a day trip to Brighton.

Alice carried her backpack down to her seat and hoisted it into the overhead locker. She sat down next to a girl who was scratching the star tattoos covering her arm and reading a Zodiac guide in an Italian gossip magazine.

New Alice would get off the train right now, she thought. She would run after him and tap him on the shoulder and declare herself. But there was no New Alice or Old Alice; there was just Alice. And she loved him too much. She simply did not have the courage to declare herself because if he did not love her back, she would not survive it, she would crack open, she would evaporate. What she was feeling was too big, too dangerous to declare. Only a fool would allow herself to be this vulnerable. In less than two days she had completely lost herself to this man. Love, she realized, was madness and oblivion. She had almost vanished. Her only hope was to stay on the train, to go to Daniel, to tell him the truth, to break off their engagement, and move on.

August tapped her on the shoulder. She looked up at him and watched him as he lowered himself to squat in the aisle next to her. He did not look into her eyes but studied the armrest next to her.

"I was thinking I should tell you something," he said quietly.

"What?" said Alice.

The tattooed girl next to her put down her magazine and looked across; clearly something interesting was about to happen.

"I . . . er . . . I've never said this to anyone," he said as an obese lady in a purple dress barreled down the aisle toward him. He stood up and stepped back for her to pass. She flopped into the seat opposite Alice, panting and smiling. He squatted back down. Ignoring his attentive audience of three, he focused on the armrest once again.

"You've never said what to anyone?" said Alice.

"That I loved them, that I had fallen in love with them."

The fat lady and the tattooed girl exchanged a look. Neither spoke English, but they both understood what was being said. The only person who did not understand, or could not take it in, was Alice. It felt to her as if time had suspended. When August eventually looked up at her, his eyes were glassy.

"So I've fallen in love with you," he said. "That's what I thought you should know."

Alice emitted two strange, startled gasps. She sank her head into her hands.

"That's such a relief," she said, "that you feel it, too."

She looked up at him, overcome and exhausted, as if she had returned home from a long journey. Plump tears sprang from her eyes, and she smeared them across her cheeks. They stood and threw their arms around each other and kissed. The fat lady and the tattooed girl looked very satisfied, as if they had brokered the deal themselves.

The carriage lurched, and the train began to move. August retrieved her backpack and hurried down the aisle with Alice behind him. The guard rebuked them as they leaped from the Florence-bound train for the second time in less than twenty-four hours. On the platform, August pulled Alice toward him and kissed her again. He forgot to think about how to kiss, or what parts to use or not use. There was no technique. There was just kissing. He pressed into her, she pressed into him, both in the moment, the long, glorious moment.

Eventually, they stopped kissing and realized the train had left the station. August started to lift Alice's backpack, but she insisted on carrying it herself and hoisted it onto her back. They joined hands and walked back down the platform.

"So what's your name?" she said.

"What?"

"I don't know your name."

He realized she was right. He felt like they had spent a lifetime together but they had, surprisingly, held to his edict that they not exchange names, e-mails, or phone numbers.

"August," he said.

"Hi, August. I'm Alice," she said, extending her free hand. He took it and they shook as they walked along.

"Hi, Alice. I'm August," he said.

"*August*," she said, playing with the word as she enunciated it. "Can I call you Gus?"

August stopped dead and looked at her.

"August is lovely," she said quickly. "I can call you August," she added, suddenly concerned that she had said the wrong thing.

August cleared his throat. "No," he said croakily, "Gus would be fine."

TWENTY-SEVEN

Leonardo da Vinci Part Two

THE LAW OF LOVING OTHERS COULD NOT BE DISCOVERED
BY REASON BECAUSE IT IS UNREASONABLE.

—Leo Tolstoy, *Anna Karenina*

Wearing an enormous pair of dark glasses, Meg checked out of the Hotel San Marco and left Alec's bag with reception. She had briefly contemplated cutting up his clothes, but she had a plane to catch and a detour to make before she went to the airport, and she simply did not have the time. She asked the doorman to instruct the taxi driver to head for the Colosseum. She did not want to go there. She wanted to go to the hotel where she and Alec had stayed almost twenty years before, but she could not remember the name of the hotel or where it was exactly, only that it was a five-minute stroll from the Colosseum. She hoped inspiration would come once she was circling the ancient amphitheatre.

In the backseat of the taxi, Meg stared at herself in the half-mirror of her window. "No more tears," she said to her reflection.

"*Scusi, signora?*" said the taxi driver.

"Nothing," said Meg.

Traveling down the Via dei Fori Imperiali, the Colosseum loomed in front of them. She marveled, not for the first time, that there it was, smack-bang in the middle of Rome with traffic whizzing around it. Something about the angle of their approach triggered a memory. She recalled walking this way, with Alec, years before and looking up at the mighty structure from a similar perspective.

"Stop," she said.

The driver pulled into the curb. Meg looked out through the front window, getting her bearings. She gesticulated for the driver to turn up the Via Cavour; they turned left, right, doubled back, took a couple of wrong turns, but Meg knew she was near. When they passed the Via dei Serpenti and glimpsed the great façade of Santa Maria ai Monti, she knew that once again Rome was delivering up her secrets.

Bronco had just seen off the two old English dames when a flash of light on the side of Santa Maria attracted his attention. A taxi had pulled into the piazza, and the sun bounced off the passenger window as the door opened. A woman got out and started to walk toward him. His blood ran cold. He could not believe it. It was her.

Meg walked toward the man standing still outside the Hotel Montini, staring at her. *It couldn't be him, surely,* she thought. She had remembered a fine-figured, flashily handsome specimen. The fellow in front of her was thick-middled, sad-faced, and looked rather unwell. Cataracts of defeat clouded his eyes. All that remained of his former glory was a luxurious handlebar moustache.

"Bronco?" said Meg.

"*Si,*" said Bronco.

"You won't remember me. I stayed here a long time ago," she said. "Almost twenty years ago."

Bronco wanted to laugh and weep. Remember her? Oh, that he could forget. She had kissed him, just once, playfully, in front of her new husband. Their lips had touched for no more than a second, but it was long enough to imprint her on some part of his brain over which he had no control. He had been, until that moment, the undisputed Casanova of the Hotel Montini. On any given day he would sleep with at least one, sometimes two, sometimes three, and on one memorable day, seven—yes, seven—adoring female guests.

After she left, he had continued with his dalliances but found himself imagining more and more that he had been making love to the willowy *Americana* with the golden curls. Eventually, she had inhabited all his fantasies. On the rare occasion that he was forced to relieve himself in the shower, she would appear before him, no matter how hard he tried to conjure the voluptuous brunette on Channel 5. At first he thought it was a sign. That maybe she was on the other side of the world, imagining him. He thought of going to America to look for her. He thought that she might one day come looking for him. He thought this for a long time, but he did nothing about it.

Months passed, then years. He let go of the silly idea that she would appear. She had never expressed the slightest interest in him. She was a creature of his imaginary world, not his real one. By what fantastical means did he think she would come? Released from the chains of hope, he made friends with gelato. He stopped refusing his *nonna*'s second serving of pasta.

He grew wide-hipped and bald. It took twenty years, but finally Bronco found peace.

And now, here she was, standing before him. He had staved off the *colpo d'aria,* but he had no idea how he would survive this.

"I think I remember," he said, pretending professional detachment. "It was on your honeymoon, *si?*"

"Yes," said Meg.

"And the young signore, *allora,* not so young anymore, I suppose," he corrected. "How is he?"

Meg shook her head. "Gone," she said.

It was only one word, but Bronco could tell that she was heartbroken, that he must have died tragically somehow, from a lingering disease, in her arms.

"Oh, I'm sorry," he said. "You haven't changed, signora."

"Neither have you," said Meg.

"Thank you for that lie," he said. "You are very kind."

"Bronco," she said, "I want to ask a favor . . ."

Minutes later they were standing in the room that Constance and Lizzie had just vacated. Meg put her vintage Gucci shoulder bag on the unmade bed and produced a small square parcel of tissue. She unwrapped the tissue and revealed the shimmering square of blue tile that matched the tiles covering the floor.

Bronco remembered now that this was why she had kissed him. She had discovered, under the rug, that one of the tiles was loose and asked if she could take it as a memento. It was highly irregular, of course, but it was under a rug, and there was a chance that she might sleep with him, even though she was on her honeymoon, so he had said yes.

"Signora," he said, "you can keep the tile. You don't have to give her back."

"Thank you," she said, "but I don't need it anymore."

Meg started to scan the floor to see where a tile was missing. Bronco flipped back the rug to show her. Kneeling down, she returned her treasure to its place and covered it with the rug. It was all over so quickly, too quickly. She pulled back the rug for one last look at this thing that had lived three lives during the nineteen years of her custodianship: the first as a talisman; the second, having incrementally lost its significance, as anonymous junk, lugged around for years in depths of various bags; the third as a mystery candidate, emerging from her jumble of samples as *the special one*. No wonder she had been convinced it was so important. It was. She was not so foolish as to lay the blame for her current troubles on an inanimate object, but if it had not been for this tile . . .

Meg gathered herself and flipped back the corner of the rug. Bronco offered his hand to help her up, and she took it. It was lovely to touch her, having worshiped her all these years, but not thrilling, not electric, as he had imagined it would be, just a little bit sad.

An hour later Meg was sitting in the business-class lounge, watching the workers on the tarmac loading and unloading planes up and down the runway. She began to think about the children, what she would tell them, when, and how. A man's hand rested on hers. She turned to see Alec perched on the armrest of the empty seat next to her. For a second, she thought she had imagined him.

"What are you doing?" she said.

"I'm sorry," he said.

"I thought you were running off with Stephanie."

"I'm not. I don't . . ." He paused, casting for a phrase that would not inflame her.

"What?"

"Love her," he said, failing to find it.

Meg's eyes wandered around the room, looking everywhere but at him. She was certain, now, that he had gone to her. And 90 percent certain that he had slept with her. She was also certain that she must let this go, that if she were to cross-examine him, she would incinerate with fury and vanish into a desire of vengeance. If they had any hope of moving forward, she must let this particular aspect of his betrayal fall away. Right here, right now.

"So?" she said.

"I'm coming back," he said.

"You're coming back because you don't love her?"

"Because I love you."

"That's not what you said last night."

"I was wrong. I was angry. I thought I meant it, but I didn't mean it. You know me, I'm . . . I don't know what I am."

"So you were right about not loving her and wrong about not loving me?"

"Yes."

"That's not good enough."

"Tell me what is."

Meg looked out the window. She could feel tears coming, but she was determined as hell not to let them escape. "I don't know," she said. "I don't know what it takes. I don't know how we ended up here."

"We screwed up, both of us," he said. "We stopped taking care of each other. It stopped being important."

"Maybe we should stop for good."

Alec said nothing.

"It's hard," she said. "And boring. Being married for twenty years. What if we struggle on for another twenty?"

Alec left his perch on the armrest and sat down next to her. He lowered his voice. "Do you love me?" he asked.

Meg did not respond. She kept looking out the window.

"Meg, look at me."

Meg kept looking out the window. If she looked at him, she did not know what would happen to her. By way of compromise, she turned slightly, looking at the lamp next to him.

"Do you love me?" he asked again.

She nodded briefly and looked back out the window.

"So let's try," he said.

Meg turned and, for the first time in a very long time, actually held his gaze. He was taken aback.

"How?" she said.

He didn't know how exactly. He knew they needed to talk. He knew what they needed to say to each other would take longer than the long flight back to Los Angeles. He knew that once they got home, children and work and other stuff would take priority and that their only chance was to not allow this to happen.

"We need to go somewhere," he said.

"Where?"

He didn't know where.

"Where?" she asked again.

And then it dawned on him.

TWENTY-EIGHT

The Gravitational Pull of Blue Tiles

THY FIRMNESS DRAWES MY CIRCLE JUST, AND
MAKES ME END, WHERE I BEGUNNE.
—John Donne, *A Valediction: Forbidding Mourning*

While Lizzie berated an airline clerk at the first-class counter, Constance stood by her side, masked by a massive pair of round sunglasses that made her look like a giant insect. She had forgotten to pack a pair of her own, so Lizzie had sent young Marco from the Hotel Montini to procure some. Sadly, his tastes were not as refined as Constance had hoped. They were, however, a step up from the monstrous red swellings through which she was attempting to see, so she did not complain.

"Please listen very carefully," said Lizzie to the beak-nosed clerk in her best terrifyingly British voice. "I am not interested in any more of your helpful suggestions. I am only interested in two tickets to London, and I insist that you put us on the very next flight. Or else."

"But, signora," said Beak-Nose, sounding like reason itself, "you are not booked."

"Then get us a booking," said Constance as if he had not explained to her five times already that all the flights to London were full. Lizzie had even condescended to fly business class but to no avail.

"But, signora . . ." said Beak-Nose.

Lizzie glanced at Constance and noticed that she was pale. "Go find a seat, girlie," she said, "and don't worry. Scary old ladies always get what they want."

Constance had never been more grateful for Lizzie's bossy streak. She retreated to an uncomfortable plastic bench and sat watching the world go by while Lizzie escalated her demands to various British Airways officials who attempted to appease her. Eventually, after threatening to have her (completely fictitious) cousin Lord Fairnsworth deregister the airline, Lizzie gave up on British Airways and canvassed every other airline that flew into London.

Half an hour later she emerged from the throng and collapsed on the bench next to Constance. "Apparently," she said, "scary old ladies don't always get what they want. The earliest we can get out is tomorrow. Sorry."

"It's this place, Lizzie," said Constance, smiling. "Roma—just when you think you've finished with her, you find she's not finished with you."

They returned, a little worse for wear, to the Hotel Montini. Bronco was nowhere to be found, but young Marco was sitting at the reception desk, lost in a video game. Constance was almost upon him when he raised his eyes from the screen. His face lit up.

"Contessa!" he said. "I thinked you go home."

Behind her, Lizzie wrangled the luggage into the foyer.

"So did I, Marco," she said, "but I'd like my room back, please."

"I beg your pardon, Contessa," said Marco, "that room is taken, but there is one next to her, almost the same."

"Our room has gone already?" said Constance. "Who has taken it?"

In the blue-tiled suite, August sat up in the bed, naked and alone. He flattened the sheet that covered him to the waist, breathed into his hand, and smelled his breath. It didn't stink, but it wasn't exactly minty fresh either. He began to deliberate whether to get out of bed and clean his teeth when Alice appeared at the bathroom door wearing nothing but a towel. His brain emptied. Had anyone offered him one million pounds to add one plus one, he would have been completely incapable of answering "Two."

His lips curled in a funny kind of half grin. Alice flashed him a brief, nervous smile in return. She walked to the edge of the bed. He took her hand and pulled her gently toward him. They lay side by side, facing each other, a sheet and a towel between them. Breathing shallow and fast, he watched the pulse beat in her neck. She ran her fingers across his jaw, his clever, crooked mouth. In one continuous movement, August ripped the sheet from under Alice, straddled her, and pulled open her towel so that their bodies were revealed to each other.

August chuckled softly into her neck. He had not kissed

her clavicle three times before they both surrendered any pretense of restraint. Quickly he slid into her, and they twisted and banged their bodies together, slippery and joyful as otters.

Next door, Marco had successfully installed Constance and Lizzie in the room that they had originally rejected, while downstairs Bronco had been roused from an emergency nap to man the front desk. He looked up to see Meg walking back into the foyer, with Alec.

Bronco felt his forehead to gauge his temperature. He was okay. He had heard of a gelateria near the Fontana di Trevi that was selling green-tea gelato. He decided to hunt some down before the day ended and focus on the promise of this to get through whatever fresh horror was about to unfold. Was this the dead husband or some new fellow she had brought with her? Professional intuition told him it was the dead husband, not so dead obviously.

"Signora!" said Bronco, conjuring a smile. "And signore!"

"Bronco!" said Meg.

Bronco looked at Alec. "You are back!" he exclaimed. Then, turning to Meg, said, "He's back!"

"I'm back," said Alec, realizing that this was indeed the same fellow who had kissed his bride eighteen years before. He wondered, briefly, why the intervening years had been so unkind to him.

"Is our old room still empty?" said Meg.

"It has just been occupied, I'm sorry," said Bronco, "but there is one next door, almost the same."

Young Marco appeared and took Meg and Alec up to a penthouse room that was indeed identical to the one next door, except for the color of the red–tiled floor. Marco was beyond thrilled with the size of his tip and lavished praise and thanks on his elegant American guests. The boy's hyperbole made Meg smile. Alec could not recall the last time he had seen his wife smile in such an uncomplicated way.

Marco left, and Meg hovered next to their luggage. Overwhelmed by the thought of dissecting their relationship, she wanted to lie on the bed and pretend that the previous forty-eight hours had never happened. Now that they had the time and place to talk, it seemed to Alec that there was nothing for him to say, except *Sorry* and *Let's give it another shot,* which he had already said. They had agreed to scale a mountain together, but both were suddenly incapacitated by the enormity and ambition of the venture.

Alec opened the doors to the terrace and walked to the balustrade overlooking the piazza. A small group of musicians were setting up their instruments on the steps of the fountain below. A complaining girl dropped an armful of music stands. A boy grappling with a double bass stopped to help her. Alec sensed a presence standing next to him and realized that Meg was by his side. He felt an impulse to put an arm around her shoulder but worried that it would seem presumptuous.

"Is it okay to . . ." He paused. "Can I touch you?"

Meg flinched. It was the saddest question he had ever asked her.

"I don't know why I . . ." She paused.

"What?"

"Why I act the way I do."

Alec had spent a great deal of time over the years being irritated by his wife's antics but had never given a great deal of genuine consideration to the cause of her behavior. Looking down at the musicians, he suddenly realized that during their lives together he had accumulated a portrait of her, of how she was formed, that actually went a long way toward explaining why she acted the way she did.

Meg had been raised on her family's outback station, larger than some European countries, with four older brothers. They were big, confident boys, and while they celebrated their little sister for her prettiness, they dismissed her usefulness on the property. Meg retaliated at first by trying to match them, mustering cattle and mending fences, just like they did. But they were bigger, stronger, older, and ultimately more effective at stock and station work. So Meg became the smart one, the funny one, the outrageous one.

He remembered, in the early days of their relationship, traveling to Australia with her and watching her work so hard with her family, to make them laugh, to sparkle, to be the star attraction. He had wanted to hold her and whisper in her ear, "You don't need to impress anyone."

But she did. And God knows, she impressed him. She was so funny and gorgeous and clever and fabulous. He pursued her like he pursued nothing else. He didn't care about his career or money or where he lived—she was enough; she was everything. Until she wasn't.

Once he had possessed her, it slowly dawned on him that he could not intoxicate himself with another person and let that be his life. Over the years, he had let her know of this epiphany in infinitesimally small increments. A restrained smile. An irritated curve of the lips. A brief but exasperated squint. Meg had collected all his feedback and dutifully collated it. In response, she became more dramatic, more outrageous, more captivating. The more he withdrew, the harder she worked.

God, he thought, *I have brought us here.*

"It's my fault," he said.

Meg turned to him, uncertain what he meant.

But he knew exactly what he meant; he had hated her family for making her work so hard to be loved. And now he realized that this was precisely what he had done.

"I'm sorry," he said.

"I think we're beyond apologies," said Meg.

"No. I really need to tell you I'm sorry."

Meg looked out over the piazza.

"I'm sorry, too," she said.

Lizzie had ordered cucumber slices for Constance's eyes, which were finally beginning to settle. In their green-tiled room, both the old ladies had retired for a lie-down. They dozed, exhausted, but buzzed in and out of wakefulness, as if they were expecting an alarm to go off or a visitor to arrive. Constance turned on her side, letting her cucumbers fall away. She watched Lizzie's lying on her back, blinking slowly at the ceiling. Gradually the time between blinks grew longer and longer until Lizzie's eyes no longer opened. Constance observed the rise and fall of her chest and was about to give thanks that at least one of them was sleeping, when an orchestra started to play in the piazza below.

Lizzie opened her eyes and listened. It wasn't a very loud orchestra. It wasn't a very good one either. They appeared to be attempting Haydn. She turned to find Constance smiling at her. Without discussing it, they each hoisted themselves up and shuffled out to the terrace for a look. Emerging into the harsh light, Constance stopped and went back to retrieve her sunglasses.

Lizzie looked down at the orchestra and immediately felt more kindly disposed toward them. They weren't an orchestra at all but an expanded string quartet: three violinists, a cellist, and double bass player, all in their early teens, struggling courageously with their instruments and the music. The poor fellow with the double bass looked like he was trying to stop it from escaping. Constance appeared next to Lizzie, observing the spectacle from behind her giant glasses. A man carrying a large bunch of burgundy roses was moving through the crowd.

"Is that Horatio?" said Constance, peering.

Lizzie recognized him immediately. He was arriving to take her to tea as they had arranged the previous evening.

Constance turned to Lizzie and saw that she was rattled. Horatio looked up at the terrace and spotted them. He waved. They waved back. Lizzie felt foolish and embarrassed, mortified that Constance's eagle eyes would be registering her heightened state.

"We arranged to meet," said Lizzie.

"That must have been some dinner," said Constance dryly.

"Oh, stop it," said Lizzie.

Constance smiled.

"I left a message with reception when were leaving this

morning," said Lizzie, "telling him I wasn't here, that I'd had to leave."

"But you are here," said Constance.

"I know. He's going to think I'm standing him up."

"*Standing him up?* How old are we? Sixteen?"

"You are in no position to be making fun of me, particularly when you are looking like an enormous fly in those ridiculous glasses."

"Better freshen up that lippy and get down there," said Constance, winking through her polaroid lens.

"Did you just wink at me?"

"I never wink."

"You must come too. Horatio would love to see you, I'm sure."

"Let's get one thing perfectly clear," said Constance. "I am not coming with you. You're flying this one solo, girlie. Now go." She pointed to the door and in her best, scariest pirate voice said, "Go!"

In the room next door, August and Alice lay on the bed, gleaming with sweat. Alice was making a study of how light interacted with the interior of August's ear to produce various shades of pink while August stared at the ceiling, wondering whether it had been finished with horsehair plaster. Alice briefly entertained the idea of covering her nakedness, but the obstacles to achieving this seemed insurmountable. Her towel was scrunched between the mattress and the headboard, and the sheet was on the floor next to August. She would have to exert herself if she wanted to reach either the towel or the sheet, and she was categorically incapable of any further exertion. Music drifted up from the piazza.

"Music," said Alice redundantly into August's ear. She watched lines at the side of his eyes crinkle into a smile. He sat up and peeled off the bed, absconding with the sheet, which he wrapped around himself as he padded to the terrace doors.

"Hey!" she protested.

August disappeared through the doors, unmoved.

Alice supposed she should muster herself to join him. She rolled off the bed in a sort of commando maneuver, put her feet on the floor, and was about to launch forth when her toe caught the edge of the rug. She tripped and fell. As her knee hit the rug, she heard a crack. She hoped that it wasn't her kneecap, which hurt but was not proportionately painful. Alice sat up to inspect her injuries. Having satisfied herself that she had fractured no bones, she pulled back the rug and discovered that one of the tiles had dislodged.

Alice wrapped herself in a towel and limped on the terrace with the loose tile.

"Look at this," said August, leaning over the balustrade, looking into the piazza. Alice joined him.

"An orchestra," said Alice.

"Not them—*them,*" said August, pointing at an old man who presented an enormous bunch of roses to an old lady and kissed her hand.

"Oh, how sweet," said Alice. "I bet they've been together for, like, fifty years."

August turned to Alice and saw that she was holding a small floor tile.

"You don't know how to fix tiles, do you?" she said, handing it to him.

"Sure do," he said and, as a joke, without giving it any thought, started to fling the tile into the air above the piazza. He was about to release it when he realized, however, that his small projectile was quite likely to brain someone below. In the final, crucial second, he pivoted on his foot and flung it the other way, up onto the roof behind them.

He had meant to impress her with his spontaneity and wacky derring-do, but he was already regretting his action as the blue tile arced through the air. It almost cleared the peak of the roof but clipped a chimney, landed, and clattered back down the tiles on a new trajectory. They could hear it land with a dull thud on something next door but could not see anything because of the vine-encrusted trellis that divided the terraces. Alice punched August on the arm.

Constance had been waving farewell to Lizzie and Horatio as they headed off to tea, when she heard on object land on the terrace behind her. She walked over to a potted lemon and discovered, sitting in the soil at its base, a blue tile. A quarter of a century had passed since it had been in her possession, but she recognized it immediately.

TWENTY-NINE

The Dream

THERE ARE MORE THINGS IN HEAVEN AND EARTH, HORATIO,
THAN ARE DREAMT OF IN YOUR PHILOSOPHY.
—William Shakespeare, *Hamlet*

The human genome contains all the genetic information you
need to make a person. The information is encoded as DNA
sequences within twenty-three chromosome pairs in cell nu-
clei as well as a small DNA molecule found within individual
mitochondria. Its total length is over three billion base pairs,
yet the differences among individual humans only vary
within a range of 0.1 percent. Further differences could be
accounted for by the extensive use of alternative pre-mRNA
splicing, but here's the take-home message: regardless of race,
color, creed, or credit rating, people are, by and large, 99.9
percent identical.

All humans are alike, and some are more alike than others.
Some humans share combinations of gene sequences that re-
main uncannily intact through generation upon generation of

reproduction. Indeed, this was the case with Alice, Alec, and Constance.

Had the dividing trellises between the penthouse rooms of the Hotel Montini magically blown away, Alice might have turned right and spotted her mother's brother, Alec, with her boisterous Australian aunt, Meg. She had not seen them since one Thanksgiving in her early teens when her mother had made a sotto voce comment about Uncle Alec giving up on architecture to become a "shopkeeper." Relations had cooled since then, and communications were limited to an annual exchange of Christmas cards.

Had Alice turned left, she might also have recognized her grandfather's sister, Constance. She had only met her great-aunt a couple of times as a child, but her mother never failed to drop their aristocratic English connections into conversation whenever the opportunity arose. Constance loomed large in family folklore.

My purpose in gathering the three of them on the roof of the Hotel Montini was merely to facilitate the efficient execution of procedure. When you are a specialist, as I am, in matters of the human heart, much of your work occurs in microcosmic realms. Harnessing the right wavelength will carry you far. Forging allegiances with certain colonies of bacteria is essential, as well as enlisting the assistance of sometimes unhelpful viruses. Inside the twisting canyons of human DNA sequences, wonders can be accomplished. For my part, it is simply more effective to work on people who share the same DNA sequences, rather like working on the same make of car. I have found over the years, however, that under these circumstances—when like is gathered with like—serendipities occur. When Constance picked up the blue missile sitting at the base of her lemon tree, for example, it was one outcome among millions that might have occurred as a consequence of August throwing the tile. But it just happened to be the right one.

Holding the small blue square, Constance could have sworn it was vibrating, very softly, in her hand. She wondered whether it was an omen. Had it returned to her for some kind of purpose? Was she supposed to put it in her bag and take it back to London? She had taken it originally for luck, and the tile had brought her luck, certainly, but the luck had been bad as well as good. She counted the years that it had been in her possession as the most tumultuous of her life. *No,* she decided, *I have done quite enough living in interesting times.*

With the tile in hand she padded back through her room into the hall and knocked on the door of the blue-tiled suite. There was no answer. Without thinking she put her hand on the door handle and turned it. The door opened. Constance peered inside. Observing the stripped and disheveled bed, she called a timid, "Hello?" Again, there was no answer, but she could see that the rug next to the bed was peeled back, revealing the space where the tile belonged. She walked into the room and, taking care not to strain her back, bent and fitted the tile into the hole.

Experiencing the deep satisfaction of someone placing the final piece in an enormous jigsaw, Constance straightened.

Hearing someone approach from the terrace, she wondered for a moment whether to stay and explain herself, but in the millisecond she had to run this scenario through her head, she realized that the truth would simply sound barking mad. She scurried to the door and had almost escaped when a man's voice said, "Can I help you?" Constance popped her head back into the room to see a young man draped in a sheet like an ancient Roman senator in need of a tailor. "Sorry. Wrong room," she said and closed the door quickly behind her.

By the time August opened his door to look up and down the empty hall, Constance had slipped back into her own suite. Alice appeared and asked what August was doing. He was in the middle of explaining about the mysterious old lady when it suddenly struck him that he may have been victim of some kind of scam. He suggested Alice check her backpack, which she did, but nothing appeared to be missing. She turned, poised to tease him about his paranoia when her eye caught the space on the floor where the tile was supposed to be missing. She rushed over to the newly replaced tile and popped it out of place with her toe.

"It came back," she said, naturally astonished.

"What?" he said.

She picked up the tile in wonder. "This," she said. "This is the tile you threw over the roof."

His lips curled, but his eyes did most of the smiling.

"I know it can't be," she said, "but it is."

And so began a long and frustrating debate in which Alice attempted to assert that the impossible was not only possible but had actually come to pass.

. . .

On the red-tiled terrace next door, Alec and Meg stood in silence watching the young musicians below sawing their way through more Haydn. Meg was accustomed to filling the space between Alec and herself with patter, banter, drivel, whatever she could come up with. In the division of labor that had developed between them over the years, this had been her job. But now she was quiet. She was not trying to force her husband's hand or make him take the lead; she had simply run out of fuel. She had nothing to offer, except an awful premonition that there may not be a future for them, that the reserves of genuine forgiveness required to move forward were not available to either of them.

They heard movement on the terrace next to them. A young woman spoke. Her voice reminded Alec of someone, but he couldn't place whom.

"I don't care what you think," said the voice. "I'm keeping it."

The low rumble of a man's voice replied, although they could not make out what he was saying. Then the young woman said, "For luck. I'm keeping it for . . ."

She suddenly stopped speaking. Meg and Alec both guessed, correctly, that this was because the source of the low rumble was now kissing her.

Alec looked down at the balustrade and saw his wife's hand next to his.

"I don't know that we could be happy again," she said.

"I don't want happiness," he said and thought, but did not

add, something that shocked him to the core with its fierce, utter, and unexpected certainty: *I want you.*

He knew, then, that he would always want her, that he would find a way back to her somehow. He let his little finger slide across the cold stone and touch hers. He was aware that she could feel it and was grateful that she did not retract.

Constance stood at the edge of her terrace. Music drifted up, melodious enough to be soothing. She closed her eyes and imagined Henry next to her. After a while she could feel him, the heat and press of his body next to hers. He had said to her once that people left but love remained. She felt, now, how right he was. Constance rested her head on Henry's shoulder, certain she could feel him bearing her weight.

Not far from Constance and Henry, Alice and August stood in almost exactly the same position, and not far from them, Meg and Alec. Three couples, surrendering to stillness, listening to the notes and the silence between the notes, oblivious to each other yet connected—standing at the beginning, middle, and end of their loves.

Some of it was my work. Some of it was not. As Nikola Tesla, engineer, futurist, and mad scientist, often asserted, it's all about energy, frequency, and vibration. The parameters around what can and cannot be achieved in the quantum realms are vast, the variables infinite. Sometimes there are consequences that I neither foresee nor plan with outcomes that surprise even me. They may crop up immediately. They may occur years later. . . .

Epilogue

Alice broke from a dream that she had married the wrong man and kicked off her sheets in a panic. She tried to wake, but the delirium of her night world stitched itself around her, tight as a collar, deadly as an anchor, dragging her back down to the murky depths of sleep. Feverishly, she swiveled her head toward the slumbering hulk next to her. He emitted a sound, neither snore nor sigh, but something in between, and rolled over.

He was the wrong man. Springing out of bed, Alice took three paces backward. The boards beneath her creaked like a traitor. She looked for an escape, but the door was not where it was supposed to be. She took in the great splash of aureolin yellow at the end of the room, as well as the canvas on which it was painted, and suddenly, blessedly, awoke.

Adrenaline flooded the vacuum that fright vacated. She had not married the wrong man; she was in the wrong life. *No, not the wrong life. A different life.* A different life from the one she had just been living in the night world. She wiped her beaded brow with the back of her hand. Light delivered itself through the slats of the shutters like a hundred thrilling envelopes: *Congratulations, you have won another morning.*

In the striped brilliance of the day, she stitched her reality back together and could see that she belonged here. Those were her canvases, her paints, she assured herself; this was her studio, her husband. She went into her shoe box kitchen, held a paint-splattered glass under the tap, and turned the handle. The faucet protested with a squeal. Pipes thumped in the wall, and cool water gurgled into the glass.

The man from the bed entered and brushed his cheek across her bare shoulder in a bristly greeting. Gus knew in theory that a time would come when he would be able to walk into a room and not touch her, but he could not conceive of it. He knew, he had seen, how lovers grow used to each other, how passion wanes, but it was beyond his youthful comprehension that this could ever happen to them. He breathed her in, feeling her loveliness next to him, and gave thanks.

They could hear the din of tourists, two streets away, already climbing the 270 steps toward the hybrid edifice of Sacré-Cœur. Three years ago, when they had first moved to Paris, she had read to him how, when it rained, the white stone released a chemical that washed it clean, maintaining the sparkling white façade. Each morning as they listened to the pilgrims passing he recalled this factoid with immense satisfaction.

Alice turned to Gus and saw his lips begin to curl. In a

moment he would smile; or maybe not. Sometimes his pre-smiles faded without blossoming, which made them all the more precious to her. They stood looking out the dirty window at a cascading landscape of gray rooftops and orange chimney pots. The stillness flowered so prettily between them that she chose not to spoil it with talk of her night world. She did not want to tell him how the darkness had once again taken her down into a different life with a different husband.

She finished her water and placed the glass in the sink, more forcefully than she had intended. The loud *clunk* of glass on porcelain suddenly ruptured a membrane to the previous evening, and she saw a dream beyond the dream about the different husband.

In this deeper dream, she was in a cellar, in Rome, sitting amid pallets piled high with tiles. She did not know how she knew she was in Rome; she just knew. She picked up a tile and looked down at it, thinking it was somehow familiar. The tile began to hum and vibrate. She had to hold tight to stop it falling from her lap. There was no aperture from which to make an utterance, but a voice rose regardless from its blue glaze.

"I am going to tell you a long and unlikely tale," the tile said.

Alice shared none of this with Gus; there was no time. She knew she must begin writing before the tale was lost. He watched curiously as she walked with great purpose to the flaking walnut table where she usually mixed her paints, cleared away her palette and brushes, grabbed a pencil and sketchpad, took a seat, and, possessed by something other than herself, began to write my story.

Acknowledgments

Thank you to my Roman friends and guides who have shared their city with me over the years—Carla Vicenzino, Tia Architto, Stefano Casu, Jeanne-Marie Cilento, Paul McDonnell, Ute Leonhardt, Marco Pugini, Michela Noonan, and Clelia March-Doeve. Thanks to my volunteer editorial team, my wife, Klay Lamprell, and my sister, Helen Bateman. Thanks to the rest of my wonderful family and friends, in particular those whose names I have wantonly pilfered.

Thank you to the gang at Flatiron—Caroline Bleeke, Liz Keenan, Molly Fonseca, Patricia Cave, Karen Horton, and Sara Ensey for the superb edit, and especially publisher Amy Einhorn, who embraced the novel so wholeheartedly. Thanks, too, to Jane Palfreyman, who furnished this tale with its title and Wenona Byrne, who introduced it to the world.

And, finally, thank you to two people for their support and inspiration: one from the past—Mr. Joseph Castley, English Master extraordinaire, who taught me at Saint Ignatius' College in Sydney, Australia, and one from the present—my agent and true believer, Margaret Connolly.